For Sue

Secrets Revealed

with best wishes

[signature]

PUBLISHING

First Edition published 2022 by

2QT Limited (Publishing)

Settle, North Yorkshire BD24 9RH United Kingdom

Printed in Great Britain by IngramSpark

A CIP catalogue record for this book is available
from the British Library

ISBN 978-1-914083-63-1

Secrets Revealed

FRANK ENGLISH

Hidden Secrets

… end of last chapter

"Your nose is broken, and you have lost several teeth," the young woman said to the young man she was tending. "How on earth did you manage to get those injuries? Fall over after too much to drink, or walk into a door, or walk into a … fist?"

"It was the latter, my dear," the foppish young man replied, eye socket swollen and badly bruised as well, and blood spattered across his white shirt and coloured jacket. "From some dashed coward, the blighter, that attacked me from behind."

"Did he steal your wallet?" she asked. "Have you any money to pay for my services?"

"He did not!" the young man insisted with a grimace and a significant wince of pain. "I do believe it must have been a *'crime passionel'* – a crime of passion I will not forget. I cannot forget that dashed ugly face, and I *will* see him again. And maybe the next time he won't see me coming either."

"You can stay here with my son and me," she went on. "But we will need money to buy the usual things that will allow us to live. Agreed?"

"Of course, my dear, of course," he replied, a knowing smile spreading.

He would not forget the disservice that had been done to his features, and he *would* return the favour, in his own good time.

And so, it continues…

CHAPTER I

"Now then, my pretty little harlot," the foppishly spoken young man said to the young girl. "Do you have a *morsel* for me?"

She stirred slowly, a sighing groan escaping her lips pitifully. No older than her companion, she drew a small black drawstring bag from under the mattress and handed it to him. He eyed it and, tossing it lightly into the air, tried to assess what it might hold.

"Feels a little … light, my dear, don't you think?" he added, eyebrow raising slowly, with more than a little tone of disappointment ringing his threat to her. He turned to face her, his mild look of disquiet changing to a sharply accusing sneer as he gripped her quivering wrist. His beard, unusually grey-streaked for one so young, masked a myriad of facial irregularities that had been wrought by someone else's heavy hand. Although foppishly uttered, his use of language was well-formed, bearing witness to an education that wasn't born of the gutter.

"Try looking inside!" she snarled, snatching her wrist away from his bruising grasp and moving away to tend to her poorly teenage son, Toby.

"Excellent, my dear, excellent," the young man hissed, a sardonic smile gracing his lips, wincing slightly as he smiled. The facial injuries inflicted by his attacker had been much more serious than he had first hoped. Apart from copious doses of laudanum to dull the pain and letting nature take its course, his medic could offer no further solution. Consequently, his only means of disguising the extensive damage had been to grow a significant covering of facial hair.

"Two sovereigns and four half-crowns will do us nicely," he went on after a pause. "This will do for *all* of us."

"I never thought I would have to resort to previous 'employments' when I invited you to share our life," she replied with disdain.

"If you would prefer that I weren't here, you only have to give the word and I will trouble you no more," he said, an unseen but serious threat underpinning his words. "I have 'associates' who would be delighted to have me stay. Shall I pack?"

"Pack what?" she sneered. "You have nothing to pack. All you possess you either stand up in or have hanging in the corner of yonder cupboard."

"But you have no idea how much I will have to spend on attire should I decide to join my other … associates," he warned. "If I go, my dear heart, you will … regret … it."

His last offering left her with no illusion as to what he meant. His steely-blue eyes pierced her to the core, leaving her in no doubt where his malevolence might take him. She winced as he reached out to touch her, expecting a slap across the face, before he flicked the end of her nose, turned on his heel, and disappeared into the night.

"For goodness' sake, Jonas! Is it really you?" his mother Louisa gasped as she opened the door to him, close on midnight. "It's been almost two years since we saw you last. Where have you been? And look at you! Beard and long hair? You look like a *real* beggar."

"I love you, too, Mater," the young man replied sarcastically. "Am I to be asked in, out of this freezingly cold night? Or shall I slink away and die in some slime-coated gutter?"

"No!" she replied sharply. "There's no need for that sort of language. Come in. Quickly now! It's freezing out there. Would you like something to eat?"

"Is Father in?" he asked warily, ignoring her question.

"He's away on business," she said. "Won't be back until Christmas Eve – day after tomorrow. Will you stay at least until he returns? I'm sure he would love to see you."

"Let's not delude ourselves, Old Thing," Jonas scoffed, waving away her offer. "We both know what *his* response would be to your suggestion. I will *not* stay. All I need is a spot of cash to tide me over for a month or two, and then I could get back on my feet. Call it a drawdown on my inheritance."

"We both know what your father would have to say about that!" she warned. "So, in this instance, you can have enough to see you through to whenever, but we won't tell your father. To be honest, he mustn't know even that you've been here. Agreed?"

"At last, my old Ma, a touch of honesty!" he laughed, not an ounce of regret in his words. "If you could see your way to cough up the occasionally dirty sovereign … or three, I'll steal away into the night and not darken your door ever again."

"Jonas!" she gasped, as tears began to well, and stretched her arms towards him.

He grabbed the money she had put on the table before

him, backed away from her and disappeared into the darkness, leaving her bereft and sobbing at his passing.

~

"Uncle Ross and Uncle Joseph?" Poppy started to ask after dinner, in that whiny sort of a way she always used when she was a little girl. It always got her what she wanted or where she wanted to be.

"Did you hear something, Brother?" Ross said, looking around, pretending to ignore her question. "I could have sworn I heard a whiny little voice quite close by."

"Ha ... ha ... very funny," Poppy muttered sarcastically. "My question was about to be something concerning the almost derelict worker's cottage halfway along the carriage-way up to the house."

"Go on then, Poppy," Joseph answered with an indulgent smile. "Take no notice of your trouble-causing uncle. I'm all ears."

"They're not that big, Brother!" Ross butted in, with a laugh.

This was one of the few times that the whole family sat down together for their evening meal at Boulders Wood. Ross and Nell Booth, Ross and Martha Booth, Joseph and Lilly Victoria McIntyre had all agreed originally to do it once every month to keep in touch with the family's news and with the running of their joint business with Tom and Lilly Garside. It was an event when any business might be raised that was relevant and of interest to all.

"Go ahead, Young Lady," Ross Senior urged. "It must be important for you to bring up something not related to your reading and writing. Or is it?"

"In a way, it is," Poppy replied, undaunted by the audience

she now faced. "As you all know, Florence and I are now eighteen years old, going on nineteen. We are very fond of literary reading and writing. However, unfortunately we can't get around to spending much time together to explore these two passions, as she lives too far away for either of us to travel unchaperoned. Our attacker of two years ago is still at large and couldn't be trusted not to try to gain access to us again. If he did, we couldn't guarantee to have our saviour, George, on hand."

She paused for a moment or two to gauge the interest her preamble might have generated. She most definitely had grabbed their attention.

"I believe I have an inkling as to where this might be leading us," Ross Senior ventured. "If I am right, I think it would be an excellent idea."

"Have we taken to reading minds, then, Husband?" Nell asked with a snigger. "Or am I, at least, missing something?"

"Carry on, Child," Nell went on. "Explain."

"Would it be possible to have that cottage converted from its present dilapidated state fit for only our pigs into something vaguely … liveable?" Poppy continued, a look of hope welling in her pretty eyes.

"By that, do you mean for you *and* Florence?" Lilly Victoria asked. "So that you might use it on a more regular basis for your budding literary ambitions?"

"Well … yes," Poppy replied quietly, scanning faces for any reactions her family members might display. "We would not only like two bedrooms, but also a reasonably large sitting area where we might read and write, and where we might entertain other like-minded people to share their ideas and writing adventures."

"Almost exactly what I thought you might suggest,"

Ross Senior said, before anyone else could express any sort of opinion. "And I, for one, would not only support such a venture wholeheartedly, I would also be prepared to sponsor you unreservedly."

"Sponsor?" Poppy queried slowly, not sure what that might mean. "As in—?"

"I will pay for all renovations to your specifications, my dear Poppy," he offered with an excited grin. "And I will be prepared to put the word around to all the writing fraternities hereabouts that I know of. Furthermore, I will employ a company to make all arrangements around your events, including catering, which I am sure would be Mary's Pantry."

"Can I mention Cousin Albert – the only stonemason in the family – to do the renovations?" Lilly Victoria suggested. "He did a wonderful job on bringing our cottage up to a very high standard, along with another we wanted doing for some of our workers to be able to enjoy a higher standard of living. And may I add that I think Poppy's idea is a wonderful one. I may even be invited to the occasional event?"

This wasn't necessarily the result that Poppy had expected. She had felt there might be a lukewarm reception to her suggestions at best, and she hadn't expected Grandpa Ross to be the one to jump on board as quickly as he had. She couldn't wait to tell Florence about the success of the ideas they had been throwing about for months.

"How is George these days?" Poppy's Uncle Ross asked, a naughty glint in his eye. "Do you still have ideas about marrying him one day?"

"Ross!" Nell interrupted. "You can't ask her such a thing!"

"It's all right, Nanny," Poppy returned with a benign smile. "The simple answer is that he hasn't asked me – yet, and I do believe that he might have his eye on my friend Annabel. We are only eighteen, Nanny, don't forget, and we have a lot to do, and hopefully to achieve, before marriage and the thoughts of raising families enter our heads."

"By 'we' you mean?" Uncle Ross asked.

"Florence and me," Poppy insisted with a nod. "We are going to be famous one day."

"I don't believe it!" Florence whooped, skipping around the living room at Boulders Wood. "Our own place to do as we wish?"

"And Grandpa Ross is going to sponsor us," Poppy explained, excitement glowing in her face. "That means he has agreed to pay for it all and provide the money for us to sustain what we will plan. For that to happen, of course, there is the small matter of permission from your parents. Is there any chance that they may not allow it?"

"They will have no choice, my dear," Florence insisted defiantly. "I will make my own decision about my fate, I'll have you know. As long as your Nanny and Grandpa Ross have no objections, I see no reason not to go ahead."

"We will at least have to mention it to them, and agree for you to see them regularly," Poppy suggested. "Will they be all right with that, Florence?"

"We'll soon see, won't we?" her friend said. "I'll speak to them tonight."

"The project will go ahead, whatever anyone else says," Poppy was adamant in her answer. "If they put any barriers in your – our – path, we'll need to find ways around them. But it *will* happen. Agreed?"

"Most definitely!" Florence replied firmly. "Can't wait. In the meantime, plans? Are we to involve our lovely man, George?"

"What would you say?" Poppy asked. "Do you think he might be … interested?"

"I should imagine so," Florence said quite convinced there wouldn't be a problem with their favourite young man. "After all, we *do* love him, don't we? And he loves us too, undoubtedly."

"Assuredly," Poppy answered quietly, a faraway glimmer in her face. "What if he – dare I say it? – wanted only *one* of us? What would we do?"

"Couldn't we … share him?" Florence suggested slowly, a wicked glint in her eye.

Poppy giggled, a pink flush growing in her face at the thought.

CHAPTER 2

"I really can't believe it!" Mary said to her husband, Geoffrey, as they locked up Mary's Pantry ready to make their way home after another record-breaking sales week. There seemed to be no end to the very high demand for Mary's wonderful baking. From mid-morning opening time to late-afternoon closing, the queues were never ending, obliging them to bake more so as not to send away any of her customers disappointed. "The more we bake, the more we sell."

"I don't really think it's anything to do with 'we'," he replied, trying to lock the back door before heading down the dark snicket to the main street. "It's more to do with—"

Stopped in his tracks by a blow to the back of the head and an arm around his neck and throat, instinctively he stamped hard on his attacker's foot with the hob-nailed boots he always wore. This drew a sharp screech of pain from his attacker, who loosened his grasp enough for Geoffrey to turn quickly and kick him in the groin. This put him on the floor writhing in agony.

The second of the two assailants grabbed for the bag Geoffrey was carrying over his shoulder. Two snips from a sharp knife and the shoulder bag and its snatcher disappeared into the gloom, but not before Mary had inflicted a hefty blow to his face from her umbrella's sharp and knotty handle.

"Are you all right, Geoffrey?" Mary asked, grasping his arm desperately to save him from dropping to the floor.

"I'm fine, my lovely lady," he replied. "But my bag is gone."

By this time, because the main street was still relatively busy and their carriage driver had been waiting for them at the front of the shop, several people had heard the commotion and rushed to their aid. The original attacker was unconscious, curled into a ball clutching his groin, with three burly men watching guard until someone summoned the police.

⁓

"So, two attackers did you say?" Detective Fred Shaw asked as he scribbled slowly into his police-issue notepad. "The one we have in the cells, and another that made off with your bag, Mr Greenstreet?"

"Yes, two it was," Mary's husband agreed. "I—"

"There was another," Mary butted in with an assured nod.

Both men turned slowly towards her, puzzled looks from one face to the other.

"Another one, you say?" the policeman said, not quite sure what to believe. "Did you get a look at him?"

"I not only saw him," Mary replied, sure of what she saw. "I recognised him immediately."

"In that dark alley?" Geoffrey gasped. "I didn't even have time to warn you!"

"Do you know his name?" the police sergeant urged.

"Indeed, I do," she said. "He is my former employer's nephew – well, the son of her niece, really. Jonas Jamieson."

"Are you sure, my dear?" her husband asked carefully.

"As sure as you are standing there," Mary insisted. "He was hiding in the shadows behind some dustbins, trying not to be seen as he directed the two other thugs to do his dirty work."

"And what did the other thug that got away steal from you?" the policeman said. "Your day's takings?"

"Not at all!" she assured him. "I have the takings here." She patted the black bag by her side with a triumphant smile. They had known for some time that other traders had been robbed, and so had been forced to take precautions.

"What was in the bag that was taken, then?" Sergeant Shaw asked, scratching his head, not quite understanding what to believe.

"Some paperwork, a sixpence piece and a couple of thruppenny bits," Geoffrey answered. "Nothing that can't be replaced. I can't see them living it up on that sort of money, Can you?"

~

"Jonas? A thief and a thug?" Florence gasped when Poppy had told her Nanny Nell's news. "But then what else could anyone have expected, given his performance when we were sixteen? Has anyone seen him since his attack on us?"

"Not that I'm aware of," Poppy said. "It gives me the shivers. I do wish we still had our protector, George Garside. I feel incredibly safe when he's around us. Is there any truth in the rumour that he's smitten with Annabel, do you think?"

"I think it's just that … a rumour," Florence replied casually. "You know how these things become *de rigeur* when there is not a grain of truth in them. I believe *we* are the only ones he thinks and feels about."

"What would *you* say if he were to ask you … you know?" Poppy asked almost in a croaky, embarrassed whisper.

"If I get Moma and Popa's blessing for our … project, we will have a lot to plan and to look forward to," Florence said, embarrassed by the thought and trying to ignore Poppy's question. "I – we – have always loved Our George and always will, but we have a lot to look forward to. Don't you think?

"When will the cottage be finished?" she went on after a moment or two of silence allowed them to clear such divisive thoughts from their mind.

"Probably four or five weeks, I am told," Poppy answered, clearing her embarrassed throat. "Though with what we need to be done, I think it will take quite a lot longer. So, you will be staying in the main house – with your own bedroom – and we will be able to do our reading and writing in the back room. You know, where the fire started all those years ago after that first Christmas that we met."

"Wasn't that going to be a preparation room for the kitchen staff?" Florence queried.

"It's been a study sort of a room for me since then," her friend added. "And now that Nanny and Grandpa Ross's main home is in Richmond, I have its sole use. Not as good or as spacious as our new one will be, but useful, nonetheless. Uncle Ross brought it up to liveable standard, although I am sure I can catch the occasional slight whiff of smoke."

"What do you think Jonas's mother, Louisa, and father, Ernest, will do about him now that he has become a thief and a violent thug?" Florence asked, not sure really why she had become interested.

"His mama would forgive him in an instant," Poppy said. "His father, on the other hand, would pitch him out of the family with no compunction, cutting him off without a further thought for forcing the family to endure such abominable disgrace."

"Why are your nanny and grandpa staying here when they have a wonderful, expensive home in Richmond?" Florence asked while her friend made them a cup of tea.

"They are here to help with Uncle Ross's wife Martha's confinement," Poppy replied. "Apparently, she is very close to delivery and having problems and a lot of discomfort. God, please spare me from ever expecting a child!"

***

"Ross!" Nell called urgently from the landing at the top of the staircase as her son bustled in through the front door. "Fetch the doctor! Quickly!"

He turned on his heel and raced out to take the little trap to find Dr Twist's whereabouts. He had been warned about the difficulties Martha was experiencing, and so he would be ready in the blink of an eye, particularly as Ross would have transport ready to bring him.

Ever since Ross and Martha had realised they were expecting, joy and delight had guided their path. Although still a fanciful dream, the thoughts of real parenthood with their own children was beginning to set the nerves dancing and reality to nudge worries into life. The problems with the birth were doing nothing to alleviate those worries.

"It's all right, Ross," Dr Twist tried to reassure him on their rather swift journey back to Boulders Wood. "Often the first child can present certain … difficulties. I'm sure we'll be able to sort it out when we arrive. Can you please make sure that all the necessaries are to hand for when they are needed?"

"My mother and sister-in-law are there already and they—" Ross answered, rather flustered.

"I know," the doctor smiled. "Don't forget that I delivered all your mother's children and grandchildren – save one – and those of your brother and his wife. So, I know your family history well. I'm sure everything will be as it should be."

The noisy approach up the driveway to the house was greeted by Joseph in the doorway who disappeared sharply inside, no doubt to alert the womenfolk of the arrival of reinforcements.

Dr Twist leapt deftly from the trap and made his noisy way to the sitting room and its welcoming, roaring fire. Significant changes had been wrought to the inside of the confusing edifice since he was here last. The walls had experienced a lick of paint and the furniture had been changed, or had it simply been rearranged? No matter. The state of the inner décor would have no bearing on the task ahead, making sure a new soul's arrival into this cold and sometimes unfriendly world would be as easy and painless as possible.

"Dr Twist—?" Ross asked the medic as he made his way upstairs.

"Don't worry, Ross. Everything will be just fine," he reassured the young man. "I would love a cup of tea in ten minutes or so, if you please. Just bring it upstairs and leave it outside the bedroom door."

Ross turned towards his brother as the bedroom door clicked shut at Dr Twist's passing. "It's just that—" he began.

"I know, I know," Joseph soothed, a reassuring hand on his brother's shoulder. "Pray to God, trust in t'medic, and it'll be all rayt. Cup o' tea, he said? I'll have one as well. It'll gi' thee summat to do to tek thi mind off things."

Ross opened his mouth but said nothing, turning on his heels as he headed for the kitchen ready to ask Mary's niece, Mary-Jane, if she'd mind drumming up tea and a scone or two for them.

As Ross reached the head of the stairs with a tray, a loud

pain-induced scream stopped him dead in his tracks. Not knowing why, his immediate reaction was to lurch for the bedroom door, but he held in check his urge to burst through into the room to make sure the love of his life was safe.

Suddenly the door creaked open to reveal Dr Twist, whose ample frame allowed Ross to see nothing beyond the threshold. The doctor relieved Ross of his tray and, with a nod and a brief smile, he closed the door behind him as he re-entered the room. Ross waited for a few moments before regaining the stairs. It just wasn't done for a prospective father to force his way into the birthing room, not even for a self-confident young man like him. He would follow protocol and regain the lounge, to pace back and forth until summoned, as all imminent fathers had done before him.

"Our twins took hours and hours to enter this world," Joseph said quietly, with a frown designed to cause concern in his brother. "I've been told since that it's quite usual for a first child to take its time to arrive. Our next took less than half as long. Don't concern yourself, Brother. Your next bairn won't hang about, I'm sure."

"Who says we're off to have any more?" Ross gabbled, panic rising in his throat, convinced that this would be the first and only child to join them. Those feelings were the ones to overwhelm Joseph when *he* heard Lilly Victoria's discomfort at the twins' arrival. And now…?

Hearing heavy steps coming down the creaking stairs, Ross jumped nervously to his feet to catch the stout body of Dr Twist just around the bottom Newell post. "Doctor?" he asked. "Is she … all right?"

"They are *both* all right," he replied with a smile. "Both your wife and your *daughter* are doing fine."

Three steps at one go up the stairs took Ross to the bedroom door in double-quick time. Knocking gently on the door, he was greeted with, "Come in … Daddy," from his mother.

Propped up in bed, looking very tired and with a suckling infant at her breast, was his lovely wife, Martha.

"My darling, thank you," he cooed softly as he slipped his loving arm around her shoulders, kissing the infant's sparsely covered scalp as he did so.

"Meet our Annie," Martha replied, turning to face him with difficulty and in more than a little discomfort.

~⁓~

"Surely she was a close friend of yours from long ago," Tommy Spence complained bitterly to his mother. "I came back from London to set up my medical practice specifically with taking up with Annie in mind, as we always said we would."

"You can't blame anyone but yourself for that, my boy!" his father pointed out. "Don't forget that we knew nothing about your 'relationship' with the girl. Let alone making her pregnant."

"Couldn't you at least have written to me, Mother?" Tommy went on, ignoring what his father had said.

"A number of young people of your age have died since you were away," his mother replied, indignant at her son's intractable and inexcusably rude tirade. "Some of them were girls. Did you want us to write to you about all of those, too?"

"I truly loved Annie McIntyre," Tommy admitted, his tone significantly quieter. "I thought you might have guessed, once you had heard. How long had you known and been associated with her mother…?"

"I assume that's a rhetorical question," his father retorted sharply. "Anyway, had we known, telling you would have ruined the rest of your life and—"

"I'm not listening to this trite gibberish!" Tommy said tersely as he made for the door. "One day you may understand."

"Wrong thing to say, Husband," Josie Spence spat at Tommy's father.

"Well, *did* you know about this whole sordid affair?" he snapped.

"Of course I didn't!" she scoffed. "Why would I? However, I was able to hazard an educated guess when I heard Annie had conceived."

"And how could you have made *that* sort of a guess when you had no idea they were seeing each other?" he sneered, a derisory grin twitching his mouth corners.

"Call it mother's intuition," she replied. "Something *you'll* never understand."

"How come *we* never knew anything about this … this affair, Josie?" Nell asked of Josie Spence, her friend of many years. "And Sally Smallshore? Who is *she*?"

"According to my son, Tommy, she was Annie's best – only – friend," Josie replied. "I've only just found out about the whole business recently."

"Then tell me again," Nell suggested as she poured another cup of tea and took one of her legendary buttered scones she had brought with her.

"Sally Smallshore was a friend to both my Tommy and your Annie, and confidante to your daughter," Josie stated. "According to Tommy, she acted as go-between in their – what shall we call it? – their relationship. He is also adamant that Annie had agreed to marry him when they were old enough."

"That doesn't surprise me at all," Nell said. "She was something of a secretive and disobedient young lady. Had her father known about her activities, he would have stopped her … physically."

The rattle of the front door's latch paused their conversation as Josie's son entered his mother's front room.

"Talk of the devil," Josie said with a smile. "This is my son, Tommy, who is a doctor in his own practice here in Richmond."

"Mother. Mrs McIntyre," the chap said as he greeted the two friends.

"Pleased to meet you Tommy," Nell said as she shook his hand. "And it's now 'Booth'. I married *my* childhood sweetheart not that long ago, after decades apart. We were talking about—"

"My Annie," Tommy said, his getting on for three decades of sadness still weighing down his shoulders. "She was all *I* ever wanted, and I think she felt the same about me."

"Tell me then, young man, what happened on that fateful night, the morning after which we found her injured and delirious," Nell urged. "Did you know she was with child?"

"That I *didn't* know!" he replied adamantly, a look of shock all but corroborating his words. "We had made love – for the first time, I hasten to add – because I had told her that my mother and father had decided to send me away to stay with my Aunt Joan in London so I might study medicine at the appropriate time at London University. I didn't want to go, but I couldn't really refuse. We promised to write to each other, but, although I wrote to her every week, I received no replies."

"I can assure you that she never received *any* letters," Nell said with a frown. "Did you send them to Boulders Wood?"

"Sally agreed to receive them and pass them on to Annie," he replied, "and then give the replies to her to send on. Sixty letters I wrote in that first year or so – at least one every week.

24

I realised to my eternal sadness that she had probably cooled and found someone else to distract her."

"Tommy!" his mother hissed, warning him that *that* was not an appropriate emotion to share, particularly with the girl's mother, who had been *her* friend since teenage.

"I'm sorry Mrs Booth, but my agreeing to do the university bit was a means of setting our futures together – for me to be accepted by you and Annie's father," Tommy said sadly. "As Annie was all I had ever wanted, two wishes only remain in my life."

"Do we know the whereabouts of Sally Smallshore?" Nell asked keenly. "She is the only one that may be able to stitch even a modicum of truth to this story. We have no other 'truth' we may rely on – other than your Tommy's version of events."

"The only two things clear in my mind that will never leave me until my dying day are why I didn't insist on accompanying Annie at least to within sight of the front door of Boulders Wood, although I did understand that she was afraid her father might see us," Tommy went on. "My other dearest wish would be to become acquainted with my … daughter."

Josie had been a close friend for more years than Nell could bring to mind, and she had always been thrilled for Nell's happiness at finding her one true love from more than thirty years earlier. Wasn't this just one of those sad but joyous happenings that she *should* support? Yet, why did she hesitate? Was she afraid she might lose the one force of nature that had kept her sane for sixteen or more years? Perhaps…

"The only person to be able to grant you peace, Tommy, is Poppy," Nell said quietly. "Talking to her is all I can promise."

CHAPTER 3

"Nanny?" Poppy asked quietly as she waited for breakfast the Saturday morning after Josie and Tommy's visit.

"Yes, my sweet child?" Nell replied. "What are you needing now? Your cottage will be ready when it's … ready."

"It wasn't that, really," her granddaughter said with a mild frown. "I know I've asked you this before – a million times – but do you think there might be the slightest of chances that we – you and Grandpa Ross – might discover the whereabouts of my—?"

"I can't promise you anything, and I don't want to get your hopes up—" Nell said slowly.

"You've found him!" Poppy gasped, jiggling her feet in excitement. "*Have* you found him?"

"Not sure," Nanny Booth replied. "We have one or two possibilities that need to be explored more fully. I can't promise anything, and our investigations might prove to be inconclusive. I don't want you to be disappointed."

"But disappointed about what, Nanny?" Poppy prodded, hoping her Nanny would repent.

"Well—" she started, but was interrupted by raised voices at the front door. The door crashed open with Uncle Ross restraining a young man in his mid-thirties.

"And I say you will not!" Ross's cross voice shouted down the young man that he had hold of, preventing him from entering the front sitting room. "This is my home, and you will enter when I say you can."

"I have a right to see my own flesh and blood!" the young man urged. "Unhand me, sir, and please let me—"

"Allow him to come in, please, Ross," Nell said quietly.

"What have we here then?" Ross insisted. "Another ne'er-do-well literary layabout that needs to return in a month or two when Poppy's cottage is ready? You know my feelings about these Tom Noddies that—"

"Poppy?" the newcomer said quietly, running out of aggression like a rapidly deflating balloon. "Did you say … Poppy?"

"Who is this, Nanny Nell?" Poppy asked, unsure of what had just happened.

"Do you remember your question that we've not been able to answer yet?" Nell tried to explain.

"About my … father?" Poppy replied slowly, as she cast apprehensive glances from her uncle to nanny. "And what has this gentleman to do with that?"

"This is Tommy, Tommy Spence," Nell explained. "He is a doctor and the son of one of my closest friends since my teenage years. We met for the first time since that time just over a week ago."

"What, pray, has this to do with me, Nanny?" her granddaughter asked tentatively, not sure what to expect.

"Your Grandpa Ross and I believe he could be – only *could* be, mind – your father," Nell explained, almost under her breath.

Poppy almost stopped breathing with tears threatening to fill her eyes, unable to comprehend what had just happened. Backing out of the room slowly, confusion rising in her face, she turned sharply and rushed into the downstairs back room, slamming the door as she disappeared.

"I—" Tommy stammered.

"You need to go, young man," Ross growled at him, forcibly turning him towards the outside door.

"Call back in two days, Tommy," Nell said as he turned to escape. "We'll sort out our next steps before then."

"What was all that about, Mother?" Ross said, not believing what had happened. "Who is this 'Tommy' character?"

"You didn't catch that he's claiming to be Poppy's father?" Nell asked, an unusually sarcastic vein slipping into the conversation.

"I did, but I dismissed the claim as preposterous," Ross replied with a sigh. "We have no probable cause to believe that. Our Annie never went out, so she can't have had even female friends, let alone boyfriends."

"Then how was it you found her outside, unconscious, early that fateful morning, in that dreadful state?" Nell said sharply. "And who knows how many times she had done that before? You knew our Annie as well as I did."

Ross sat back with his cup of tea, a faraway look in his eyes, running over that fateful night in his head, as he had done so many times before.

"There has to be a father … somewhere," Nell went on, almost to herself. "Otherwise, how would Poppy be here? Magic?"

"There is no way this … this Tommy can prove his

involvement in her conception," Ross argued.

"Other than by the say-so of others that knew at the time," Nell offered. "It seems that Annie's only friend can offer second-hand 'evidence', I am told. She is called Sally Smallshore."

"Smallshore?" Ross gasped disbelievingly. "Not Jim Smallshore's daughter?"

"I don't follow," Nell puzzled. "You know of them?"

"Jim Smallshore and his wife, Joan, had a daughter of about Annie's age," Ross explained. "They worked for us and lived in the very cottage we are refurbishing for Poppy's literary gatherings. They left – Jim and his daughter – shortly after Poppy was born, after the death of his wife. They went to live in a little town not too far away. Guisborough, I think it was. Not that far from Saltburn-by-the-Sea."

"But that's one of the seaside places we visited with Poppy and her friends on the twelfth anniversary of her birthday, all those years ago," Nell gasped. "The point now, of course, is whether Sally is still alive?"

"Or even, does she still live in the area?" Ross added. "Perhaps I need to make a few enquiries?"

"Hello, Poppy my sweet girl," Nell said as she turned at the creaking hinges of the back-room door. "Coming in to join us? Cup of tea?"

"Are you all right?" her Uncle Ross asked, as Poppy sat by him a look of confusion still sitting in her eyes. "We were just talking about you and—"

"Has he gone?" Poppy replied, ignoring all her nanny and uncle had said in their attempt to engage her. "That … person – Tommy?"

"Yes, my lovely, he has," Nell said carefully. "We are about to make further enquiries in an attempt to uncover the truth."

"Not sure that I want to know the … truth," Poppy

muttered uncomfortably. "How could it possibly make any difference to me now?"

"To be honest, little one, it's been a truth *you've* wanted to uncover for at least the last decade," Ross added carefully with a benign smile. "However, we will abide by your decision as to whether you would like us to pursue enquiries or … not. All right?"

Poppy sat in thought for a while, eyes flicking from side to side in utter confusion until she burst out passionately, "Yes!… No!… I *don't know*, Unca Ross!"

Covering her face, she burst into a heartfelt bout of frustrated sobbing, unsure what she wanted to do. Ross slid his arm around her shoulders and drew her mildly resisting body to his. This is what she needed – understanding support in her hour of desperate need.

A creaking of the stairs drew their attention to Martha's unsteady form descending to them, a muling and puking infant shrouded in swaddling clothes clutched to her bosom. Ross leaped to her and immediately his loving arms wrapped urgently around them both.

The effect on Poppy was startling. A smile lit her face as she extended her arms in the hope of welcoming little Annie into *her* world. As soon as the baby entered her arms, she fell silent as if a button had been depressed, looking up at Poppy with awe in her eyes.

"I've made up my mind," Poppy declared bravely as she nursed her mother's namesake. "I should like to find out about my father once and for all. I think we both owe it to each other, no matter the circumstance of how we came about."

In the following days, because Poppy's close confidante,

Florence, was away with her parents visiting relatives, Poppy spent much of her days either writing or nursing and walking Baby Annie. She could spend only as much time outside as the North's doubtful weather would allow. She crunched the noisy driveway and skirted the large lily pond in her joyously safe circuits, nursing, rocking and holding one-sided conversations with her tiny cousin. She was, however, unaware of the malevolent and lascivious eyes set on her every step from forest eaves on the ridge on the near horizon above Boulders Wood.

She still awoke occasionally in the early hours, the revulsion of those leering eyes she had encountered an age ago but a blink away from hers, choking her as she started from her sleep. That was not an experience she wanted to live through again. She would always worship George Garside for his timely rescue.

George? Why hadn't she seen him for more than … two weeks? Was he working so hard on his father's farm, or had he discovered a new love in his life? That *latter* observation consumed her with loathing and jealousy; to think after all they had been through, *that* could be a real possibility. No, surely, not he…

"Good afternoon, Poppy," a deep, resonant male voice, dear to her heart and entrenched at the very centre of her being, washed over her. She turned sharply to see her ideal man.

"George!" she gasped. "You startled me. I – we – haven't seen you for an age. Are you well?"

"Indeed, lovely lady, I am," he replied with an easy smile. "You're not—?"

"Most definitely not!" she urged, a pink suffusion colouring her face. "This is Annie – Uncle Ross and Auntie Martha's new baby. Just giving her some exercise and attention."

"No Florence today?" he asked.

"Afraid not," she replied. "Family business, I fear. Always a nuisance when it interferes with more important … things."

"Are you still … writing?" he asked pointedly. "I don't seem to have been asked around to see 'my girls' for quite some time. Boyfriends a-calling, eh?"

"Not really," she answered cautiously, a tremulous catch in her throat betraying how she felt about him. "Just … busy. You?"

"Farming, morning to night, really," he said slowly. Their stilted conversation was leading them nowhere. How things had altered since their halcyon days when they were young teenagers and they spent most of each day in each other's company!

"Did I hear that you and Annabel had become – what shall we say – 'friends'?" she asked carefully, not wanting to have some unsought truth jump out at her.

"Since you ask," he explained, "I wanted to tell you that I have asked her out, with her father's permission, of course."

"And?" Poppy asked, desperately not wanting to hear his answer.

"She has agreed," he went on. "Time to be set. To be honest, you and Florence seem to have become so engrossed with your 'literary' stuff that there is no room for the likes of your erstwhile friend – namely … me."

"Oh," she gasped, unable to grasp what she was hearing. George? With someone else? And to cap it all, someone that was one of her reasonably close friends.

"I am obviously not able to have either you or Florence – both of whom I have secretly loved dearly," he went on, slightly embarrassed. "Annabel was willing so … Got to go. Another field to plough."

Utterly dumbfounded, she could not even iterate her

feelings for him as his broad, muscular back disappeared around the corner of the closest cowshed. Now what had she done? Her George in the arms of someone else! Life didn't get any worse!

~

"So, young man – Tommy, isn't it?" Ross Senior said, as his young visitor sat in the high-backed armchair near the sitting room's great oak table. "We have asked you back to discuss your claim to be our Poppy's father."

"Yes, sir," the young man replied. "All I want is to become part of my daughter's life. I would have loved dearly for it to have been Poppy *and* her mother but…"

"We have contacts that might prove to be fruitful in the long term," Ross continued. "But that might take some time. Although I understand your urgency, you will have to be patient, and abide by Poppy's view and decision. She is a young lady of real quality and firmly held opinions who will not relinquish her status quo on any account. If it were to be proven as far as possible that there is a possibility that you *are* related, you would need to plead your case with her. Her word would be final, you understand."

"I understand what you are saying, Mr Booth," Tommy Spence replied, resigned to the stated rules. "And I agree – but would it not be possible to speak to her, in your company, of course?"

"Not yet," Nell butted in adamantly. "Once it has been established beyond reasonable doubt in the circumstances, we will ask Poppy *if* she would like to speak to you. As my husband has said, the last word is hers alone. We'll let you know in due course, Mr Spence. Good day."

The day was sunny, if a little breezy, but fresh enough to

expel any doubts as to the next steps. Why was it that he had the feeling that he had just undergone a sharp cross-examination with him well and truly in the hot seat? Still, there was nothing he could do about it but hope they would come up with irrefutable proof that he was indeed *this* young lady's sire. When that happened, he would be able to relax and try to enjoy the years left with his daughter – if she wanted to spend them with him.

"Seems genuine," Ross Senior observed once the slam of the outside door had stopped reverberating throughout the ground floor. "At least, I feel he believes his convictions."

"Not sure yet," Nell pondered. "He *seems* genuine, but there are doubts in my mind. Why isn't he married with children? Thirty-two or thirty-three should be an ideal age to have bairns, but—"

"Not found the right girl?" he offered. "After all, I gather Annie would have been a hard act to follow."

"Maybe," she said, "but he only got to know about Annie relatively recently. So, why hasn't he found anyone else? He is quite a good-looking chap, and he is a doctor. Surely he couldn't have held a candle for her all this time? Why didn't he seek her out once he had qualified and left university? Something doesn't resonate truly here."

"*I* did, my lovely," Ross replied bluntly with a slight tilt of his head. "And mine was thirty years or more."

Nell fell into a reminiscent silence, shuddering almost imperceptibly with thoughts of those times crashing about in her head. Since Ross had strode back into her life, she had come to realise that she couldn't have carried on with Joss. But what would she have done? It didn't bear thinking about.

CHAPTER 4

"How do you mean lost him?" Florence burst out forcibly. "And Annabel? How could we have allowed her to get her inept claws into him? He's ours, Poppy, and always has been."

"Not any more, my dear friend," Poppy urged. "I have it on good authority that she is – what is the blessed word? – smitten with him."

"We'll see about that," Florence sneered almost under her breath. "Our George needs to be brought back into *our* fold, and quickly. Is our Wuthering Heights anywhere close to completion yet?"

"I have been told by Uncle Albert – Lilly Victoria's stone-mason cousin, you know, the one that refurbished *their* cottage – that our cottage will be ready in two weeks," Poppy explained. "*Then* we can start to show the literary world what we are made of."

"Our first guest will be—" Florence suggested with a demure smile.

"George Garside!" they chorused, dissolving into helpless

giggles as they collapsed into their one acquisition towards their literary refuge – a settee.

"On his own, so we can explore the full extent of our 'project'," Florence sniggered quietly.

"Naughty!" Poppy replied with an understanding smile.

"How are we going to decorate and furnish, do you think?" Florence asked. "As authentically literary as possible, in my view."

"Think of the houses we have read about in our favourite writings, and we'll try to use as many ideas as possible, don't you think?" Poppy suggested. "Most of them seem to be dark inside, with sumptuous furniture and—"

"Won't that be … expensive?" her friend interrupted. "I have very little—"

"Grandpa Ross has given us virtual *carte blanche* as far as setting up is concerned – as long as we don't break the bank," Poppy assured her. "We have to be careful not to appear to be either living below or above our position as far as furnishings and furniture are concerned. In Mr Charles Dickens' *Our Mutual Friend*, one of the characters said that because he had acquired a reasonable fortune, it would be proper to do what was right by that fortune, to be acted upon reasonably quickly.

"We are not *vastly* rich, so I think middle of the road would be the best way forward," she added after a moment's pause.

"Employing an interior designer, perhaps?" Florence suggested.

"A good idea, methinks," Poppy agreed. "Perhaps also taking hints from some of the literary houses we have visited over the last year or two?"

"Do you think that it might be an idea to find out who are the prominent writers that live in these parts?" Florence replied.

"A letter in *The Times* might be a good idea for that one," a deep male voice joined their conversation.

"Grandpa Ross!" Poppy said with joy, although startled to hear him so close by.

"But we don't know anybody at such an august newspaper," Florence groaned. "Or even at one of our local ones."

"Maybe not but I … do – at both," Grandpa Ross explained. "How about if I drop a line to my contacts at *The Times*, and the *Darlington and Stockton Times, The Newcastle Guardian,* and the *Durham Chronicle*?"

"Goodness!" Florence gasped. "That would be wonderful. It all now depends on dates and times, I suppose."

"They'll want to interview you both, so you ought to be prepared well in advance," Ross advised. "A written piece ready, perhaps?"

"We shall get on to it today, Grandpa," Poppy said, clapping her hands excitedly. This was wonderful, and something she had not expected. What was to be next? Fame? Fortune?

Recognition for their skills as both writers and social beings was all they desired, purveyors of strong literary culture in an area that was devoid and sterile. Their society needed their new and exciting approach, drawing in like-minded young people who wanted to improve their outlook on life with thoughts, feelings and intellect that needed to grow.

"Something I didn't tell you about when George called a while ago," Poppy said to her confidante, Florence, as they sat sipping tea as if it were too hot for the mouth and absent-mindedly nibbling on biscuits. Grandpa Ross had left them alone.

"George? *Our* George?" Florence asked, trying to seem nonchalant about this new revelation when the sheer mention of his name brought excited goose pimples to her flesh. "What might that have been that needs to be brought up now?"

"He intimated that he had always *loved* us – both," Poppy

explained. "And now that we had become engrossed with our literary intrigues, we seem to have shut him out. I was dumb-founded and horrified to think that he considered we didn't want him with us any more."

"My God! That's desperately upsetting!" Florence gasped. "A world without *our* George! Can I assume that *that* is the reason he's taken up with that … that hussy, Annabel?"

"Indeed," Poppy agreed. "We have to *do* something to rescue him from her desperate clutches. What if we…?"

~

"Oh, is that my husband, Joseph McIntyre, I see creeping through our bedroom door?" Lilly Victoria said sarcastically. "Not seen you close up for an almightily long time."

"There's no need to be sarcastic, Lilly Victoria," he replied, flopping on the bed next to her, an exhausted sigh escaping his lips. "I have been up since dawn and now it's about seven o'clock."

"Try *nine* o'clock, Husband," she emphasised disapprovingly. "How long do you think this state of affairs has been going on?"

"I don't know," he sighed, his eyes closing with utter fatigue. "Don't forget that I haven't had a break for some months now, and—"

"Don't forget that we haven't even been *pretending* to be husband and wife either, for virtually that length of time," she said, ire rising in her throat, and a caustic edge betraying her sadness. "You are close to me only when we are asleep, and you never pay any attention to our children either."

Joseph fell silent, eyes closed, dangerously close to uncon-sciousness as he struggled to stay awake. What had this life brought him to? Little did he know that Tom's near-death encounter through his heart attack would plunge Joseph into such a maelstrom of overwork and mind-numbing exhaustion.

"I can only … say that … I'm sorry … Lilly Victoria," Joseph gasped in his now vain attempt to stay awake. "We never could have foreseen Tom's demise. I *had* to take ower completely or we would have gone under significantly."

"I suppose," Lilly Victoria replied with a non-committal shrug. "But why didn't you employ somebody like Annabel and Alice's father, who has been with us for many years? Anybody to give us a break – together. Your own children are beginning to forget who you are and no longer enjoy the times we *used* to share."

"Then what am I supposed to do?" he pleaded.

"Employ someone who can help until Tom is able to take up his duties once again," she suggested simply. "Somebody who you can trust to allow you a break from the monotony of perpetual work and tiredness."

"And if I can't – don't?" he asked pointedly.

"We won't be around long enough for you to find out," she stated bluntly, to his stunned silence. Concerned that she had been too harsh, she looked over at him to find that his eyes were fast shut and he was breathing slowly and deeply. He had succumbed finally to an exhaustion-induced, profound sleep that his brain wouldn't relinquish for several hours.

What had she done? Had she been too harsh with him, this man whom she adored? She knew that he had been thrust into an impossible position following his business partner's demise. However, even before Tom Garside had fallen ill, she had recognised the signs of Joseph's immersion in his work – at the expense of their family life. She needed to start setting ground rules to save their life together! Where would she be, and what would she do otherwise? A curse on the circumstances that had brought them to this!

"John Stafford," Ross said, as he and his brother sat with a mug of tea and a home-baked buttered scone on one of their very rare breaks from their daily chores running a busy farm. "He is semi-retired but is one of the best herdsmen around, with forty years' experience second to none. I also believe his knowledge of dairy cannot be rivalled."

"What's wrong with our existing workforce?" Joseph replied, puzzled why Ross hadn't approached them first.

"Not interested," Ross explained.

"Not interested?" Joseph gasped, not able to believe what he was hearing. "A golden opportunity, I should have thought. What—?"

"Family commitments, they all say," Ross grumbled. "Though I believe it *is* to do with money – not enough offered for the responsibility and the extra time they would be working."

"What's the matter wi' 'em *all* these days?" Joseph snarled.

"Perhaps they look at you and don't want to be dragged into doing nothing but work all day and every day," Ross offered. "They don't own a farm like you do. Can't blame 'em really, I suppose. Even I don't spend enough time with *my* wife and child, and I don't do anywhere as much as you do. You need to be very careful. Tom is a prize case of how careful you have to be. How does Lilly Victoria take your eternal absence from the family hearth? I would say that she is astoundingly patient but long suffering."

"Thanks, Brother!" Joseph tutted disappointedly. "But you are right in your thinking, of course. Do you know, I fell asleep the other night while she was telling me how upset she was that our family was non-functional. I didn't hear the last part of what she threatened, and she refuses to repeat it."

"Threatened?" Ross gasped. "Then you must do something about it!"

"If I don't know the substance of what's upsetting her, how can I possibly respond to it?" Joseph complained lamely. Positive thinking had never been his forte.

"You'll need to explore what you must do as a matter of importance, old chap," Ross urged. "Surely you'll be able to hit on a solution of some sort, even if it becomes short-lived. If you don't, you could find yourself without a wife and family."

"Where could she possibly go?" Joseph scoffed, unable to comprehend what his brother was suggesting. "Surely a wife's place is by her husband's side, and—"

"A wife is probably the most important element in any marriage," Ross insisted. "Particularly one like Lilly Victoria. She has had a lot to put up with in the time you have been married. Besides, she has her parents' place close by she could go to, hopefully to nudge you to do the right thing."

"But how can we get workers to *want* to come to us?" Joseph replied, his ample shoulders slumping in abject resignation.

"Up the financial offer, perhaps?" Ross suggested with a resigned shrug. "By a small but significant amount. You could even encourage John Stafford to stay on a part-time basis. Something to think about?"

"We have always been interested in literature," Poppy replied to the local newspaper reporter's question.

"By literature, do you mean children's stories by Beatrix Potter … and the like?" he asked rather dismissively, a smirk on his face.

"No," Poppy said sharply. "I had already started reading the Brontës, George Eliot, Louis Carroll, Charles Dickens and Robert Louis Stephenson by the time I was twelve. My friend, Florence, and I want to share our love of such esteemed writers with other like-minded young people."

"But why this and why now … Florence, is it?" he asked, displaying no real interest or understanding of such elevated concepts as 'literary appreciation' or 'the love of non-everyday expression' or 'intellectual understanding'.

"You don't really expect me to explain our innermost thoughts and feelings for something that is essentially and intrinsically personal, do you?" Florence said calmly but with a degree of sharp scepticism he would neither have expected nor would understand. "Well, do you?"

"Well, er, I just wanted to try to find out—" he stammered, set back on his heels.

"If we are real?" Poppy butted in. "Sorry – Mr Smith, is it? – this is not what we wanted at all. We will have to leave you now, as we have a real reporter from *The Times* coming to see us later this afternoon at Mary's Pantry round the corner. Thank you for your time."

The door of the newspaper's front reception slammed shut as the friends took their leave of one dumbfounded and stunned provincial newspaper reporter who had no idea what had just befallen him.

"Not quite what we either expected or needed, Florence, dear," Poppy said with a shrug.

"I hope the lady from *The Times* fares better this afternoon," Florence sighed, a look of disappointment dancing in her eyes. "Will everybody think of us as that … that buffoon just did?"

"He's probably reasonably fine at reporting on lost pets

or Friday night disturbances outside the local hostelry or the twins Mrs Goodwin has just delivered," Poppy added. "But nothing that needs a degree of intellect or understanding about or feeling for the written word."

~

Mary's Pantry was busy, with a significant queue formed for a table in the tearoom. Folks waited patiently and good-humouredly because they understood how lucky they were to be able to sample Mary's famously delicious afternoon tea, even if they had to queue for it.

Her husband, Geoffrey, had put in place a booking system to try to control the ad hoc visitors that thought they might be able to circumvent the system. So far, it had worked, although there were still those that thought it didn't apply to them. He had posted notices in the Pantry's window for several weeks, warning of the new system, and although there had been initial teething problems, things seemed to be working. Most customers were repeat visitors, and they appeared to have taken on the role of self-appointed monitors to make sure no-one got above themselves.

"I think she's in the corner by the window," Poppy pointed out as she nudged her friend.

"She certainly looks more the part than the one we've just dismissed," Florence said. "This could be good."

"Good afternoon," the young lady said as the two friends approached. "You must be Poppy and Florence. My name's Abigail Green, and I'm—"

"From *The Times*?" Florence said. "Pleased to meet you, Miss Green."

"Call me Abigail, please," she replied with a widening smile. "Are we able to talk here?"

"Indeed, yes," Poppy assured her. "The owner, Mary, is a close family friend."

"How wonderful to have close friends with premises like these!" Abigail Green observed. "How I wish I had a place like this where I live."

"Miss Poppy! Miss Florence!" a very familiar, very warm voice greeted them.

"Mary! How lovely to see you," Poppy said, greeting the lady she knew so well with a kiss and a hug. "Is everything all right?"

"Indeed it is, as you can see," Mary replied. "Your afternoon tea will be with you in a moment or two. Does your friend require *your* usual?"

"Please, Mary," Poppy agreed, as Mary turned to wave to one of the serving girls.

"I didn't expect *this*!" Abigail gasped as she gazed at what had been placed before her. "This looks divine."

"Only the best for a lady who has taken the trouble to come all this way to interview two eager young ladies who have the deepest desire to share their love of literature," a deep, melodic voice interrupted the party.

"Grandpa Ross!" Poppy whooped as she flung her arms about his neck. "Thank *you* for coming."

"Good afternoon, Ross Booth," Abigail said, holding out her hand. "It's good to see you again after all this time."

Poppy and Florence stood dumbfounded, puzzled looks leaping from one to the other, not understanding what they were witnessing.

"I have known Abi's father for many years, Poppy," Ross explained. "*She* is a very smart and learned young lady who shares your joint passion for the arts and literature, in particular. I dropped in only to say hello, so I'll be off to see to my

44

businesses, and leave you to enjoy each other's company. I will be at the bank for the next couple of hours, so if you would like a lift home, please drop in.

"By the way," he said as he turned for the door, "afternoon tea's been settled." With that he was gone.

"Settled?" Abigail asked, not sure what he meant. "What does that mean?"

"He's already paid the bill," Poppy explained. "Now, to business?"

CHAPTER 5

Tommy Spence sat in the front room at Boulders Wood, a roaring fire consuming the pile of logs that had been set in the enormous fire grate. His stiff, upright frame was supported by umpteen unyielding cushions on the huge settee close to the stone hearth.

He was unsure why he had been summoned *now* by Nell and Ross Booth, when he had expected to see them more than a week before. That room hadn't changed in essence since Nell was a young mother overwhelmed with two healthy and demanding bairns to look after, along with a household and seriously sexually demanding and overbearing husband to satisfy.

Even the fire that had consumed the back room umpteen Christmases before had made little difference to the overall downstairs layout. It was, after all, still a busy working farm that was not given to ostentation or fancy decoration. The only change had been the refurbishment of that room to accommodate Poppy's needs, as far as her personal arrangements for her literature project were concerned. Her plans for the cottage close by would, to her delight and youthful impatience, hopefully soon come to fruition.

Tommy Spence didn't really know what he might be letting himself in for, although he wished deep down that he did. He had missed so much that he had always wanted, losing count of the times he had run through his life that wasn't to be with his beloved Annie. He had wished beyond endurance that one day she would be his. Now all he had left to celebrate her memory was a beautiful daughter – if he was given the opportunity to become part of her life.

His eyes were jerked away roughly from the depths of the red-and-yellow tongues in the fire grate by the click of a door sneck to his left, jerking his attention to the back room next to the kitchen. His involuntary gasp at seeing the elegant form of a beautiful young lady standing by that door surprised him and drew his Annie back to his mind. This second sight of *his* daughter, Poppy, brought tears to his eyes, a dithering smile to his lips, and a fear into his mind.

As his daughter stood by the door, eyes downcast to the book she was holding between nervously fiddling fingers, not knowing really what to say, Nell entered purposefully from the kitchen. She halted by the foot of the stairs, obviously there in quiet support of her granddaughter. A heavy, pregnant silence hung in the air like the unexpected spectre at the feast as Tommy Spence stood up nervously.

"Good morning, Miss McIntyre," he started, clearing his nervous throat. "It is good to see you. Thank you for inviting me to have the chance to meet you officially."

At an almost imperceptible nod from Nell, Poppy moved forward, like an automaton whose lever had jerked it into disjointed action.

"You are very welcome, Mr Spence," she said haltingly.

Although she had always wanted to discover her roots and find her sire, this situation didn't sit comfortably with her. It felt to her like it had been manufactured as a sop to her incessant questioning of her ancestry.

Looking over at her nanny, Poppy said quite simply, "Why are you here?"

"Possibly, like you, Miss McIntyre, I have felt something of a gap in my life that I should like to fill," he replied quietly. "All I would like to do is to become a part – even a small part, should you wish – of *your* life, and for you to be able to call me 'father', insofar as we are able to establish that you are my daughter. Your mother was the love of my life, although we were no more than sixteen years old when we spent what were our last moments together. I never met nor wanted to be with anyone else, and I was devastated when I learned the worst possible news about her demise."

"Why did you not come before now?" Poppy asked as she sat down in one of the high-backed, winged easy chairs.

"We promised each other on that last night we spent together that we would wait until we could wed," he began. "Unfortunately, my parents guessed that something was not right, so they sent me away to stay with my aunt Oxford way on, to 'improve' myself. I realised too late they weren't going to allow me back until I had gone through university and had a sound job that that paid me a reasonable amount to live on, which would allow me to ask your mother to be my wife. I bought myself into a medical practice up here.

"It was only recently I was made aware that I was more than twenty years too late. I was devastated. It wasn't until recently that I discovered Annie had given birth to … you."

"But why didn't you even write to her?" Poppy insisted, tears glistening.

"I did. I wrote every day for a year with no reply," he explained with a heartfelt sigh. "We'd had an arrangement with a friend that I would send my letters to her and she would make sure your mother received them without anyone else knowing."

"And?" Poppy asked.

"She didn't receive them," Tommy said. "She can't have, because I got no reply."

"Who? Your friend?" Poppy puzzled.

"No," he went on. "Your mother – and I don't know why. If we could only find our friend—"

"Sally Smallshore?" Nell butted in as she joined them in front of the glowing fire. "Your Uncle Ross has found out where she lives, or at least where she and her father moved to when they left here."

"So?" Tommy asked, hope rising again.

"If we find her, we will know one way or the other what substance there is to your story, and whether you could be Poppy's father … or … not," Nell finished.

"Parky out there," Ross Senior said to his wife as he began to remove his overcoat and gloves. "I should like you to meet … Miss Sally Smallshore, now from Guisborough, formerly of Boulders Wood. Along with her … father, Jim."

A stunned silence settled on Nell and her son, Ross.

"Jim Smallshore!" Ross woke up finally to greet the man who had worked for them years before. "How are things? Long time no see."

"Good to si thi, Master Ross," Jim Smallshore replied, shaking him vigorously by the hand.

"Sit down, both of you, please," Ross Senior suggested.

"I'll go and ask our cook to rustle up something to eat. It's been a long journey."

"We were very sorry to see you leave all those years ago, but obviously we understood the reasons," Ross said. "You were the best of the best with our herds, and we have never found a herdsman of your quality to replace you."

"That's very kind of you to say so," Jim acknowledged. "I had to get away because I knew I couldn't give the time to look after Sally *and* work full-time here."

"We would have been able to accommodate your needs, I think," Ross said.

"Maybe *you* would have, but your master wouldn't," Jim said, snarling at Joss's memory. "I also had to get Sally away from under *his* gaze before he laid hands on her. If'n he had, I wouldn't have been responsible for my actions."

"We didn't know *that,* Jim, and I'm sorry for it," Ross assured him. "What do you do now, then?"

"Fishing, mainly, and Sally has a job in one of the big houses nearby," Jim said. "My job isn't full time because of the state of fishing in our neck of the woods, and Sally has to travel too far."

"Not much reward for you to live on, then," Ross added.

The door to the back room next to the kitchen clicked shut quietly as Poppy entered the room almost unseen.

"This is our granddaughter Poppy," Ross Senior announced as he re-entered the room. "The young lady for whom we are desperate to find a father."

"Not just *a* father, Grandpa Ross, but *my real* father," Poppy butted in, a serious look underlining her strong feelings.

Jim Smallshore and his daughter turned towards the newcomer.

"She's the image of her mother," Sally burst in, tears

50

beginning to gather. "Annie was the only friend I ever had, even now."

"The all-important question, Daughter, is does Poppy resemble in any way the man who is supposed to be her sire?" Jim added quickly.

"She could be no-one else's but … Tommy Spence's," Sally replied slowly, after a moment or two of silent thought. "Eyes, nose, mouth – they are all his."

"But I thought—" Ross puzzled.

"She has features of both parents, which leads me to believe Tommy is her dad," Sally emphasised.

Poppy sat in quiet disbelief at what she was hearing, that at last she had found her father. Should she accept what this woman had said? How could she be so sure? Was it because she sensed that Poppy clearly wanted to know, or was what she said as true as it could be? In her heart of hearts, she wanted *desperately* to believe, but could she – *should* she – jump in with both feet? Perhaps she needed more time to think it over and to rationalise…

"Why didn't you send the letters Tommy said he had written to you that you had agreed to make sure Annie received?" Ross asked. "She never received anything."

"But I never received any letters," Sally insisted. "He said he would send them to me by this new-fangled penny postage thing, but none ever arrived. So, I couldn't pass them on."

"How are you finding things now, Jim?" Ross asked, changing tack to give Poppy some time to think as she left them to regain her room. How was she going to rationalise all that she had heard, and arrive at a decision that might impact upon the rest of her life? Could she ever accept Tommy Spence as her father on the scant proof of a complete stranger? Was Sally Smallshore dependable enough for Poppy to allow an unknown into her life? What if she was wrong?

"So, so, you know Master Ross," Jim replied with a grimace and a shrug.

"Come on, Dad!" Sally butted in. "Why don't you tell him the truth?"

"Sally!" her father hissed, warning her not to go any further.

"Sally nothing!" she went on. "You know as well as I do that we can barely make ends meet."

"Here's the thing," Ross went on. "Do you remember John Stafford? He worked for us as head herdsman when you were around. He's now semi-retired and we were thinking of asking him to join us again as a temporary stand-in. Might you be interested in joining us on a permanent basis? There's a cottage on site at a nominal rate."

"Dad!" Sally urged. "I can get a job anywhere…"

"Can I think on it for a bit?" Jim replied.

"Course you can," Ross said with an ever-hopeful nod. "But it would be good to shake on it here and now."

"My God! Jim Smallshore!" Joseph's voice accosted them all. "Why are you here?"

"Master Joseph," Jim acknowledged the man he hadn't seen for many years.

"Come on, Jim, less of the formality," Joseph replied. "How long did we know each other?"

"I've offered Jim the permanent job as head herdsman with the cottage down the driveway," Ross said. "Subject to your approval, of course."

"Good shout," his brother agreed. "And who is this young lady?"

"My daughter Sally," Jim offered as he shook Joseph's hand. "If you've any space for her, she's a good worker and—"

"Dad!" Sally urged her father with a quiet hiss.

"How does working in our dairy in our sister farm a short way away sound?" Joseph offered. "Tom Garside isn't well enough to fulfil his obligations, so Jim would be taking over from him. We will need to replace his missis, Lilly, because she is looking after him. Any takers?"

"I'm in," Jim said with a relieved grin.

"Me too!" Sally added quickly. "When do we start?"

"Excellent!" Joseph sighed, punching the air. "We can offer you both…"

Nell turned on her heels and went into the kitchen to organise a celebratory tray bearing its usual to help the agreements on their way.

"Stroke of genius, my man," she said as her husband joined her. "This amount of progress never happened until you came into our lives. We have a lot to thank you for, and—"

"Nonsense!" he replied. "Logical and sensible outcomes. That's all."

"What are you going to do?" Florence asked Poppy, a concerned look invading her face.

"I … don't … know!" Poppy insisted.

"You did want a father figure, didn't you?" Florence replied. "Though I don't know why. Mine has been nothing but a nuisance ever since I was able to understand the vagaries of parenthood. God forbid I shall ever wish to invest my valuable time in offspring! So much easier to be free to decide what *I* want to do with my life."

"Not quite as simple as that, my dear," Poppy said. "You have both your parents still, and so you know your origins and consequently from whose loins you spring. On the other hand, I have neither. You could say that I am a lone soul in the wilderness, not knowing which parts of my make up belong to me, and which elements I have inherited from where."

"Do we know anything much about him?" Florence waded in again, unable to leave her good friend to sort out things for herself. "Are we any closer to being able to analyse his character, his characteristics as a human being and, most important of all, his motives?"

"In a word, my dear Florence – no!" Poppy said adamantly.

End of conversation, and definitely the end of Florence's attempted analysis of Poppy's prospective father's morality and reasons for wanting to associate himself with her and her future.

"Do we know if he—?" Florence started again after a short respite from her persistent probing.

"Enough, Florence!" Poppy insisted forcefully. "I will think on it at some other time, and *then* I will tell you what I decide."

Silence descended as they both sat deep in thought, neither alerting the other as to what was running through her mind.

"Are we to—?"

"Shall we—?"

They both started at the same time, descending into hilarity as they did. A knock at the door settled their humour quickly.

"Hello, Cousin Albert," Poppy said on opening the door. "Please come in."

"I'll not, thank you, Poppy," he said. "I have another very pressing engagement to attend to imminently. I simply wished to inform you that your new cottage is ready for you to inspect at your leisure, and here are the keys."

He held the jangling lumps of shiny metal out to her on their brass retaining ring. She took them with a growing look of awe, overcome with a mixture of joy, excitement and emotion.

"Thank you, Cousin Albert," she gasped as he turned to leave. "You have no idea what this means to me – to us."

"This is a difficult one," Poppy said slowly, once Cousin Albert had left.

"Difficult?" Florence puzzled, not sure where *this* line of reasoning would lead them. It seemed lately that her dear friend had become uncertain as to how her life was about to unfold. "What is difficult about taking a set of keys to your – our – own property where we can do as we planned, and—?"

"We'll have to be careful not to appear to be living either below or above our position as far as furnishings and furniture are concerned," Poppy remarked carefully. "In *Our Mutual Friend*, Mr Dickens said 'We have come into a great fortune, and we must do what's right by our fortune; we must act up to it'. *We* are not vastly rich, so I think middle of the road would be the best way forward."

"Also bearing in mind that, although funds are plentiful," Florence added, "those funds have been supplied by your Grandpa Ross, and we weren't born into them."

They both laughed at that observation that they had already reached and articulated.

CHAPTER 6

The night was dark, drizzly and cold. Indistinct barely human figures drifted quickly from dimly lit doorways to black alleys like phantoms, leaving no trace of their passing. Few people shared these lost paths with them, hurrying from legitimate business to safer homes, hoping to reach them without incident or interference.

A door catch snicked as a crack of dim light pierced the gloom and as quickly disappeared, leaving a vague, almost indistinguishable, imprint in its passing.

"Well, my man?" A muffled voice punctured the silence in the grim, dirt-encrusted room where a crumpled bed, two rough chairs and a table littered with overturned glasses and empty liquor bottles heralded some haphazard existence. "Did you do as I asked? What have you got to show for it?"

"Yes, Boss," the dishevelled ruffian replied, as he dropped a few blood-stained notes and the odd sovereign into the man's grubby palm.

"What's this? Blood?" the boss man asked, annoyed at the state of the money he had in his grasp. "How did you come by this, my man? Physical violence? Is that what I asked for?"

He dropped the money into a small wooden box that was half-filled with coins already. Fastening the box's lid deliberately, he caught the ruffian a hard blow across his face with the back of his clenched fist, drawing blood from his nose and mouth. The man bounced off the table corner, knocking over a chair as he hit the floor with a groan and a shake of his head.

"Although useful enough, it wasn't about filching paltry sums and drawing attention to our existence, dear boy," the master said, stroking his ample facial hair gingerly, wincing gently as he did so. Some former injury inflicted by an earlier adversary, perhaps?

"Your brief, old boy, was to follow and observe *unobtrusively* and *not* alert your quarry as to our intentions." The tone and volume of his malevolence became sharper and more threatening as his cold, steely blues threatened to pierce his henchman's eyes to the core.

The henchman winced slightly at what he knew his boss might do, but he was taken aback when he offered his genial hand to help him to his feet.

"We are here to plan our next moves, and while this cash will help us to pay for us to nibble at some of the necessities of life, we have much bigger fish that we will ultimately come to gorge on," Jonas added almost jovially.

His henchmen were always aware of what he might do if they got it wrong but were never quite sure what his *immediate* response might be, or what he might have in mind for the future. As far as they were concerned he was unpredictable, although *he* knew to the last dot what he would do throughout his every – planned – waking moment.

Dealing with George Garside still remained at the top of his 'to do' list.

"How are you getting on, Tom?" Joseph asked his good friend and partner as they sat down together in the Garside's front room, a mug of tea and one of the cupcakes that Lilly had taken to baking to hand. "Any better?"

"Yon medic 'as warned me that I need to be wary abaht tekin on too much too soon," Tom said. "And that means even stirrin' mi own tea!"

"I'm sorry to hear that, old friend," Joseph said, genuinely upset for his neighbour. "You must take your time getting well. In the meantime, I have brought back in a chap that worked for us over ten years ago and…"

As the logs in the front room's fire grate reduced to dull embers and sparks escaped up the chimney back, Joseph explained what he had done and how he planned to fill the void that Tom and his wife had created by their withdrawal from their workforce.

"That's removed a worrisome burden from mi shoulders at two fell strokes," Tom sighed. "And this chap, Jim Smallshore, is good at what he does?"

"Aye, he is that," Joseph replied. "None better. I have offered him the cottage down the driveway, not a hundred paces from Boulders Wood's front door, at a nominal rent as a further incentive."

"But … can we afford him?" Tom's final question had Joseph smiling, knowing of old his friend's pragmatic financial sense.

"Paying him the good wage I have offered makes better financial sense than letting thy side of our joint endeavour disappear," he replied. "If we don't replace thy skills, we effectively lose half of our business, and that would lead to financial ruin."

"And 'as 'e got two pairs of 'ands?" Tom asked.

"Does tha know," Joseph grinned. "I was about to tell thee about Lilly's replacement. I know she was never wholeheartedly settled on running the dairy side, so I've gone and replaced her with – and don't get thissen in a lather abaht this – Jim's daughter. She's called Sally. She was Annie's best friend, and she has no family to bother her except her dad, Jim. She may need a bit of training, like, but she's a bright lass who is quick to learn, and who will be an asset to our growth."

"Bloody 'ell!" Tom gasped. "Thy 'as bin busy! But thank you, my friend. I knew I could rely on you. Lilly, I am sure, will be happy that you have found a competent replacement for *her*."

Joseph smiled, understanding Tom's double meaning, while Tom was happy that he didn't have to endure Lilly's caustic comments about *her* situation in the dairy that she had never taken to.

"When do they start, Joseph?" Tom asked. "We don't have to fork out for any bugger else, do we?"

"I'm getting John Stafford in to cover for a short time, until Jim and Sally have sorted out their stuff and the cottage is made habitable and comfortable for them," Joseph explained. "He can stay onny a short while, so it's on us to get stuff organised with, and for, Jim and Sally."

Late autumn at Boulders Wood was always something of an enigma, with most people unable to understand how differ-ent the weather could be from one day to the next, or even in successive hours. The whole neighbourhood seemed to become shrouded in mystery, puzzling all that lived through its vagaries.

Poppy and Florence felt its overpowering atmosphere at almost the same moment; it affected their sensibilities at the same time. Flurries and showers of red-and-brown leaves were carried to ground by winds of varying strengths to form deep drifts, almost as harbingers of the colder snows of winter not far behind.

"I love this cottage," Poppy said, ensconced in her new favourite armchair by the huge living-room window.

"I can't believe we are here," Florence added from *her* chair opposite her friend. "Here, finally, as ladies of leisure in our own right. Your grandpa treats us well, and for that I shall be eternally grateful. All we need now is someone like—"

A genteel knocking at the front door interrupted her as Poppy made to answer it. With the living-room door leading to the entrance vestibule closed against marauding chill winds from the outside door, Florence could hear only the vaguest of mutterings that conveyed nothing to her until—

"Guess who we have here, Florence?" Poppy said teasingly as she led into the room—

"George!" Florence gasped as she leaped to her dancing, excited feet. "What brings you here? Just passing?"

"Actually, no," he said, once he had sat down in the third chair positioned exactly between the other two.

"Don't tell me you came to see—?" Florence went on slowly, only to be interrupted quietly by their male friend.

"You two," he said making them prick up their dainty ears in anticipation of what deliciously tasty morsel he might be about to treat them to. "I haven't seen you for quite some time and I have—"

"Missed us?" Poppy asked. She moved to one end of the

three-seater settee in the middle of the room facing the huge, ornate chimney breast where a roaring fire celebrated its ostentation. "*Have* you missed us?"

"We have missed you, too, our George," Florence added as she took up the other end of the same settee with a warming smile. As she sat down gently, she patted the remaining space between the two young ladies as an invitation for him to join them. This he did, hesitantly at first, but once his muscular frame had filled the space between them, both ladies shuffled slowly sideways towards him. Kissing them both in turn on the lips, he slid his arms around their shoulders and drew them slowly towards him. An anticipatory look grew in each face as heads snuggled to his shoulders and eyes closed.

The fire crackled and spat as a pregnant warm gloom invaded the room, growing from corners to be joined by low giggles, the occasional contented sigh, and a close intimacy that each of them had yearned for as they had matured.

A cold grey dawn revealed a deep sprinkling of white, covering the ground. The first snows had arrived early, along with an unwelcome and alarmingly solitary set of inordinately large footprints that circled the cottage close to its walls and marched off into the eaves of the wood quite close by.

Poppy and Florence lay soundly asleep in their separate beds, dreaming, no doubt, of their evening the day just past. George had risen early, breakfasted, and laid and lit their sitting room and work-room fireplaces. Sure that the wonderfully comforting and enlivening warmth would have spread to every corner of each room, and that guards had been strategically placed to prevent sparks and burned wood from escaping, he set off quietly to start his day's work at *his* family farm a fifteen-minute walk away.

Thoughts, memories and feelings that swamped him during the long evening coursed rapidly through his now over-active mind. He never felt in a million years that he would ever experience such a wondrous time with his girls. Yet now, he was convinced he needed to settle down and raise the next generation of Garsides.

His feelings and hopes for life with Annabel had evaporated forever once he had found out she was seeing some-one else. Not wanting to be caught in a fidelity trap again, he had returned to his girls whom he knew would never use him like Annabel had. Where should he go from here? He couldn't marry both of his wonderful friends, and he knew that neither would be interested in marriage at this time, if ever. They had too much to accomplish in their young lives. Might the indeterminate future hold better plans for him?

"Footprints? Around and from the cottage?" he muttered, mildly concerned that a long-dead ghost might have surfaced to plague them once again. He searched the horizon with his keen young eyes, aware of movement at the top edge of the forest field around a quarter of a mile away. He had seen such movement there some ten or more years before. That particular ghost had been exorcised long ago. Had another arisen to take its place?

Gone. Perhaps a trick of the light in this stark landscape.

Casting such thoughts to the back of his mind, he marched off to his daily toil, unaware that a pair of unblinkingly evil eyes were watching his every step.

"Well, don't you know, old chap," the figure muttered to itself from the dense copse nearby, "your hour is fast approaching. Very soon you are going to be mightily and unbelievably sorry that you ever encountered the name Jonas. And he will enjoy showing your two little girls what a real man is capable of without interference or interruption from a nobody like you."

George slowed and stopped as he reached the corner of Joseph's cottage, a warning crawling into his head that all was not perhaps as it should have been. He turned slowly, scanning the stark white landscape to see if he could detect any untoward movement.

Jonas inhaled sharply, not sure whether, in his arrogance, he had been heard, but as George drew away a relieved breath escaped his lips. "There you go, old chap," he muttered again. "Don't know I'm here? You undoubtedly will do so in the near future, when you are least expecting it. My vengeance will be extensive and you, old chap, will bother me no more."

CHAPTER 7

"What do you mean you are moving out *permanently*?"
Florence's father spat at her as she began to gather
all her belongings together. She'd had her bedroom almost
since birth, and it had become … adequate, although not as
'adequate' as the one occupied by her brother.

They had never got on very well because he was their parents'
blue-eyed boy, destined to do well in finance or law or some
other equally nebulous and boring field. Florence, on the other
hand, was just … a … girl with little prospect other than to be
somebody's wife, able to bear children to no useful purpose.

"I am old enough to look after myself, Father," she stated
remarkably calmly … for her. She was the one with a caustic
wit that her father had often railed against, ostensibly because
of what he called her lack of respect, but not so secretly because
he had always wanted another son. This she knew well, and
had looked forward to this day … forever,

Most fathers in his position looked towards the day when
they would no longer be responsible for their daughter's
upkeep, with their only aim to secure a suitable suitor.

"And what do you consider other people are going to think about this move?" her mother chipped in. "Are they not going to think that it is … strange?"

"Mother, since when have I cared what others think about *me*?" Florence scoffed at her mother's obvious meaning. "As far as husbands and families are concerned, I have no doubt that opportunities will present themselves whenever, if ever, I wish to consider them. Until then, my good friend and I will indulge in our true love of literature, which we will share with other like-minded souls."

"Don't think you'll be getting anything from your mother or from me to support you!" her father snarled at the perceived lack of thought or feeling from his daughter, "And—"

"I will have *no* need of *your* support or care," Florence replied with conviction, cutting him off sharply. "All our needs will be attended to without any problems."

"So, you are to become a … kept woman?" he sneered, to gasps of horror from his wife.

"Indeed, if that is how you want to put it," Florence said with a pityingly sarcastic smile. "Unlike you, Poppy's Grandpa Ross is supporting us entirely, allowing us to decide our own future and to pursue whatever literary opportunities might cross our path."

Mother lifted her lace-edged handkerchief to her face, as if to gather some errant invisible tear, while Father blustered and huffed, not knowing how to deal with what his daughter had said. Florence simply smiled having delivered her final verdict in calculated and measured tones that her father, no doubt, would ponder upon for a short while, before dismissing with disdain.

"Ross!" Florence called from the front door to Poppy's uncle as he waited in the pony and trap, ready to transport her entire world to the cottage she was to share with his dear niece. "Would you be so kind as to give me a hand with my trunk?"

"Indeed I will," he answered as he strode purposefully towards her, a welcoming smile plastered across his face. When he saw the trunk she was to take with her to Boulders Wood, he called back, "Are you sure you wouldn't like me to fetch a bigger two-shire-drawn wagon to load the *whole* house?"

Florence laughed, happy that there was someone pleased to see her and be ready to offer her assistance. How wonderful were all the members of Poppy's family; very different from her own in every respect.

Their new project and her very different lifestyle excited her enormously. How she was looking forward to striking up new relationships and doing the things she had always wanted to do! She couldn't help but cast her mind back to that Christmas Eve, when she wasn't yet ten, when she had arrived at Boulders Wood for the first time to spend the festive period in the company of another youngster of the same age who had become a sister to her in all but blood.

"Your parents not too excited about your leaving home, Florence?" Ross said to her.

"They never were excited about having a daughter in the first place," she said with a grimace. "Father, certainly, would have been significantly more animated had I been a boy. No time for female offspring, I'm afraid, as has been seen in his attitude towards my brother."

"A new life in all respects then?" Ross replied with a knowing shrug.

"Looking forward to it very much so," she agreed.

Although it had always been too far to walk from her parents' home to Boulders Wood, the journey by pony and trap seemed to last only minutes. The joyous crunch on the deep pebble-laid driveway welcomed their arrival.

"There's Poppy now at your cottage doorway, milady," Ross said as he slowed the pony to a steady walk.

"Thank you, my man," Florence replied in the same vein, with an indulgent smile as she waved to her friend.

"Here we are, Poppy," Ross greeted his niece. "House guest, at your service."

The sky was clear blue, with only the occasional patch of darker cloud to warn of what might develop at a later stage in the day. The early morning's fine sprinkling of virgin snow still lay on the ground around the cottage but was now crunchier because of the dropping temperature.

"Beautifully warm in here," Ross gasped as he dropped Florence's trunk in her bedroom. "Much as I would love to stay and help you to install or rearrange your furniture, I must away to my work. I have a farm to help run."

Poppy flung her arms about his neck and kissed his cheek in thanks for his help with her friend's belongings. "Cup of tea, Uncle Ross?" she offered.

"No thank you, my lovely," he said as he turned to leave. "Love to, but there's lots to do. As long as you are both settled, I'll away. Another time, maybe?"

"Florence," Poppy sighed as she embraced her lifelong friend and co-writer.

"Poppy," Florence replied with a reciprocal hug. "You all right?"

"I am now," Poppy said. "Now our new life can begin…"

Their voices faded as they re-entered their inner sanctum, ready to prepare for their first literary soirée where they would be able to announce their arrival onto the literary stage of the area. Now the interesting part of their life would begin in earnest.

"So, you are still set on this ridiculous idea of spending time with this ... this young woman – your supposed long-lost daughter?" Sam Spence said to his son, Tommy.

"No need for sarcasm, Father," Tommy replied sharply. "She *is* my daughter, of which I am convinced, and I fully intend to pursue my wish to its ultimate conclusion, whether yea or nay from you."

"No good will come of it, mark my words," his father warned. "Then you'll not only have to accept what is thrust into your lap, but a positive outcome will give you a hell of a lot more responsibility, and a negative one will destroy your wishes and hopes."

"No matter," Tommy said sharply. "I have to know whether there is anyone out there who has my blood coursing through their veins. If that is so, then my life is complete, and I will take whatever responsibilities are deemed in order. If not, I have lost nothing and will return to 'normal' living, whatever that might be.

"Today is the day I might take one step towards my goal," he continued nervously, after a moment or two of quiet indecision. "Now, I must away."

The journey from Richmond to Boulders Wood was probably the most difficult he had ever undertaken, bearing in mind what was at stake. The thoughts of being able to experience closeness to his beloved Annie were overpowering, after so many years of not having her physically next to him, feeling the rise and fall of her bosom, the scent of her hair in his quivering nostrils and the softness of her skin on his. The product of their union in his arms, their daughter as beautiful as Annie had been all those years ago, was almost beyond belief, beyond hope. Was this to be taken away from him when he was so close?

"Come in, Mr Spence – Tommy," Nell greeted him at the entrance to the great doors. "Thank you for coming. It *is* good to see you."

"Hello, Mrs Booth. Thank you for asking me," Tommy replied, beginning to relax after that first greeting. He hadn't been sure what direction his reception might have taken. Was this greeting the positive start to the rest of his life he had dreamed about for the last umpteen years? Was he about to be accepted by his daughter at last?

"Can I get you some refreshment?" Nell suggested as Mary brought in a tray of goodies and tea. "A drink, perhaps, and some home-made scones?"

"That would be wonderful," he enthused. "Haven't had proper home-baking for many a year. Mother was never much of a baker."

"Indeed," Nell giggled. "Her pies were a little lacking in … substance and taste if memory serves. Mary here owns Mary's Pantry in Richmond, which you really must visit. She's filling in here today because it's one of her niece's days off."

"Mary's Pantry?" Tommy gasped. "Then it is indeed a pleasure to meet the owner of such a wonderful tea house. I have partaken of your exquisite baking many a time, Mistress Mary. Lunchtime wouldn't be the same without your fruit-and-walnut scones."

"If you need any more, please shout," Mary advised as she headed for the kitchen door.

Almost at that same moment, Poppy entered the room, causing Tommy a sharp intake of breath that interrupted what he was about to say. "Miss McIntyre," he said quietly, once he

69

had gathered his scattered senses. "It's so good of you to allow my visit, and it is good to see you again."

"It's Poppy," she replied firmly. "Please call me Poppy, Father dear."

Those two soul-uplifting and long-awaited words were enough to persuade tears to threaten. He had neither heard nor expected anyone to utter those two sacred words. 'Father' was almost as much as he could bear.

Handing over a small box, he said, "I have recently received these from our new-fangled post office, and I thought you might like them. They are the letters – all sixty of them – that I sent to Sally Smallshore, your mother's friend, from my incarceration at my aunt's home in London, so that she might get them to Annie. Sally never received them, and they have only just resurfaced from the post-office depot, where they have lain hidden for the last two decades or more. I should be extremely happy for you to read them because they will obviously set our relationship into a context that will allow you to understand how we felt about each other."

Poppy's response was unexpected. She walked across to her father, flung her arms about his neck and burst into tears. "At last!" she sighed. "The father I have yearned for so long. It now hurts to hold you to make up for all those empty years. Welcome into my – our – life."

Tommy couldn't believe that at last he had found his blood link to his beautiful Annie, the young lady that had promised to be his forever wife and partner. Now there was no doubt that Poppy was his – and Annie's – daughter. The fact that they were unable to share her together was just too much for him, and he broke down as he embraced his daughter.

"Of course, I don't know how things will turn out," Poppy said to her friend Florence in their cottage that night. "I've read about a quarter of the sixty letters my father wrote to my mother, and I was reduced to tears. I don't know how I'm going to cope with the remaining forty-five or so."

"Were there any replies, from your mum, I mean?" Florence asked, overcome by this story.

"As she never received any of them because they were stuck in some little cupboard since before I was born, she never wrote back," Poppy explained. "If there *had* been replies, they would have been too heart rending to even open, let alone read."

"They could form the basis of a wonderful love story, rather like *Wuthering Heights* or *Rebecca*, don't you think?" Florence suggested.

"Now *that* we would have to think about seriously," Poppy said with a smile. "How did your parents take your moving out?"

"As you would expect, really," Florence replied. "Father was concerned only about how the public would view two young women living together. They were also concerned about our being 'kept women'."

"Kept—?" Poppy gasped. "Ah yes, of course. Grandpa Ross's financial support. Weren't they pleased for *you*, that you wouldn't have to go into service or some such thing?"

"I think their main concern centred on their future welfare," Florence sniffed.

"Does that mean what I think it means?" Poppy asked incredulously.

"Mother believes fervently that I should be working towards husband and children and planning to look after *them* when they are no longer able to look after themselves," Florence scoffed. "Imagine *me* spending all my time looking after two old people that can afford to pay for care! No fear!"

They both laughed, easy in each other's company, glorifying in their next steps into a world that each had held dear to her heart for as long as they could remember.

The logs in their ornate fire grate cracked and spat as they launched yellow tongues and a myriad red sparks up the chimney breast, and cascaded waves of welcoming heat into a sometimes-chilly living room. They had derived a singularly exciting degree of joy from choosing period furniture that they had decided would enhance their living and literary aspirations. Although unnecessary, they felt they needed to be mindful of the cost implications for Poppy's Grandpa Ross, despite his setting up a nigh-on bottomless pit of finance for their use. Whatever they considered they might need they should have, he had assured them on more than one occasion. Poppy was his only grandchild, after all.

Chapter 8

"What have you there?" Nell asked her granddaughter as the latter rushed into the front room at Boulders Wood and slammed the door on the usual sort of a snowstorm for early December. The fire, which was never allowed to die, urged its waves of heat to fill the area corner to corner in an attempt to spread comfort in this inclement weather.

"These, Nanny, are the letters we have received in response to Abigail Green's *Times* article on our literary group's activities in the run up to Christmas," Poppy replied, a frisson of excitement coursing her body. "Ten letters in all."

"I read those articles and I thought they sounded exciting for anyone who has an interest in literature," Nell observed. "I suppose that access to books of today is somewhat restricted for ordinary people."

"Hopefully, one day that won't be the case," Poppy answered. "And that is why we would like to embark upon this our dearest project – to spread the love of writing and reading wonderful books. Funnily enough, one of the responders has the last name of McIntyre."

"Really?" Nell said, her interest jumping to the fore. "What's the Christian name?"

"He's called Hal," Poppy replied. Her nanny gasped. "Hal McIntyre. Why, Nanny? Do you know him?"

"Thereby hangs a tale," Nell explained with a grimace. "Grandpa Joss's father, Alexander, so I'm given to believe, had four illegitimate children by different women, but only one of them survived past the age of five. *That* one bore the name of Harold, or Hal for short. He was brought up by his mother with a little help from Great-Grandpa Alexander, but it was touch and go whether he would survive into adulthood largely because of the rough crowd he mixed with. He had an illegitimate son, also called Hal. At twenty-three, *he* found his calling in life when he became an explorer. He is ten years older than you and has spent much of his time exploring in Africa."

"Heavens above!" Poppy exclaimed, hardly able to believe she had such a well-travelled cousin.

"What does he want?" Nell asked, a little perturbed by this information.

"He wants to talk about the book he has written about his travels," Poppy explained. "I think his driving force has been the exploits of one Dr David Livingstone.

"Anyway, Nanny," she went on, "would it be possible to have our first soirée the Saturday before Christmas when Mary may be able to cater?"

"Mary has been primed by Grandpa Ross to be ready," Nell explained. "So, you only have to give the word and she will spring into action, as only Mary can do. She will also organise some of her staff to wait on. All you have to do then is to pay her out of the money he settled with you in your bank account."

"Excellent!" Poppy exclaimed, with her usual leg jiggle. "I

will speak to her at the beginning of next week," she went on, elated that their show was about to hit the road.

~

"How exciting!" Florence giggled once her sister-in-arms had returned to their cottage to break the news. "I could never have imagined that this would happen for and to us all those years ago when you introduced me to reading *Middlemarch* and *Mill on the Floss*. That's getting on for ten years ago."

"I had thought for quite some time before that, once I discovered the wonderful stories that were around, that writing and sharing the stories that *I* had written was what I wanted – needed – to do with my life," Poppy said, settling in front of their roaring fire. "And it's all been made possible because a certain gentleman entered our lives."

"That would be Grandpa Ross, of course," Florence agreed. "I have never met anyone quite like him in my all-too-short life. Your family contains the most extraordinarily wonderful and exciting people. Whereas mine is—"

"Mine, my dear heart," Poppy interrupted her. "Don't forget that family is what you choose, not necessarily what you are. *You* are part of *my* family, just as if we were *born* sisters."

"Hello!" An immediately recognisable voice drifted in from the hallway. "Anybody home?"

"George!" they both exclaimed, casting excited glances at each other as he strode bootless into their living room.

"How lovely to see you, dear friend," Florence uttered. "But you are bootless! Have you been robbed en route?"

They all laughed as they hugged.

"Deep in snow out there, and parky too," George replied. "Left them by the door – inside of course – so as not to cart muck and wet into this lovely home."

His ordinary use of language and its sound was very different from that of the two girls. They had tried to slough off the common usage that they had grown up with from birth to bring out a more acceptable – in their view – level of pronunciation and articulation in line with what they were intending to do.

George's view on his speech and language was entirely the opposite. He considered that the speech he had developed from the time he had learned to talk was the one he would keep, without alteration, until he booked his plot in the local cemetery. That was a view held by most real, proud Yorkshiremen. Ifn folks wanted to converse wi' 'em, they'd 'ave to learn 'ow to talk like one on 'em, si thi.

"You … staying?" Florence asked, flashing him one of her seductive smiles as she reached for his coat. "It's warm and … welcoming in here, and cold out … there."

"Well, go on then," he agreed, relinquishing his outer coat. "But I've onny ten minutes. Got to call off at Joseph and Lilly Victoria's – although she's no longer there."

"No longer … there?" Poppy puzzled, a deep frown furrowing her brow. "Is there a … problem?"

"Don't know," he replied. "She's staying at ours wi' their kids and has been for a while. Just dropped in to ask you if you'd like me to give you a 'and with your soirée, whenever you plan to hold it."

Florence had already gone to the kitchen to put on the kettle and to bring out some of the delicious cakes that Mary's niece, Mary Jane, had made.

"Probably the first Saturday in December," Poppy replied tentatively. "You would be more than welcome. Have a look at the guest list, if you like."

"Tea's up!" Florence called as she placed the tray on the living room table.

"How's Sally getting on, Tom?" Ross asked the old farmer one rather chilly Friday afternoon in early December. "Has she learned the ropes yet?"

"Learned the ropes?" Tom scoffed. "She's not only learned the ropes, you'd have thought she'd written t'instruction manual! She not onny gets on wi' t'job, she gets on wi' our lasses. They think the world of her."

"A good appointment then, would you say?" Ross replied with a satisfied smile.

"Not only is she working well, both production and profitability have increased by fifty per cent," Tom added. "Tha'll not get our Lilly to come back now, si thi. Nor would I want her to, with how much of a natural yon lass had proved to be."

"I've found t'same with her father, Jim," Ross said. "I think we fell on our feet when we brought those two on board. How are you feeling now, Tom?" Ross went on after a few minutes. "Any improvement?"

"Yon medic reckons it could be some time before I get back to approaching normal," Tom tried to explain slowly. "If ever I get there, I'm afraid."

"No problems with the farms, Tom," Ross pointed out. "So, tha needs to tek it easy and get better when tha can. Slowly, slowly, catchee monkey. In fact, we have a farmers' meeting in Northallerton this evening to look at fluctuations in markets and the ways forward according to public demand, and such like."

"Aye lad, I wish I could accompany thee," Tom said. "I do miss mi usual pint in t'Swan and all them tales shared wi' t'other lads. Tell thee what; 'ows about if our George comes wi' thee?"

"Would he be all rayt wi' that?" Ross asked.

"Course 'e would!" Tom exclaimed. "'E's mi son, int he?"

"Job's a good un, then," Ross replied with a nod.

~

"So, what did you think about yon meeting, George?" Ross said once he had ordered two pints of bitter at the Swan's bar.

"Interesting if a little inconclusive," George replied. "It seems to me that a bit more footwork needs to be undertaken with our customers."

"How do you mean?" Ross asked, wiping away the first froth from his lips.

"It's all well and good taking orders to customers reasonably close to where we operate, but what about the communities further afield?" George answered, once he'd had a much-needed gulp of his liquid refreshment. "Like Richmond, Pickering, Sherriff Hutton, Bowes and Castle Howard, for example. We need to be extending our range – permanently – to all the outlying areas where there are communities that need our services. Larger towns like Thirsk and Scarborough, where we went a year or two ago. Big then, but much larger now."

"How would you go about doing that, bearing in mind that your dad and Joseph did that sort of research to ascertain demand," Ross pointed out.

"But that was ages ago," George insisted. "There is now a much greater demand for what we have to offer. We need to expand by employing drivers of a few more wagons to take out deliveries, after doing research out in those areas – which I would be more than happy to tek on."

"Bloomin' 'eck!" Ross gasped. "You have thought this through, haven't you! How about if I talk to Joseph tomorrow with you present, to see which way we go?"

"Excellent!" George agreed. "Now I must away."

During this conversation, a darkly clad hulk of a man with collar upturned, flat cap pulled down over his forehead and long greasy hair tucked into its back, had been listening, though not really understanding much of what was said.

He caught George's last words, downed his pint and left the pub quickly. This news had to be interesting and worth carrying off to his master. Hadn't he always been going on about anything to do with George Garside?

"And are you *certain,* old chap, that this body is on his way home, alone, to Garside's farm," his master insisted, drawing his face closer to that of his lackey slowly, threateningly.

The ruffian flinched as the boss man flicked his nose lightly, leaving him in no doubt what his 'reward' would be if he were relaying erroneous information.

"Sure beyond *all* possible doubt?" the Boss Man insisted.

"Well, er, yes. I think so," the ruffian replied, now not so certain.

"Indeed. I hope that your feelings prove to be correct," Boss Man warned, a dire threat wandering through his steely eyes. "For your … own … sake."

Those words bore a dire, frighteningly clear warning that left the man in no doubt what any mistake would cost him.

"JoJo and Bango, follow the quarry with Pete here. Stop him and bring him back here to me," Boss Man urged. "Mess up and you will be … sorry."

⁓ ⌁ ⌐

"I've never done that before," George admitted.

"What? Had a pint of ale in the Swan?" Ross asked, quietly surprised.

"No. Been there umpteen times," George explained with a snigger. "Attended a meeting and given my opinion on what needs to be done. What I said earlier on makes complete sense, and I am prepared to do what I said. It's—"

"Get 'im!" a raucous voice called out, as both George and Ross were grabbed from behind and dragged out of the pony and trap. "Get 'em both and strap their arms and legs so they can't escape. T'master wants 'em both alive."

~⌒~

"Our George not home yet?" Lilly Garside said to her husband, a worried look surfacing.

"His first time at the Farmers'," Tom replied, referring to the meeting he had attended with Ross Booth. "Let 'im be. He needs to experience the atmosphere and all that goes wi' it, along wi' t'social afterwards."

"If you mean sending copious amounts of beer down his throat, that won't do him any good. I can't call that socialising," she snapped.

"It won't happen, my little poppet," her husband offered in his son's defence. "He's wi' Ross Booth, our Martha's lovely 'usband, and 'e wayn't let it happen. Be rayt."

They were interrupted by the snick of the front door. As both turned to confront the intruder, George tiptoed into the room to a warm glow from the fire grate and his parents' shadows flickering on the wall to his side.

"Goodness gracious!" his mother gasped. "What happened to you?"

"'As tha bin in a fairground boxing booth, our George?" Tom laughed. "What's to do, then?"

"We were attacked – from behind, I hasten to add – on t'lane just outside t'turn off to Boulders Wood," their son explained. "There were three on 'em, and at least one I've seen before. He's associated with Jonas Jamieson, Poppy's cousin – and my, would I like to get my hands on *him!* It's a pity he has to resort to employing thugs and ruffians to do his dirty work."

"I see you've had a crack to the side of your head," his mother observed. "That'll be sore tomorrow."

"You should have seen the one that Ross dealt with!" George went on. "He had Ross round the neck and throat from behind in the cart, when Ross simply stood up with this … this human *scarf* still around his neck, lifted him above his head and threw – yes, threw – him down that steep rocky edge, bouncing off boulders and several trees in his journey south. My attacker's face was a picture of shock and fear when he saw what Ross had done with his mate. I simply took advantage and socked him in the jaw three times. Went out like a candle in the wind."

"What are you going to do now?" Lilly asked, still shocked.

"We have them securely tied – wrists, arms and legs – in the back of the trap, fast asleep," George said. "Ready for—"

"Won't they freeze to death outside in the cold?" she gasped, again concerned but for different reasons.

"A trip to the local police station tomorrow," he continued unabashed. "And don't concern yourself, Mother, as the trap is in the shed, next to the pig sty."

Tom Garside burst out laughing at the picture his son had just painted, and the feelings of joy his assailants would experience when they awoke to the 'dainty' atmosphere their lodgings had provided – at no extra charge.

"And the third ruffian – the one I recognised – hot-footed it like the hounds of hell were within snapping distance of his sad arse," George sniggered. "I can just imagine the welcome he will receive from his master when he breaks the news of their failure once again to bring the prize Jonas has so desired for all these years, since the last time I brought home to him the error of his ways."

CHAPTER 9

"Tell me again," Jonas urged the ruffian thug in a corner before him, who had blood oozing from a broken nose and his eye socket swelling rapidly enough to close down his vision. "Or else, once again, you ... will ... be ... sorry."

"JoJo and Bango attacked as we had planned, when Garside reached the rocky slope where the track breaks off to the McIntyre Farm," the ruffian started to explain. "But we didn't expect that he would have a companion for protection."

"Companion? For protection?" Jonas asked, more than a little surprised. "Who was this ... companion? Description, please old chap. I might know him."

"You would certainly know him if you saw him," the ruffian explained. "Physically enormous by anybody's standards. Well-known in farming circles, he simply stood up still in the cart with JoJo around his neck, lifted him above his head and threw him down a rocky ravine."

"Did he ... survive?" Jonas snarled. "Quickly, man. Did JoJo survive this ... encounter?"

"I don't see how he could have. I mean..." the ruffian

replied, cowering even further into the corner.

"And Bango?" Jonas continued. "Did he at least do as he was bidden?"

"Three massive blows to the jaw from Garside and he was out," the ruffian responded quietly.

"Arghhh!" Jonas screeched in a violent fit of rage. He kicked out at the ruffian, catching him on the side of his already battered head as he slumped unconscious in a distasteful and useless pile in the corner of this refuse-strewn room.

"Damn! Damn! Damn! Thwarted at every turn!" Jonas exclaimed, kicking a broken chair into the corner almost as a tombstone for his unfortunate henchman. "Will I never be granted the revenge due to me because of inefficient and inept people?"

He gathered his scant belongings and stamped out of the room, leaving nature to take its course on his former companion. Cheap lodgings such as this were available at a moment's notice – should you know where to find them. Fortunately for Jonas, he could always rely on Jenny Bott to provide him with somewhere to lay his head.

"Oiy! Anybody aht there?" Bango Ruffian yelled from his restraints in the cart next door to a rather smelly pig sty. "I'm cold in 'ere! 'Ave you no 'umanity? Oiy!"

The door to the small shed creaked open slowly to allow entry to two large men whom the incarcerated ruffian didn't recognise in the very cold light of a snowy winter's day.

"You're awake then," the shorter of the two said with a sarcastic sneer. "Hungry and cold, eh? How on earth did you find your way into here? Bit of a strange – and smelly – lodging place, don't you think?"

"Are you going to release us, then?" the ruffian responded. "We've been kidnapped and imprisoned illegally in this cold cell. My friend here—"

"Is dead," the taller of the two boomed, his deep rasping voice almost grating on the ears. "And has been for some time."

"Just a minute…" the ruffian puzzled the faces before him began to swim into focus. "You're not the—!"

"Ones you were supposed to rough up last night?" the shorter man offered. "Didn't do such a good job after all, did you? Met more than your match, eh? I recognise you, Mr Bango Allen, and your worse-for-wear buddy, JoJo O'Neal – two of the most inept strong arms in the business. Your boss left you to it, then? Left you to pick up the tab on this murderous attack, which will see you behind bars for many a year. Your jailers might even be encouraged to misplace the key to your cell."

"Now wait a minute!" Bango complained. "I have rights! And who did we kill? And who are you to keep me prisoner here?"

"We are the police, and we are here to provide you with accommodation in a lovely cell that you will be sharing with seven other miscreants," the shorter one said. "Detective Sergeant Shaw and Detective Constable Green, at your service. As for why, the two gentlemen that have just joined us were attacked last evening by you and your pal, who I think is a little stiff with the cold. Now, here's the thing. If you can see it in your way to give us your boss's name, we might – just *might,* mind you – see fit to be a little more lenient with you."

He turned to Ross and George for acknowledgement, to nods and thumbs up from them.

"As our transport for criminals is somewhat limited, I'm afraid, would it be possible for you to drive the living and the dead to the police station with us?" the sergeant asked.

"Of course it would," Ross returned. "But it would be good to know for sure who is the mastermind behind this fiasco. We've a feeling who it *might* be."

"We've only ever known him as 'Boss'," Bango responded quickly, ever mindful that his relative freedom depended upon his memory. "But I know that his real first name is Jonas. Like as not, he will have left our other friend, Pete, in a state little better than JoJo here. I don't know his other names."

"Just as we thought," the Detective Constable retorted. "We have found your other pal in a deserted dwelling in the town. He is now in hospital, close to death."

"Well, gentlemen, if you wouldn't mind?" the sergeant inquired as Ross and George drew the trap out of the shed into the startlingly cold winter morning.

"I'll take it from here, George, if you want to get back to breakfast and work," Ross offered. "We'll talk about our other stuff later on with Joseph,"

~

"Is it true about Uncle Joseph and Auntie Lilly Victoria?" Poppy asked her Nanny Nell as she stood by the front window of Boulders Wood one Friday morning, gazing at the incessant snow blizzard.

December had come in like the proverbial lion, roaring and blustering as if it needed folks to notice that it was there. Nothing was ever achieved outside in this sort of weather except making sure the animals were safe. Their very hardy flocks of sheep could withstand a certain amount of harsh weather, but they needed food and unfrozen water to survive.

"In what respect, my poppet?" Nell asked, as she turned from outside's inclemency to the gloriously roaring fire that no house could manage without, particularly this one.

"Is it true that they are not living under the same roof?" Poppy answered, never short of an honest riposte.

"A minor readjustment of living conditions because Uncle Joseph—" Nell started to reply.

"Works too hard? Poppy suggested. "I know it's not my business, but is that really a reasonable solution to what every farmer does? I mean—"

"You are right," Nell replied. "It is not any of your business."

"Come on, Nanny!" Poppy sneered. "I'm not six any more. Even I can realise there must be problems. I know them very well as a couple, and I have spent a lot of time with their youngsters."

"To be *really* truthful," Nell went on, "I am hoping things will sort themselves out once Jim and Sally Smallshore have settled in, along with George Garside—"

"George?" Poppy asked quickly. "Why? What's George about to undertake?"

"He's made a lot of very pertinent and obvious observations about the wider circulation of ordering and delivering our meats and dairy produce throughout the North Riding," Nell explained. "So, he's going to take over all of that from after Christmas."

"Does that mean he will be away much more?" Poppy asked carefully, not wishing to give away her feelings for him. "I mean—"

"Indeed, it does, at least in the short term," Nell assured her. "He is getting to an age when he may well be looking for a wife. To do that, he needs to begin earning a good wage, and this is one way of doing it. He is a bright young man who must start to spread his wings."

Poppy sat down with a bump in front of the fire and

reached for a cup of tea and a nibble on a piece of fruit cake that Mary-Jane had just brought in. My, that cake was good; as good as everything else she did. It was almost as good as the stuff Mary produced when she lived at Boulders Wood.

George to be away more, travelling? Did that mean she would see less of him? Did it mean also that he would find greater opportunities to snare himself a … wife? Problems that she would have to share with Florence.

～

This took Joseph back a year or two: waiting in the Garside's front room, hoping to catch sight of the lovely form of Tom's eldest daughter, Lilly Victoria. Same place, same emotional wait to catch sight of her, but would she feel the same? Not only did he want to see and hold her – his wonderful wife – but he needed to be able to hug and rough and tumble with his three children, too.

Having kept him on tenterhooks for fifteen minutes, she finally slid around the door frame, whereupon he walked purposefully up to her, took her in his arms, and kissed her passionately. She responded as she had never done before, leaving him in no doubt where she wanted to be.

"Are we ready for home together, my wonderful wife?" he asked, still holding her tightly. "I am ready to take my family home, but only if they want to come with me. Jim and Sally Smallshore are functioning well, along with John Stafford, and that will allow me to have a goodly amount of time away from work to spend with my family. What do you say? Is it time to become a family again, like we used to be?"

"You've no idea, my lovely man, how long I've waited for this moment," she responded with a quiet sigh of contentment. "I've regretted being away from you every moment since we walked out and—"

"Don't blame yourself, Lilly Victoria," he replied softly, kissing her on the forehead. "The blame rests squarely on my shoulders because I was too busy working to see the effect my not being there was having on my beautiful family. I promise that it won't happen again. Shall we go back to our cottage, which is cold and soulless without you all?"

"In this weather? Cold? I hope not!" she replied. Upon seeing the puzzled frown flicker across his face, she burst into a heartfelt giggle, showing him the sense of humour he had missed, a good dose of which he really needed at this moment to replenish and reinvigorate his feelings and emotions.

Almost immediately a whirlwind of young arms and legs burst through the adjoining door, heading unerringly for Daddy. Overwhelmed, Joseph's tears flowed down his cheeks as he embraced his youngsters as if he hadn't seen them for ever.

"Your carriage awaits milady," he said, turning towards his wife to beckon them all to join him for their short ride home.

Unlike his brother, Ross made it in his way to spend a significant amount of time with *his* wife and their daughter, Annie. In hindsight, this would be the most important part of his life as time wasted without them could never be recalled or replaced. Every minute of his waking hours spent in *their* company enhanced *his* existence, and he couldn't wait to return to them at any time during each day.

Consequently, work never became a chore or a bore because he was working for his family's good. His ultimate reward? Family time at the end of each day when he could bathe his daughter before her bedtime and spend 'catching-up' time with his lovely wife thereafter.

For the wider family, time seemed to stand still *and* to move on frighteningly quickly when, within the blink of an eye, bright morning became stark and claustrophobic dusk.

Nell and Ross Senior had taken to spending a significantly larger slice of their life in their lovely home in Richmond, close to the countryside they both gloried in. There, even at this time of year under a blanket of pristine snow, the smell and feel of living nature was ever present. They visited and stayed at Boulders Wood only when necessary, either because of family need or business opportunity.

A goodly part of her time, Nell allowed her mind to drift back to opportunities missed and to things she regretted not having done. Uppermost during much of her time alone was the overwhelming loss of her two bairns, Jamie and Annie. How would their lives have turned out? Would *their* presence have enhanced *her* life any more? Would things have been any different had Joss not turned out to be the monster he was before his untimely death?

Mary also spent only as much time there as she or her niece, Mary-Jane, felt was important or necessary. Now the consummate businesswoman, Mary was able to spend her days whenever and wherever she considered she was needed. Her marriage to Geoffrey had proved to be a gloriously successful and shrewdly important move; not only did he love her to distraction, he also supported her in all her endeavours to make a success of their life together. Her one regret? She could never have children. Not because she didn't have the desire, but because physiologically it was not … conceivable.

⁓

"You seem very pensive today, Mother," Ross said at break-fast early one morning in mid-December. "Anything troubling you?"

"I have a lot on my mind just now," Nell returned with a stretch and a yawn.

"Anything you'd like to share?" he offered. "I'm all ears."

"They're not that big, my son," she said with a slight giggle. "Festivities for the coming winter season, for example. Do we invite family here to—?"

"Not your family home any more, Mother dear," he remarked baldly. "And so not your decision to make. We all assumed you would be away to somewhere where there's no white stuff and no extended family, but certainly plenty of warmth – and I don't mean Scarborough. Don't forget that your ageing bones need warmth."

"Is that your way of telling me I'm getting too old to be concerned with organising Christmas?" she laughed.

"Actually, we all thought that our small family might like to celebrate the coming events quietly here at Boulders Wood for the one day, which would be—" he went on.

"Christmas Day?" Nell ventured.

"Too right," he agreed. "Joseph and I would like to decorate our own places to celebrate with our own children for that morning, with perhaps a meal in the afternoon here for us all, bringing in the likes of Florence and Poppy with her father, along with Sally and Jim Smallshore. We should invite Mary and her Geoffrey, and Mary-Jane and her young man, Trevor. Outside caterers would be important, too."

"Mary and Mary-Jane – and me, of course – wouldn't be at all happy with that one!" Nell warned. "If it's to be only one meal, that sort of thing *has* to be done by us, and I am sure Mary would agree. Don't forget that the only family she has is Mary-Jane. It wouldn't be a problem because we could rest at some other time. Agreed?"

"Do we need to run it by Mary first?" Ross said, knowing that there was more here than met the eye.

"Already done, my son," she replied with a self-congratulatory grin.

"Mother!" he exclaimed. "Walked right into your trap, eh?"

"We have had exactly the same ideas as you, except for the catering," Nell laughed. "Only, we had them earlier. The other thing on my mind was why we seemed to have a deepish set of footprints around the house," she added. "They were there when I arose at six o'clock, when no-one else had been up, and they disappear into the distance towards the woods up past the lake."

CHAPTER 10

"So, you are about to embark upon a new adventure, eh, George Garside?" Poppy asked. George's Monday off had guided him towards his favourite place of all time because of the tea and eye-watering cakes – although the company of his two favourite ladies might have had something else to do with it.

"I felt simply that it was about time I raised my head above the parapet to shout about what I thought," he returned with passion. "Fortunately, Ross agreed with my ideas, and Joseph gave the go-ahead for early January."

"Is that the best time to undertake something like that?" Poppy puzzled. "I mean, bad weather and all that?"

"Don't have any problems wi' that, bearing in mind I shall be getting a brand-new wagon and shire for my trouble," George replied with a puff out of his ample chest. "It'll allow me to visit places I've niver seen before, like Hawes and Richmond and Pickering and Bowes. A veritable exploratory adventure!"

"Oo, hark at you with your chic language!" Poppy

exclaimed with a giggle. "By the way, will you be at our launch soirée this coming Saturday?"

"Try to keep me away, young lady!" he stated categorically. "You'll need *someone* to keep order, I feel. You never know the sort of people you are going to attract until they stagger through yon door. They do know how to *get* here, I suppose?"

"Trust me, George Garside," Poppy assured him. "If they can't find their way here after all the instructions I have sent them, then the door will remain shut and they don't deserve to be here."

"And Florence is—?" he said, to be interrupted by a very familiar, light, well-spoken voice.

"Here!" Florence announced cheerily.

"Slept in?" George teased her playfully.

"Not really," Florence replied confidently. "I've been writing, deciding where my *magnum opus* might take place and what characters might catch the reader's eye."

"Story time, eh?" George asked, an enthusiastic grin decorating his face. "Come on then, let's hear what you have to say."

"I don't think so!" Florence said, her demeanour warning him to back off. "We writers don't divulge our sources and our ideas until the finished product is in print. In other words, dear George, keep your nose out."

"All right. Just off to finish my cake and tea, then I'm away," he said sternly. "I know when I'm not wanted." With that he drained his cup, wiped his lips on his pristine, white serviette and headed for the door.

"George! Don't—!" Poppy urged, but the outside door clicked and he was gone.

"Could have been more delicately put, Florence, my dear," Poppy remonstrated with her friend. "We probably won't see him now for goodness knows how long. We were having such a lovely, intimate conversation, too."

"Are we going to fall out over a … man, Poppy, my friend?" Florence said sharply. "Had he known what he was asking, I wouldn't have minded, but … *that*?"

"I should imagine that there is now a distinct possibility he won't even turn up for our soirée on Saturday after your outspoken outburst, my dear," Poppy reiterated, irritated at her friend's unnecessary sharpness.

"If he comes, he comes," Florence muttered, dismissive of her friend's criticism as she slipped into the kitchen to make tea.

Poppy could not rationalise her friend's startling change in attitude. Was this a new Florence, or one that had always been there but she hadn't experienced before? Or had something happened that she wasn't talking about? Only time would tell. Poppy would have to be on her guard, particularly as they had a very important event to host the following weekend.

"Do you really not care about … anything any more?" Poppy asked her friend pointedly, not sure of her answer, or even if she would answer at all.

"Just not sure whether I can be bothered with other people's thoughts and opinions now," Florence replied moodily. "Nobody cares about mine, so why should I bother about theirs?"

"But we *do* all care about you," Poppy said, trying to persuade Florence of her value, particularly to her … and their dear George. "There is no-one – not even our dear George – that I would rather share my time with, you know. I have been, and still am, very much looking forward to our first soirée, and I won't be able to see it through on my own."

"Sorry, *dear* Poppy," Florence's apology drew tears to her eyes. "I don't know why, but I was feeling a little fragile and, well, unloved, really."

Poppy slipped her arm round Florence's shoulders and drew her to her bosom in a fulsome hug. Her friend's welfare was her most important concern, not only because of their impending literary event, but because her friendship had always made Poppy feel they were more like sisters.

"Shall we have a look at the piece we were mulling over the other day?" Poppy suggested with a fond grin. "I've had a few ideas that might – 'might', I say – carry some bearing and engage more than one or two of our guests."

⁓

"Uncle Ross?" Poppy's voice crept over his shoulder while he was having a break in Boulders Wood's living room from his chores of the day. As usual, red and yellow tongues were intent on escaping up the chimney as well as sharing their overwhelming heat with the living room and its occupants.

"The answer is … yes," he said, raising Poppy's eyebrows with his unduly sharp answer.

"Yes?" she queried. "You don't know what I was about to ask you, unless you are a psychic."

"Ah, but I do, and I can't profess to be psychic, either," he replied, putting the daily newspaper on the settee next to him. "But I do know what's so special about this day."

"Go on then!" Poppy scoffed. "Shock me."

"You and Florence would like me to take you to the woods to choose a Christmas tree for your cottage to decorate before your first literary soirée, which is this coming Saturday," Ross replied confidently.

"How did you know that, Clairvoyant Ross Booth?" Poppy giggled.

"This is the day for the last several years – exactly – that we have brought in a tree for Christmas decoration, under your direction," he crowed, sticking his chest out.

"Well, smarty pants, do we have a deal?" she sniggered. "We will be having our soirée this coming Saturday, so there is not much time."

"It will be my pleasure to take you both on Florence's first Christmas tree hunt," Ross agreed. "The choices will be yours, bearing in mind the height and width of your living space, and the time you have to decorate it."

"And now, here we are, only four days to go, and we have all the other decorations to do as well," Poppy said, a slight curl of worry appearing at the corners of her mouth.

"Tomorrow's Wednesday, my day off," he replied with a smile. "How about if we do it mid-morning, then? Will Florence be with us?"

"She's not that enamoured, but with a bit of persuasion we may get her to join us," Poppy replied. "She's very wary, not only about paddling about in deep snow, but also about her safety."

"Safety?" Ross puzzled. "In what respect?"

"She was concerned about the recent attack on you and George that we just heard about," she explained. "Also, she doesn't really respond enthusiastically when confronted with temperatures lower than seventy degrees. She doesn't feel safe when there is little heat. Don't ask!"

"Hello," Florence's enthusiastic voice joined them.

"Been writing, ready for our event?" Poppy asked as Florence sat near them with a deep sigh.

"Not really," she replied. "I've been tidying my bedroom, ready for decoration. Do you know what we need?"

"Could it be a Prince Albert tree?" Poppy cast a glance at Ross's smiling face.

"Prince Albert?" Florence puzzled. "What is he to do with decorations?"

"Did you never have a Christmas tree to decorate?" Poppy said. "Do you remember the one we had that first Christmas you came to stay?"

"Never had one of those at home," Florent reiterated sternly. "Father didn't believe in that sort of thing, really, although I did like the one when we were eight."

"Would you like to have one in our cottage?" Poppy asked eagerly. "Ready for our soirée which is … four days away?"

"That close?" Florence gasped. "We'd better get a move on, then! Unfortunately, though, my delicate feet and all that deep, cold white stuff don't make easy bed fellows. Even as a child I couldn't stand the stuff. Consequently, if it's of little concern to you both, I'll wait in the cottage and help you carry it into the sitting room when you get back."

They all laughed at the face Florence pulled while describing her non-love affair with the winter climatic conditions that most – children, at least – loved to experience, if only for a brief moment.

Florence liked comfort and excitement. She had come from an uncomfortable and mundanely controlling family experience, particularly as a teenager. She couldn't believe the freedom that had leaped into her lap once she had taken up with her cousin and best friend, Poppy McIntyre. Very similar in outlook and literary ambitions, but not so in tastes and feelings, they got along famously. It would be safe to say that, without Poppy's support and friendship, her life would have followed a sadder and less fulfilling path.

"I must be away back to work," Ross said, leaping to his feet. "Just off upstairs to see Martha and Annie before I go. See you tomorrow."

"Why tomorrow?" Florence asked, once Ross had disappeared into one of the very large bedrooms upstairs that had been converted into another sitting room for his family's sole use. They certainly had no need of five bedrooms – for the time being, anyway.

"His day off, and we're going out for another reason," Poppy answered. "I'm hoping you'll change your mind and join us in searching for our tree. Think about it? It'll be good fun, and then we could decorate it together."

"Where would we get the decorations from?" Florence queried. "I know nothing about that sort of stuff."

"I have them already," Poppy assured her with a giggle.

"And I suppose you have just the place for the tree as well?" her friend said.

"Just the *perfect* place," Poppy smiled.

"What did I tell you?" Poppy said, as the friends and Uncle Ross set off for the high field where all the pine trees grew.

"I am already cold, and we've only just closed the front door!" Florence shivered. "Do you know where we're heading?"

"Trust me," Ross reassured her. "We are heading for the same field Poppy and I visited when she was eight and had never seen a Christmas tree before, and that was—"

"Great fun!" Poppy whooped. "I had no idea what all this decorating was about and was convinced that that well-known parasite plant was called 'middle toe'."

They all laughed, giving Florence the opportunity to grow accustomed to the chill and the damp snow around her booted and stockinged feet. Afraid that her feet and legs might drop off because of the cold, she was impressed with the rubberised, waterproof, knee-length boots that kept *all* the wet out, allowing her feet to stay reasonably warm in the thick woollen stockings she had never worn before. Lots of layers of under-clothing beneath a lengthy, thick coat persuaded her that this wasn't such a bad outing – as long as it didn't last forever!

The outer edges of the wood, where the trees brushed the north field, glowered moodily as if they too would have preferred to be somewhere warmer. The swishy long grasses at the margins between the two fields at lower levels were completely hidden by a deep, extensive white blanket, with only the very occasional bedraggled blade tip visible. The three intrepid adventurers broke through the hedge at its thinnest, ready to enter the only field where the magical Christmas trees grew in abundance.

"This could become our Christmas field," Poppy announced through the muffling clothing, scarves and hat that virtually covered her body and head.

"Christmas field?" Florence queried. "Is that because the field appears only at this time of year?"

"Nooo!" Poppy reiterated. "How could that be? No, because all the foliage decorations we *need* for Christmas décor grow only here in this hallowed field."

"Not much idea what you are talking about, really," Florence replied, with a vague hint of sarcasm.

"Just look!" Poppy urged as a small field appeared magi-cally before them. It contained fir trees small enough to cut and grace their cottage sitting room, holly bushes in full berry, 'middle toe' growing through the branches of its host trees, and ivy a-plenty. "This is all we need to provide us with all the Christmas cheer we will require to host a very success-ful soirée."

Ross smiled indulgently at the two young ladies' earnest discussion. They had been so well-cocooned from the sharp edges of society at large, and, in general, that both pleased and concerned him at the same time. He needed to keep a handle upon everything they wanted to achieve and provide security when needed to fend off the unpleasant side of a generally depraved and undesirable society. He had just the man in mind upon whom he might rely to help him with these two beautiful young ladies.

"It puts me in mind of Brigadoon, the legendary village in the highlands of Scotland," Poppy began.

"Brigadoon?" Florence retorted, a deeply puzzled look crossing her face. "Not heard of that one, I'm afraid."

"Me neither," Ross chipped in.

"It is believed that the village of Brigadoon 'disappeared' in 1754," Poppy explained. "A spell had been cast over the village to protect it from the advancing English Redcoats during the Jacobite Rebellion of the mid-1700s. The village is supposed to exist still, and to reappear only for one day every one hundred years. Outsiders could visit during that day only. The only problem was that *no* inhabitant was allowed to leave, or it would disappear into Highland mists, never to reappear."

All this she recounted with a straight face, urging her friend to believe the story.

"Is that really true?" Florence asked, not quite comprehending the term 'myth'. "I mean—"

"I think the clue rests in the word 'myth'," Ross suggested, trying valiantly to suppress his mirth. "This takes me back to the time *we* first did this, Poppy," he said as he pointed and scanned the eaves of the distant woods.

"I assume you mean that you have seen that body dressed in black that's trying to hide from the snow up there?" Poppy replied, pointing to the line of trees at the edge of the trees. "He's looking down here."

"You said almost the same thing the first time we were here together," he sighed. "That is indeed what I meant."

"And, now he's gone," Poppy observed.

"His demeanour was familiar, but I can't recall where I've seen him before," Ross puzzled.

Florence had no idea what they were talking about.

"Jacobite Rebellion?" Florence went on, trying to ignore their words about this ghostly observer miles away. "What *were* Jacobites? What does that name refer to?"

"Followers of James Stewart," Poppy explained. "Jacobite comes from the Latin for James – Jacobus. So, 'followers of James'."

"You've decided upon the tree, then?" Ross asked, raring to get back to his family. "You two cut the holly, ivy and 'middle toe' you need, while I take down the tree."

CHAPTER 11

"Goodness me!" George gasped as he entered the sitting room in Poppy and Florence's cottage. "That tree has to be six-feet high if it's an inch."

"Do you like the decorations of the *whole* room?" Poppy asked, a joyous jiggling of her feet betraying her excitement.

"Shall I start at the top and move downwards eating all those hanging sweets, fruit, nuts and cakes?" George offered eagerly – he *was* always hungry, was George. "They *are* edible … aren't they?"

"I wouldn't try those transparent balls!" Florence laughed. "They are made from glass. The angels and candles are real as well."

"Real, as in?" George puzzled.

"The angels come alive after midnight, and then they light up the candles," Poppy replied with a smile.

"You're having me on!" George said, an unsure grimace ushering in his doubt. "Aren't you?"

"Of course we are!" Florence laughed again. "Similarly with the Nativity scene at the tree's base. We *have to* have a

Nativity scene. Christmas wouldn't be the same without it."

"When did you say the hordes will be arriving for your literary soirée?" he asked, genuinely interested.

"As today is Friday, the fourth of December, that would be … tomorrow, mid-afternoon," Poppy replied. "Everything is set and ready. You *will* be coming, won't you?" She slipped her arm through his as she rested her head briefly in his chest, eyes looking upwards into his face and telling him that she desperately needed him to be there.

"The catering has been arranged by Mary and her niece, Mary-Jane," Florence butted in, latching on to his other arm. "You can't surely miss that—"

"Spread?" he interrupted. "No fear! How could any right-thinking man forego the sort of a spread that undoubtedly will be exquisitely extraordinary?"

"Hark at you, George Garside!" Poppy chided him playfully. "Using big words like … 'forego' … and … 'spread'."

"You always did know how to pull my leg, Poppy McIntyre," he said. "Or is it soon to be Spence? Will you be taking your father's name? Has Mr Thomas Spence asked that question yet?"

Poppy remained quiet for a while, a pensive look overtaking her pretty face.

"Not sure yet, George," she responded slowly. "I've worn the name 'McIntyre' since I entered this world and I have a mind to keep it. Although when – *if* – I become an author, I wonder if it might be advantageous for my name to become P. Spence?"

"Why P. Spence and not Poppy Spence?" he asked.

"Unfortunately, history has shown us that female authors have been less well-received than their male counterparts," Poppy explained. "For example, George Sand, the French female author, was actually named Amantine Lucile Dupin. The three Brontë sisters wrote as Currer, Acton and Ellis Bell. Mary Evans used George Eliot as her pen name."

"And we can heartily recommend *her* novels *Mill on the Floss* and *Middlemarch*," Florence butted in.

"The American author Louisa May Alcott – author of *Little Women* – originally wrote under the pseudonym A. M. Barnard," Poppy added. "There were many others who were refused publication by recalcitrant publishers."

"Crikey!" George gasped. "How do you know all that?"

"Reading, dear George," both girls chanted with a grin.

"It can do you nothing but good," Poppy explained.

"Particularly when you have nothing else to do," Florence added. "You will never be bored."

"You will be coming to our soirée, then, won't you?" Poppy cajoled again as she snuggled up to him.

"Please?" Florence said, supporting her friend and doing the same on his other side.

~

George thoroughly enjoyed the close contact he had with 'his girls', Poppy and Florence. Even if he had an enormously generous amount of work to wade through, he wouldn't have missed their inaugural event for the world. Consequently, he rose early, shaved and bathed, breakfasted and prepared himself for what he deemed might be a trying, if enjoyable, time.

He also felt that it was his duty to provide a degree of security for his lovelies that might not be forthcoming from elsewhere. Although held in a relatively safe environment, no-one could guarantee that interlopers would *not* infiltrate, particularly with Mary's catering laid out for the taking.

The room was warm, but the welcome for George from

the hosts of the gathering was even warmer. The Christmas decorations and baubles around the tree added a further *je ne sais quoi* to the surroundings, with lush, thick curtains draped at the windows to encourage the heat generated by the glowing logs in the fire hearth to remain in the room. Each guest arrived, swathed in appropriate clothing to ensure survival in the dire winter conditions that only the North Riding could inflict on its inhabitants.

Horse-drawn carriages arrived and deposited their fares at the door. Their drivers were given express instructions to return at precisely eight o'clock sharp in the evening to whisk away hopefully happy guests, with their literary aspirations fulfilled to a certain degree, ready for the next soirée in the near future.

By four o'clock, all the guests had arrived, the gas wall lights were glowing, the inviting spread of deliciously looking and smelling foods had been laid in the dining room, and enjoyment was afoot. Poppy had made card name labels attached to safety pins so that guests might know to whom they were talking, thereby allowing more convivial social interaction.

"Hal … McIntyre?" George asked of a bluff, bearded young man who bore a well-travelled air. "Does that mean—?"

"I am related to our host?" the man replied. "Indeed, it does. As far as I am concerned, we share the same blood to some degree on the male side of the family. I am theoretically, if not legally, her first cousin once removed. To me, legitimacy is merely a technicality. An intensely practical person, I need as many *real* relatives as I am able to secure."

By this time the whole group had gathered around them, plates of delicious food to hand, as they listened to Hal McIntyre's exploits in Africa. Many discussions over tasty morsels worked their way around the group after introductions had been made and talks about their individual works

106

of literature had been delivered.

Poppy turned around to see her father standing by the inner door. She strode over to him purposefully. "Father," she said quietly as she embraced him. "I didn't know you were coming. You should have let me know and I would have been here to greet you. Let me introduce you to my group."

"No, Poppy, it's all right, really—" Tommy urged.

"Everybody!" she called. "Just one minute, if you please. I should like you all to meet … my father, Thomas Spence."

Both Florence and George acknowledged Poppy's delight at being able to introduce her father publicly, something she had desperately wanted and needed to do for many more years than she could remember.

"So, your name, my friend, is Pieter van de Behr?" Hal said to a strangely muffled, heavily bearded and moustachioed fellow who had mysteriously kept himself to himself throughout. "Where are you from?"

"I am Dutch, and I am from the Hague in Holland," de Behr replied in a curious accent.

"That's a very strange accent for a Netherlander," Hal McIntyre observed. "I have spent a lot of time in the Netherlands in the company of the natives of that country, but I have never come across anyone that has called himself 'Dutch' or has called the city of Den Haag 'the Hague, or the country 'Holland'. To a native it could be only 'Netherlands'. Are you sure you are a Netherlander?

"Hello," he said abruptly, turning to talk to a young woman whose eyes were covered by dark spectacles beneath a large-brimmed hat pulled down level with her eyes. "Don't I know you from somewhere?"

He turned back to his 'Netherlander' to find he was no longer there.

"Abigail?" Poppy said, recognising the young woman's voice. "Abigail Green? Is it really you? Why didn't you let me know it was you?"

"You know as well as I do that women are – how should I put it? – not as well received in literary circles as men," she explained. "J.J. Whiteside was my maternal grandfather – a lovely man – and I thought his name might bring me luck. This is a fantastic gathering, by the way. It will make a fabulous article for the coming week's paper."

"I recognised that man who just left," George said to Poppy, taking her on one side. "The one that your cousin Hal was taking to task over … something obscure. There was just something about him I—"

"You mean Pieter van de Behr from Amsterdam?" Poppy replied.

"It was Jonas Jamieson, from No Fixed Abode, actually," George whispered to her, almost in an aside. "As soon as he had gone, I knew who he was – with that arrogant demeanour. Pity I didn't work it out before he left, otherwise he wouldn't have bothered you again – ever. It was your cousin Hal that started the ball rolling with me. A good chap, that Hal."

The shocked look on Poppy's face said it all. His close proximity to her and to Florence brought back that horrendous time that, had George not been on hand to dish out an incredible beating all those years before, what *could* have happened had given her nightmares for months. Her dear George!

～～

The Shady Lady Inn, as usual, was subject to a slow, swirling thick atmosphere of tobacco smoke and hemp, where lamps were dim and conversations were whispered. This was no gentlemen's watering hole! It was a renowned hostelry where shenanigans, skulduggery and criminal dealings were the order of the day.

Tables in alcoves could barely be seen, along with their occupants and the deals that were being arranged, discussed and agreed upon. This was where the likes of Jonas Jamieson held court with the thugs and reprobates he called associates, and this was where he planned every detail of his reprehensible predatory excursions into law-abiding society at large.

"So, your recent outing into gentry was unsuccessful, then," the landlord, Pieter van de Behr, growled at him as he replenished tankards all round. "The mistake you probably made is a mistake you English make all the time – not knowing how to become a credible and bona-fide Netherlander in both accent, general aura and knowledge of the people."

"No matter, no matter," Jonas returned, sweeping the criticism away with his arm. "There was nothing there of worth anyway."

"Don't use my name again!" the landlord spat at him, stabbing an accusatory finger towards his face. "You'll be getting me a bad reputation."

The small group around the grime-encrusted and ale-swilled tabletop laughed at the concept.

"Anything else in mind?" van de Behr asked sharply. "If you haven't already done so, you need to reassess your 'office' accommodation, mi thinks. Well?"

"We have one or two real possibilities in hand, old chap." Jonas fobbed him off with a foppishly dismissive wave of his hand in his usual non-committal way.

"And they are?" van de Behr insisted.

"Can't reveal the detail, my friend – yet," Jonas went on. "Needless to say, you *will* know when the money drops into your grubby paw."

"Why, you—!" the landlord growled, moving towards him threateningly, to be stopped in his tracks by the enormous bulk of one of Jonas's heavies.

"Don't harm him, Johnny, dear boy," Jonas said with a condescending smirk. "I feel sure he means us no harm. I'm afraid Johnny here is somewhat … protective of his boss man, my dear van de Behr. Any move towards me seems to trigger an immediately 'protective' response in him. As I said, when success has been achieved, you will be paid. Have no fear. How *much* is very much open to discussion, don't you think? Now, if you don't mind…"

He waved away the barman dismissively as he turned towards his gang of ruffians, who bore nondescript unemotionally ugly visages The degree of loyalty they shared was proportionate to the financial return that would be forthcoming.

"Now then, my lads, to business," Jonas started again. "Boulders Wood could be our next target, depending on the amount of cash returning to the fold after trade has been done each day. We will maintain a watching brief. If it's not worth it, we won't waste our time … unless it involves Master George Garside, of course. *Then* it will become priority. But I have to warn you that either of the two families – McIntyre and Garside – may be difficult to nail down. Be aware, eh, old chaps? Now, drink up. We have people to visit and money to raise."

Chapter 12

"Was that a *real* person we saw at your soirée?" Tommy Spence asked his daughter. "Only, you seemed totally terrified when your young man, George, mentioned him after his very quick departure."

"One of the most evil young men in our orbit, unfortunately," Ross replied, as his niece was still overcome by Jonas's audacity at calling in to *her* life once again.

"Yes, Father, unfortunately he is," Poppy answered finally. "He has been a blight upon our lives since he was a teenager, even though he is part of our extended family." She explained briefly what he had done and threatened to do, insisting that they would never be totally safe until he was no longer with them.

"Can we not alert the police that he is causing mayhem in your life, and get them to … arrest him?" Tommy suggested.

"Not that simple, unfortunately," Ross went on. "They have been on the lookout for him for some considerable time, but have no idea where he might be. I can assure you that if either George Garside or I were to find him, there would no longer be a threat."

"How can you know that? And why are you wishing to become involved other than that Poppy is your niece?" Dr Spence asked pointedly.

"He has arranged – twice – to have his thugs 'take care' of us, fortunately unsuccessfully," Ross replied. "We were strong enough to dispatch them both times, but who knows if *that* will be the case if he tries again – and assuredly he will."

"He can't be too bright, this Jonas person," Tommy went on. "Trying to impersonate someone from the Netherlands without either knowing the accent or the names of places, according to the natives."

"He won't make the same mistake again," Ross replied. "Criminals like him usually learn from their mistakes, or they go on to spend a reasonable slice of their lives behind bars. We *are* taking steps to make the cottage more secure, particularly with the doors and windows – triple locks and bolts, and shutters for the windows, along with locks and such like."

"Count me in wherever costs are incurred," Tommy added.

"No problem with all that," Ross explained. "*My* father is sponsoring Poppy and Florence's literary aspirations to include everything."

"*Your* father?" Tommy puzzled. "I thought Joss McIntyre was … dead."

"He wasn't my father," Ross replied, going on to explain the situation. "Ross Booth *is*. Anyway, nothing much we can do about that now. Would you like to come with me? There's somebody I think you ought to meet."

"*Me*?" Tommy replied, puzzled at Ross's change of tack. "Where are we going?"

They left Poppy's cottage and strode down the crunchless, snow-covered driveway. The sky was clear, but threatening clouds gathered from the west, a possible harbinger of more inclement weather to visit the area. That sort of weather in that part of the world at that time of year was nothing unexpected. It would be a strange change in weather patterns if snow *didn't* arrive when habitually expected.

Ross knocked on the door of the next cottage down from his niece's, probably a hundred paces or thereabouts. The door opened slowly to reveal—

"Sally Smallshore!" Tommy gasped, not expecting to see his friend from all those years gone by. "I knew you were hereabouts, but I never expected to have the luck to see you."

"Tommy Spence!" she reacted, quietly surprised, her palm covering the lower part of her face as tears began to gather. "Poppy's dad, and now a reasonably close neighbour."

"I'll leave you two to reacquaint, but I'm off back to the house," Ross said as he turned. "It's Sally's day off, Tommy, so enjoy your time together," and with that, he was gone, striding purposefully back to his wife and daughter.

"Don't just stand there," Sally urged. "Come in and warm yourself. Dad will be back in an hour or so. Kettle will be on the boil in just two ticks, with a mashing of tea in the pot shortly after."

"Not heard that expression for many a year, Sally," Tommy said, once the door had been latched firmly to keep out the piercing chill. "Twenty years or more since we last saw one another, perhaps?"

"Certainly is," she agreed. "Just over twenty-two years, and you with a bairn that I had no idea was on its way. Lost time to make up, eh?"

"Also lost time to make up with you, perhaps?" he answered. "Don't forget, although you and Annie were best of friends, you and I were friends also. I wouldn't have asked

113

you to act as go-between otherwise."

"I know," Sally said with a sigh. "A lot of water under the bridge, and many sadnesses to embrace, I fear."

"I've thought about you a lot since that dire day I was obliged to leave by my parents," Tommy explained. "I can assure you that I didn't want to leave but, at sixteen, I had no choice. Realising I would be able to return once old enough and settled in work. I needed to acquire enough financial backing to live other than in the Oxford area. So now, here I am."

They sat for a few moments, sipping tea and looking out at the snow-covered landscape. "You?" he asked, drawing back his thoughts to the here and now.

"The last twenty years have not treated my dad and me well," Sally returned, slowly turning to face him. "Mum died when I was about fifteen, leaving Dad in a dire state. He felt that he couldn't keep up to the work under Joss McIntyre – a very hard and unforgiving taskmaster – *and* look after a bairn as well. So, he did the only thing possible, uprooted us from this very cottage and moved us to the Guisborough area where his sister lived. She had four children already and was more than happy to take on another so Dad could find work. To keep a roof over our heads and food on the table, that was largely in sea fishing."

"I had no idea," Tommy said quietly.

"Annie and I had already been friends for a couple of years, unbeknown to anyone else … but you," Sally continued. "We left Boulders Wood, shortly after you were sent away to Oxford. It was only a little while later that she had her 'accident'. She discovered she was expecting, and that *you* had no idea about it. She hadn't even shared that bit of information with me, her best friend."

"When I didn't hear from her for the whole of the next year,

I began to accept that she might have had second thoughts about us – her and me," Tommy said. "But I still held on to the hope that she might have wanted me. Little did I know, eh?"

"So, who is this, Sally?" a deep, resonant male voice joined them in the living room. "Not come across him before."

"It's Tommy, Dad, Tommy Spence," Sally explained. "He is Poppy's father, whom we helped to find."

"I've seen you before, haven't I?" Jim Smallshore replied, his eyes narrowing in concentration. "Weren't you with a youngish woman who had a little lad in tow, Richmond way on?"

❧

"Thank you for letting me stay over, Poppy," Abigail Green said to her hostess. "It wouldn't have been possible to find anywhere to stay locally – that I could afford, anyway. That room was beautifully comfortable, and I don't feel I would like to leave it … yet."

"Then don't," Florence suggested, to a positive nod from Poppy. "If you would like to stay a few more days, you might be able to do your piece about our soirée – if you so wished, that is."

"Stay as long as you like," Poppy agreed. "It would be lovely to have your company longer. I can't see there is any point in trying to get into work as this snow certainly won't allow it. I could introduce you to my Nanny Nell and my grandpa, although you know him already."

"If you're sure, that would be wonderful," Abigail replied. "Although it was an enthralling soirée, there are perhaps one or two points we should talk through. Another three days then?"

"Excellent!" Poppy agreed enthusiastically. "Now, our cook is called Mary-Jane and she does a mean goose dinner, and that's what's on the menu for this evening. Interested?"

"Rather!" Abigail retorted eagerly, almost drooling at the thought. "Don't get much chance to dine as well as that, so it will be an absolute pleasure. Changing direction slightly, the bearded chappy, you know, the one that hot-footed it out of the event, who was he?"

"He's the one who…" Poppy's voice faded into the details of her history with him. The story drew startled 'Ohs' and almost disbelieving 'Ahs' from Abigail, who found it hard to believe a family member could behave in such a brutally calculated manner towards two ladies, one of whom was a blood relative.

"I know it might sound calculating and harsh and dismissive, but there has to be chapter and verse in there, somewhere," Abigail suggested.

"I don't follow," Poppy replied, a slightly perplexed look accompanying her words.

"Stories these days – or any other day, for that matter – need to be picked up and worked wherever they present themselves," Abigail went on. "What better way to weave a character such as that into a novel? You have the experience, the skill – don't forget that I have read some of your literature already – and the inside knowledge of such dire people and how they developed into what they have become. Think about it, Poppy. This could form the backbone of a thrilling, exciting and gripping story."

"She's right, you know, Poppy," Florence waded in. "God-sent opportunity. I'm already reviewing *my* upbringing!"

They all laughed at her words and facial expressions, knowing full well that she was entirely serious.

"I never thought of that experience in any way other than gross and, hopefully, forgettable," Poppy replied thoughtfully. "Food for thought, eh? Talking about food, time for dinner?"

"Dinner?" Abigail gasped, startled at the thought. "We haven't had lunch yet!"

"We actually call lunch 'dinner' in this neck of the woods," Florence butted in, "and dinner – the evening meal – is 'tea'. Don't forget that this is the North Riding, and next stop is … Scotland."

"Lord a mercy me!" Abigail exclaimed. "This I will have to remember, especially as I have been reassigned to Richmond to cover a much greater area of the North Riding."

"You can stay here with us, then, on a more permanent basis." Poppy whooped for joy. "The room you are now staying in could become yours for as long as you wish to stay here. Any money you save on renting could buy you a carriage, perhaps?"

"I couldn't really!" Abigail insisted. "That would be—"

"Absolutely wonderful!" the two girls chorused loudly, very excited that they should have a literary journalist and prospective author living with them.

"That's a done deal then," Poppy said finally, as they trooped up to the big house for 'dinner'.

"We have been thinking seriously about doing a watered-down version of the Grand Tour," Poppy said over a cup of tea and a scone. After eating, they were sitting in front of the habitually roaring log fire. "Not a 'coming-of-age' thing, as with most rich young men, but because we would like to visit some of the sites where some of our European brethren derived *their* inspiration – Victor Hugo and George Sand, for example."

"George Sand is one of our cases in point, of course," Abigail pointed out.

"Cases in point?" Florence queried. "How do you mean?"

"Using a male pseudonym because of the lack of perceived credibility accrued by female authors in a male-dominated world, of course," Abigail explained.

"Louisa May Alcott is another, as we mentioned at the soirée." Poppy added. "Paris and Rome are the two places we would love to visit."

"Perfect!" Abigail joined in, clapping, quietly excited. "I have family in and around both cities, two brothers in Paris and aunts and uncles very near Rome."

"Dare I ask an impertinent question?" Poppy ventured after a few moments of pensive silence.

"The more impertinent the better!" Abigail laughed. "Fire away."

"If we were to do that – travel in Europe for a couple of weeks, I mean – would you be available to accompany us. All expenses paid, naturally," Poppy suggested, more in hope than in certainty. "You could act as our chronicler and chaperone, maybe?"

"Hmm," Abigail hummed. "Let me think about it?"

"Take your time. No need—" Poppy replied, fully aware that Abigail might have to ask permission from her employers to leave the country.

"I've thought about it long and hard," Abigail returned with a snigger. "And … I'll do it!"

"Excellent!" Florence gushed.

"Fantastic!" Poppy exclaimed. "You sure? Because if you are, we can get on with our planning, which will involve the three of us."

<hr>

"And where have *you* been?" Jenny Bott said to her teenage son, Toby. "It's late."

"Do you care where I've been?" he replied curtly. "You never have before."

"You're my only son," she retorted sharply. "And I need to know. You can never be sure who's out there watching, particularly at this time of night. It's close to midnight."

"If you must know, I now have a job," he insisted disdainfully. "Somebody has to bring in the money, as you do it only occasionally."

"*That* was unnecessary!" she exclaimed. "Don't forget that I *am* your mother, and it's been me that's brought you up and provided a roof over your head and food for your belly."

"Not the most comfortable or exciting of upbringings," he grumbled accusingly. "And you were very often not there when I needed you most. Anyway," he said after a moment or two fiddling about in his britches' pocket, "this is for you – for us."

He pulled out a coin, which he squeezed into her palm gently. Her jaw dropped as she examined it in the room's dim light. "It's … it's a sovereign!" she gasped "Not seen many of those recently. Where did you get it?"

"Does it matter where I got it from?" he responded dismissively. "It's money, and that's summat we don't see a lot of. Wherever it came from, it'll pay for us to eat and to be a bit warmer than we've bin in t'past winters."

The room they were in was dingy and sparsely furnished, with a dark settee and an unmatched easy chair where Jenny Bott sat uneasily, wary about who might enter. Thick, ill-fitting curtains half-covered the single grimy window, letting in a scant amount of light, given that most of the daylight couldn't escape the cloying filth of the town's non-salubrious back streets in which their accommodation nestled uncomfortably. Personal cleanliness wasn't an issue for most of the wretches who found themselves in this dilemma of a situation because there was neither bathing facility nor money to pay for one. Consequently, this habitation, where umpteen other folks precariously existed, stank of filth, stale urine and an overpoweringly unpleasant odour of old sweat.

"The sack in yonder corner contains a few chopped logs to help feed yon fire," Toby said, making a move to set flames where none had existed for many a month. "There is also a sack of foodstuff in the other corner."

"But, Toby," Jenny said after a few moments of silent concern, "where has it all come from? We never—"

"Mother!" he urged. "No more questions! No matter on its origin, there's at least a week's worth of raw vittels yonder. All it needs is … cooking. I assume you can do that? If you must know, I've become a runner for a businessman in town – a messenger, in other words. Somebody that brings and takes vital information between certain businesses to help to keep industry functioning well in this good town."

"Whatever it is that you do, please be careful," she went on warily. "You never know what's waiting for you around the next corner in *these* alleyways."

"I can look after missen, Mother," Toby assured her almost arrogantly. "*You* always did, and you're a female."

"Where are you going now?" she asked urgently as he turned to leave.

"Places to go and business to attend to." He touched the side of his nose with a grubby forefinger as he sidled out of the latchless door.

"Please be … careful!" she sighed, once he had disappeared to goodness knew where.

CHAPTER 13

"Someone at the door, Poppy!" Florence called out from the kitchen.

"Hal! What a lovely surprise!" Poppy enthused, surprised at seeing her cousin-once-removed. "I thought you were on your way back to Africa. Please come in. Tea? Or something stronger?"

"Thank you," Hal replied as he removed his boots. "Tea for me, please. I don't drink alcohol. I have been teetotal since becoming an adult."

"Teetotal? What does that mean?" Poppy asked, never having heard the term before.

"Ever heard of the Temperance Movement?" he asked, not surprised that having led such a sheltered life she would not understand either the need for its existence or the reason behind its formation.

Their surprised faces told him volumes about their lives and their present hiding place.

"The demon drink has played an enormous part in the development of society's problems, and it prompted the

Temperance League in the 1830s to found a movement for which the over-riding desire was to rid society of alcohol-based beverages," he explained.

"Is that something that's ever bothered you, Hal?" Poppy asked carefully. "My Grandpa Joss drank the odd glass of beer now and again but railed greatly against its use while his workers did what they were paid to do."

"My father, Harold, who incidentally was illegitimate, had an over-fondness for the stuff and his antics persuaded me to have none of it … ever," Hal returned. "From age fifteen, when he forced me to drink a glass of whisky, I never touched a drop ever again."

"Didn't you like it or—?" Florence asked naively.

"It made me vomit violently, my dear Florence, to the point that I couldn't even eat for three days," he explained loudly. "*That* did it for me because, as you no doubt could tell from my predilection for mi vittels at your fabulous soirée the other night, I love mi fodder."

Both girls laughed at the wild faces he pulled before sitting down with a bump and a huge sigh.

"Can we offer you something to eat and drink, then, dear Hal?" Poppy offered.

"Do you know," he replied with an enormous grin splitting his face, "that is the most wonderful thing I have heard today. I should be delighted to join you in dining in your splendidly attractive and comfortable cottage." He stopped abruptly as their friend, Abigail, entered the room. He followed all her actions almost without breathing as she clapped her gloved hands together to try to re-stimulate her slow circulation to her extremities.

"Very cold out there today," she observed, stripping off her bonnet and outdoor coat. "Oh, hello … Hal, isn't it? How lovely to see you."

Poppy and Florence's couldn't fail to notice the effect that Abigail's entrance had had on their male visitor, enthralled as he was simply by her unexpectedly exquisite appearance.

⁓

"Nice chap, if a bit quiet," Abigail observed once Hal had departed and they were sitting round the fire enjoying a cup of hot tea and a petit four.

Poppy looked across at Florence, and both smiled knowingly.

"What?" Abigail said, with a growing look of surprise. "What's so funny? Have I got a nut stuck between my teeth?"

"Actually, no," Florence answered. "You have no idea how voluble our friend Hal is usually."

"Then, what?" Abigail said, even more puzzled.

"It's you, dear Abigail," Poppy explained. "He was holding the metaphorical fort big style before you walked through the door. As soon as that happened, the mental and emotional shutters descended. He is smitten with you, my good lady."

"That's ridiculous!" Abigail protested. "I've only seen him twice. How could he possibly—?"

"Don't denigrate your allure, my friend," Florence interrupted quietly. "Even *I* can see that you were meant for each other."

"Preposterous!" Abigail reiterated, her face flushing to a bright red. "How could that possibly happen in such a short space of time?"

"It only takes a moment, or so some of our romance stories tell us," Poppy re-joined with a knowing smile. "He's a lovely and very interesting chap. His writing's none-too-bad either, and now he's about to set all his exploits and experiences in Africa to typescript. Do you know anyone who is able or agreeable to setting his words to type?"

"Indeed, I do!" Abigail said, eyes twinkling in anticipation. "If you give me an address, I'll contact him. In the meantime, I have a publisher interested in *your* literature."

"Which one?" Florence said with an apprehensive shrug, well aware that her friend was a better writer than she was.

"Both!" Abigail exclaimed, catching them unawares.

"Woohoo!" Florence hooted.

"Yes!" Poppy exclaimed, punching the air joyfully.

"I'll introduce you to her shortly after Christmas," Abigail said nonchalantly.

"Her?" Poppy said with a frown. "I didn't know—"

"That there are female publishers around?" Abigail interrupted. "She is called Jenny Wilton, and she's beginning to make a name for herself. Excellent time for you three to meet. Female writers are at last getting noticed. It'll take a lot longer, though, to have females as well received as their male counterparts."

"Hear, hear to that one!" Florence added.

"It will happen only when more women of talent take to the quill," Abigail explained. "Unfortunately, history tells us erroneously that we are not as good as men, and most people have been persuaded that *that* is the truth. Most ordinary women don't have the wherewithal to buy books, let alone read them. Sixpence doesn't seem a lot for a good book but doing without food to be able to read a book they probably wouldn't understand wouldn't cut it at all for them. Still, free public libraries are beginning to make their presence felt, and they cost … nothing."

"What was that?" Poppy said sharply, hearing a noise outside. "There it is again! Sounds like somebody's trying to get in."

Abigail reached for the heavy cast-iron poker as she followed Poppy and Florence to the door. Although it was locked and bolted, it sounded like someone was trying to gain entrance to their warmth and well-stocked pantry.

As they reached the inner door leading from living room to vestibule, the outside door gave way with an almighty crash, allowing quick-thinking Abigail to duck behind the wall next to the inner door. Realising instantly that there was nothing friendly about their appearance, as the first ruffian opened the inner door and strode into the room Abigail swung the poker with deadly accuracy at his head, causing him to collapse unconscious to the floor, a gash on his forehead pouring blood.

The other two ruffians stepped back sharply, not expecting that sort of a ballistic greeting, to be levelled by another behind them who was not part of *their* gang. The second intruder was felled by a hefty adze handle to his knee, causing it to shatter sideways and pitching him to the floor screaming in agony at his shattered knee joint. The third ruffian tried to flee, but a large fist to his face persuaded him to remain where he was.

"A nifty piece of work, that one, Abigail," the newcomer said. "I don't think he will recover from *that* for some time."

"George?" Abigail gasped. "How come you are here? How did you know they were going to break in?"

"I didn't, but I have seen footprints in the snow around both the big house and the cottages for a while now," George explained. "I'm glad I was on hand on *this* day. You all right, Poppy, Florence?"

"We are, and we can't thank you enough," the girls said, hugging their friends for their swift response to being invaded by three ruffians.

"Could one of you get Ross and send a lad to the police station to fetch Sergeant Shaw?" George suggested. "I'm off

to have a little word with the groaning lummox on the floor
– t'onny one that's conscious."

"Well now, you lot've been busy," Poppy's uncle's very
familiar voice chimed through the door. "What have we here?
Christmas revellers?"

"I bet they wish they were," George replied. "Two unconscious – one levelled by this tiny young lady here – and one I
am just about to have a word with."

"Be my guest, George, mi owd mate," Ross said with a nod.
"If you need any help to persuade him to talk—?"

"Be rayt, Ross," George answered. "Now then, matey," he
went on, flexing his ham-like fist, "who sent you? If you don't
answer, you will end up like your two pals."

"You can't—!" the ruffian complained, to be shut up by a
hefty slap across the head.

"Shall we try that one again?" George warned, clenching
his fist. "Preferably with a different answer?"

"OK. OK!" the ruffian said, flinching at the thought of
losing another few teeth. "We was told to frighten 'em and to
see what we might lay our hands on."

"And your boss's name is?" Ross urged, picking up the
ruffian by the scruff of the neck, ready to 'persuade' him
even further.

"All right! All right!" he capitulated. "It was …
Jonas Jamieson."

"He's wanted for a whole range of criminality," Detective
Sergeant Shaw pointed out, once their prisoner had been
secured in the back of the horse-drawn police wagon. "We've
searched his usual known haunts, but he is like the proverbial
Will o' the Whisp – a ghost. The worst thing about it all is

that we have never had any proof to hang around his neck, because he almost always gets his henchmen to do his dirty work. We'll just have to hope he runs out of accomplices in the not-too-distant future."

"Cup of tea and a cake, Sergeant Shaw?" Poppy offered.

"No thank you, Miss." He reacted politely, remembering the generosity of her grandma's hospitality in past years. "We've a lot on, so Constable Green and I need to be away. We'll let you know if we sniff anything out about Jonas Jamieson, his being a relative and all."

"Thank you for being on hand and attentive enough to keep a close eye on Poppy, Florence and Abigail," Ross said as he shook George's hand warmly.

"Nay, Ross. I shouldn't enjoy being on the wrong side of yon Abigail in a mood!" George laughed with the others present. "But, like you say, it's having somebody around when I'm not. I think we need to mek them doors and windows much more secure as well. Doors and windows that can't be kicked in. Shutters perhaps?"

"I'll see to it, old chap," Ross agreed. When he had departed, George turned to the others with a sigh.

"Close call, ladies," he said. "Fantastic response, Abigail, but if I'd not been close? There were three ruffians who would have had no compunction about causing you untold harm. It's a sad day when you're not safe in your own household."

"Cup of tea, George?" Poppy offered, nestling up to him. "You are our saviour."

"Don't forget that what Abigail did to the first entrant set the tone for the others," George replied. "Had she not wiped him out, goodness knows what they would have done. Hopefully that Jonas Nobody will realise and accept he has no way he can get at you all, not while I'm here, anyway. I *will*

127

catch him, have no fear, and I *will* see to it that he will never do anyone else any harm – ever!"

———～———

"Damn! Damn! And damn that blessed beggar called George Garside!" Jonas raged in a quiet, run-down shack in the back of beyond, not far from Darlington's south-west. "Tell me once more, Bruiser, old chap, what happened," he asked again, keeping his anger in check.

Bruiser told him again, in his very slow manner of speaking, what had happened to all three ruffians who were in Jonas's employ, sparing no detail of all their injuries and arrests.

"Two of 'em will be in hospital for some time, and the other likewise but in a police cell," Bruiser carried on. "He's up before Judge Dreadful, who will slap a stiff sentence on 'im."

"Enough!" Jonas muttered, realising that there would soon be no muscle left to employ, and his nemesis would walk the streets unmolested and unafraid. Why was this happening to him, and how could George Garside manage so easily to keep one step ahead of him? Fate? Better organisation? Second sight? "We need to work something out to stop this … this upstart pest."

"You can count me aht," Bruiser insisted, becoming slightly uneasy and a little agitated once the slow thought entered his mind at what could happen to him should he be drafted in to 'see to' Jonas Jamieson's enemy. "I aint tekin 'em all on! T'McIntyre clan goes way back, an' I want nowt to do wi' 'em. So, I'm off."

With that rush of bravado, he was up and out of the door before Jonas could do anything but heave a huge sigh of disappointment. *Now* what was he to do? Confront Garside and the whole joint-family clan on his own? Not likely, because he had shown himself to be a consummate, dyed-in-the-wool, fully-paid-up … coward, who always employed somebody else to do his dirty work.

CHAPTER 14

"You are, aren't you, Hal?" Poppy asked her first cousin once removed five snowy days before Christmas in front of a roaring fire in her cosy cottage.

"I am what?" he puzzled, his backside having discovered a very comfortable easy chair within direct warming distance. A bone-china cup and saucer containing a steaming beverage of infused tea was to hand and a buttered scone rested on a small occasional table by him.

"Rather keen on Abigail," she sniggered provocatively.

"I don't know what you mean," he blustered, uncharacteristically embarrassed as his complexion turned to a deeper shade of pink. He had been out of Africa so long that his deeply weathered look had faded to a vaguely sepia tinge. Time he was back there? That depended upon certain factors he needed to sort out before his decisions could be finalised.

"I have a feeling, a very sure feeling, that you have cultivated – how shall I put it? – a certain … regard for our good friend Abigail Green," Poppy pointed out. Trust the young not to beat around the bush when dealing with matters of the heart.

He gave her no immediate reply, but simply stared into the flames before speaking.

"Is it *so* obvious, my dear cousin?" he replied slowly, trying hard not to either overstate or underemphasise how he felt. "I could offer this only to you when I say that I find her exquisite in all respects and would like nothing better than to become her preferred companion. There. Said it."

"Bravo, my dear Hal! Well said," Poppy congratulated him. "Then, why don't you tell her? She is a lovely person, and it's fascinating to be associated with her – a feeling I am sure you share."

The lock of the outside door snicked and the brass hinges squeaked slightly, turning their heads towards the inner vestibule door. Both doors had been repaired and made more secure, and the spattered blood cleaned since the ruffians had been dispatched by Abigail and George. It was always a little fear-inducing for Poppy, as dear George had now taken on his new duties in dispatch and delivery for the two farms' rapidly developing dairy trade.

"Florence … and Abigail!" Poppy whooped with joy as her two female friends bustled into the warmth from the sub-freezing temperatures outside.

Hal's eyes fixed on Abigail's face, longing for her to *notice* him and see the way he felt. He may not have recognised that similar look in her eyes, but Poppy had. *She* was immediately set on a course to unite their kindred spirits without further ado, before Hal decided he had to return to his adventuring in exciting climes.

"You'll never guess to whom we have been speaking today," Florence gushed excitedly as they both divested their outdoor clothing and closed in on the fire's all-encompassing warmth.

"We won't if you don't give us a tiny hint," Poppy laughed, eager to hear Florence's news. "Come on then! We have no idea. The Aga Khan? Queen Victoria herself? We give up!"

They all laughed, joyful to be in each other's company, cocooned from the deeply searching chill of winter in the North Riding.

"You remember James Hawley Weeks, our erudite poet from our first soirée a short while ago?" Florence enthused. "His poetry was so … so *de rigeur* that he needed to be published as soon as possible. Well, he turns out to be a well-to-do aristocratic businessman with significant and widespread contacts."

"Really?" Poppy asked, a feeling of excitement growing.

"He has strong contacts with – wait for it – a large publishing house in the South—" she went on.

"Egremont Publishing," Abigail butted in eagerly. "I know it well."

"He has suggested that he likes our thoughts and writings so much that he will facilitate our move towards publishing!" Florence burst out, unable to contain herself any longer.

"He also said that Hal's work was so impressive that he should produce a 'readable' manuscript as soon as possible," Abigail added. "How about that, Hal?"

"I think I might need a modicum of help with the 'readable' bit," Hal confessed. "I have enough ideas and experience to fill the proverbial encyclopaedia, but expressions and sentences I need help with."

"That isn't a problem, Hal," Abigail assured him. "I have enough expressions and sentences and words to fill out your manuscript several times over. We'll get together soon after Christmas and sort things out. All you need to do is to make sure all you want to say is written down for us to look through together."

Poppy smiled inwardly, mentally punching the air with satisfaction. 'Way to go, Cousin Hal!'

———✦———

"Sally!" Tommy gasped as his friend walked through his surgery door. "I wasn't sure I would see you again after your dad's aggressive questioning the last time we met."

"I have to apologise for his abruptness, and that he seemed to accuse you of something of which you obviously had no knowledge," Sally said as she sat down. "He was out of order, but he was only looking after my welfare."

"The young woman and little boy were my sister and her son, Joseph," Tommy explained. "Joseph had bumped his head, so she brought him to me. It was only a slight bump, but mothers sometimes tend to think the worst. He's fine now, and it was a little while ago. I marvel at your dad's ability to remember so much detail."

"I just felt that I needed to apologise, that's all," she added.

"There was, and is, no need," Tommy went on finally. "As luck would have it, I am just about to close up shop for the day and wonder if you might accept my invitation to afternoon tea at Mary's Pantry. I don't know whether you have ever been there?"

"No, I haven't, but I would be delighted to accompany you," Sally agreed with a smile. "We can have a much better chat without my father's prying ears flapping close by, causing a draught in our face."

Tommy burst out laughing at the picture she had just cast into his head. He put on his velvet-collared overcoat over his new three-piece suit – all dark, according to the fashion of the day.

"I'm sure I haven't been to Mary's Pantry before," she said as they strolled along High Street, her arm linked in his as if they were an old married couple. "How do *you* know it?"

"Mary was employed as cook and housekeeper at Boulders Wood, I believe, until her cooking and baking became more widely known and appreciated," Tommy explained. "Encouraged by Poppy's Nanny Nell, she felt she needed to widen and diversify. She was supported by Nell's new husband, with whom Nell had a child as the issue of a clandestine romance years before, a bit like Annie and me, I suppose. I am sure you will agree about the quality, because here we are. It's now three o'clock, and they don't close until five."

"That was the most wonderful two hours I've spent for many a year," Tommy sighed as they prepared, reluctantly, to leave afternoon tea – all of which they had consumed unapologetically. "Where did the time go, Sally? And now I have to wait another week to see you again. *May* I see you again, Sally, please. I mean—"

"No need to qualify what you have just said, Tommy," she answered, cutting short the qualification of his feelings that she understood already. "I would be delighted to see you again … and again, should you so wish."

"I couldn't think of anything that I would rather do than to spend more time with you," he added quietly, gazing into her green eyes. "This has been heaven. I'll drive you back to Boulders Wood. My carriage and pair are back at the surgery. Shall we?"

He held out his hand to her which she grasped eagerly.

"How's things then, mi owd cock?" Pieter van de Behr, the landlord at the Shady Lady, said in a mock jovial greeting to Jonas Jamieson.

He had approached carefully initially, bearing in mind their last altercation when he had been confronted by Jonas's henchman. Now that he had seen – and heard – that the cocky lad no longer had any supporters, he could afford to be sharper with him.

"No 'friends' wi' thee today?" Pieter sneered. "Nobody offering to buy thee any drinks? I have heard on sound authority that the police would give anything to know where one certain Jonas Jamieson might be found. Now, I wonder what that 'anything' might amount to?"

"Get me a tankard of ale, and be quick about it, old chap," Jonas said, ignoring the landlord's last comments.

"Show me thy means of paying for that, and I'll consider thy request," the landlord answered, feeling a degree of bravery crawling onto his shoulders. "Or should I summon *my* friends to show thee 'politely' to the door?"

He turned to face his associates, and on return to await Jonas's response, he was mildly surprised to note his chair was empty. "Well, my little man," the landlord muttered, "too hot for you in here, eh?"

"Excuse me, mister," a young voice drew his attention.

"Aye, lad, what does *thy* want? Would it be a tankard of ale tha's after, or would it be a jar of milk?" the landlord asked with a sniggering sneer.

"Could you tell me where Mr Jamieson is, please?" the boy asked. "Onny, I was supposed to meet him here, and he's … not."

"No idea," the landlord offered. "The local slime pond, perhaps?"

"But—" the lad answered quizzically.

"No buts," was the landlord's quick response. "T'way out is t'same as t'way in. Now bugger off or tha'll be sorry."

As he turned to leave, the lad hurled a largish pebble at the landlord, hitting him squarely on the head just above his ear. Pieter rushed to the door, cursing as he went, to find the streets empty and a hefty mist descending.

"Young bugger!" he muttered as he returned to his bar. "I know who thy is, and woe betide thee when we meet again."

⁓

"Psst!" a low, urgent hiss nosed its way into the lad's hearing as he stopped under a dimly lit gas lamp. "Toby! Over here!"

The lad spun round to see his master beckoning him from a nearby doorway over whose step oozed a dull light from within. "Mr Jamieson, I've been looking for you," he urged quietly. "Mr van de Behr told me you'd been and gone. I've a message for you."

He handed over a folded and sealed note, which had become somewhat crumpled in his pocket.

Jonas read it eagerly. "Excellent!" he uttered, screwing up the paper and lobbing it onto the roof. "Good man. Just what I wanted to know."

"Might I help with anything else, sir?" the lad offered enthusiastically, hoping to be of further assistance to the boss, who had only ever treated him with respect and kindness.

"I don't know … yet," Jonas replied quietly. "It may well be that you can play a vital part in the plans we are developing, but in the meantime here's half a sovereign to tide you over. All I can say is keep yourself safe and in readiness for the biggest pay day of your life. *Then* we will begin to improve our lifestyle considerably."

⁓

"I haven't seen him for a longish time," Jonas's mother, Louisa, said to Nell over a cup of tea and a slice of early-baked Christmas cake that Ross Senior always loved.

The snow that had plagued their rustic existence in the North Riding had largely disappeared, following a mildish period attended by torrential rain. The deep snow had been superseded by equally impressive yet destructive flood waters throughout the area.

"What do you mean by 'longish'?" Ross Senior asked. "And why come to see you at all, when you and his father don't seem to be his priority lately?"

"Twice in the last year, and only then to ask for money," Louisa responded, an anguished look invading her already worried face. "He doesn't even seem to want to stop to talk."

"The unfortunate news about your son will take a lot of swallowing, I'm afraid," Ross started to explain.

"I know he has taken to spending time with – how shall I say – undesirable … riffraff, but—" she went on naively.

"Police Sergeant Shaw said that he is wanted by them for a whole range of criminality, from burglary to physical assault," Ross explained further. "None of which he has been involved in perpetrating. He leans more towards Charles Dickens's character Fagin in that he gets others to do his dirty work."

At this character assassination of her once dearly beloved son, Louisa broke down into floods of soul-destroying tears.

"I never … believed all … that about him!" she sobbed, distraught that her little baby Jonas could have grown into the evil, manipulative and predatory character that had been laid before her. "He can't be! Can he? His father has never liked him, even from an early age. *He* thought he would grow up to be a worthless layabout. Not far from the truth, eh?"

"He seems also to bear a grudge against Tom Garside's lad,

George, although George has only ever protected folks from *your* boy," Nell added seriously, only wanting to protect Louisa from her son. "I believe it's a grudge Jonas has carried from an early age, though I can't really be sure why."

"What can I do?" Louisa pleaded, lifting her tear-stained face in supplication towards her Aunt Nell, feeling that there must be something positive that might be done to help her son.

"I know this may sound harsh," Ross added, "but have you ever considered that this may well be Jonas's choice of lifestyle? He may well think only that he's been unlucky."

"How? In that he has been unfortunate in his choice of acquaintances, and things have happened badly for him along the way?" Louisa said, plucking at straws in her endeavour to give reason to his behaviour.

"Not really," Ross said, his iconoclastic statement about to punch holes in her gentle thoughts. "Unlucky in that he believes he hasn't succeeded in achieving his heinous aims through simple misfortune and mischance. He is probably the sort of person who will continue at the expense of others until he succeeds in either punishing his fellow human beings or making lots of money so he doesn't have to involve himself in honest labour."

Louisa fell silent then blustered, "Does that mean that you think he is … using *me*?"

"Probably … yes," Ross agreed quietly. "What you have to accept, Louisa dear, is that he can only succeed in his life by using *others* to achieve his aims.

"And probably will always be the same," he added firmly after a brief silence.

"I have to go!" Louisa burst out urgently, knocking over the small table next to her chair as she stood up sharply. "My husband doesn't know I'm here, and I don't want him to. While ever my boy is alive, there is the chance that he might change."

She hurried out of the door and climbed urgently into the brougham that was waiting on the gravel driveway. Once inside, she was away at reasonable speed.

"She is going to be very disappointed, I'm afraid," Ross commented with a knowing shake of his head. "I have come across a lot of lads like Jonas in my time, with almost all of them descending to the darkness. She needs to share all of this with her husband."

CHAPTER 15

"My, what a wonderful home you have here!" the young lady gushed as she sat down to a celebratory cup of tea and a slice of glorious Victoria sponge.

"They designed it with significant financial support from Poppy's grandfather," Abigail Green explained. "Living, working and social space for everything these two young authors hopefully need to set themselves on the road to literary nirvana. Hello? Anybody at home?"

"Abigail! Welcome home!" Poppy retorted as she popped her head around the door from the vestibule. "Tea just mashed?"

"Mashed?" the young visitor asked, a puzzled frown descending. "Isn't that to do with … potatoes? Are we having potatoes as well as Victoria sponge cake? Intriguing."

"The expression for making a pot of tea by boiling water infusion," Abigail laughed. "Particular to Yorkshire. Lancashire, for example, a close neighbour to the south and west, uses the term 'brew' to describe the same process."

"Never heard that before," the young woman commented with a shrug.

"Poppy," Abigail said as her friend re-entered the living room, a steaming cup of tea to hand. "I should like to introduce Jenny Wilton, the publisher I was telling you about, who likes the sound of what you hope to achieve here. She would be ideal for Hal, too."

"Lovely to meet you finally," Poppy replied, greeting this important newcomer to their life. "You are welcome here at any time. Have you had far to travel?"

"Not really," Jenny said. "I'm based in York, although I was born in Oxford. These new-fangled trains make it a lot easier to access parts of our green and pleasant land that would have afforded lengthier and much less comfortable journeys before they were invented."

"Whenever you are in our area and need somewhere to stay, you should come and stay here with us," Poppy offered, genuinely welcoming.

"But you've only three bedrooms and … three people are using them," Jenny answered, pleasantly nonplussed by her offer. "How—?"

"Florence and I can always move in together," Poppy assured her. "The rooms are large enough to accommodate two bodies each. So, you could have your own space without a problem. We also have *two* flush lavatories."

"Two?" Jenny gasped. "Who designed your ablutionary facilities? That sounds amazing! Talking of which—?"

"Into the vestibule and through the door labelled 'WC'," Poppy explained.

"WC?" Jenny asked, not recognising the term.

"'Double-vay-say' as the French would have it," Abigail butted in.

"Or 'water closet' as we say in this country," Poppy added. "We have all mod cons here, I think you might say."

They all laughed as Jenny sought solace in the ladies' powder room.

"When would you like to set up your next soirée, Poppy?" Abigail asked eagerly. "It's just that my next review is due into *The Times* by Wednesday 23rd December. So, if you would like publicity second to none, let me know … soon."

"We were thinking Saturday 16th January 1892, if that's all right?" Poppy replied.

"That sounds about right," Jenny Wilton added as she re-joined them in front of the glorious log fire, together with Florence. "If you have anything close to a manuscript, I would love a copy to be looking through so I might make suggestions."

"We both have stories close to fruition, Jenny," Florence suggested, a note of excitement entering her tone. "Mine is a romance and Poppy's is a detective story."

"Good gracious!" Jenny gasped. "A veritable take over! I can't wait to see them both."

"And before you ask, my nom de plume will be F.T. Smythe," Florence went on.

"And mine, P.P. McIntyre," Poppy added, both smiling broadly at the decision they had taken jointly.

"The main reasoning being?" Jenny queried, although she thought she already knew.

"I think you probably know better than the ordinary person in the street why," Poppy replied. "Several reasons are uppermost in our thinking."

"One has to be that the ordinary person doesn't read books because he can neither read nor afford to buy them even if he can," Florence added.

"The most striking thing, though, is that female writers are not as *acceptable* as their male counterparts," Poppy went on seriously. "And so, *disguising* their gender is perhaps the only way good female writers might succeed."

"The Brontë sisters, George Sand and George Eliot are cases in point," Florence added. "Consequently, we will be writing not as males but as clandestine females. This will not affect our writing, but it will allow us to be judged by our story-telling abilities and not by who we are physically."

"Then, with that mindset, you *will* succeed," Jenny avowed. "I will see to it personally. I can't say that it will be instant – nothing is in these days of uncertainty and stiff competition – but watch out ye glorious world of clever literature!"

⁓

"This is a wonderful tea room that I've never heard of until now," Hal said in his self-conscious, halting sort of a way.

"Florence and Poppy brought me here the first time we met, just before I wrote the first article about their escapades as literary figures," Abigail returned, quite nervously for her. "So, where to next for you, Hal? Venturing into pastures new in fresh lands to explore?"

"Don't know, really," he said, uncharacteristically unsure of what he could say. "I think I would certainly like to explore putting my adventures into print, but I am not sure of how to do it … both the writing and where to go and what to do to have it published."

"As I said to you before, that's where I come in … if you would like me to?" Abigail responded slowly, awaiting his positive response. There was a brief, unsure hiatus which saw him struggling to form his answers. "If you would prefer—?"

"I *would* prefer to have your help," he blurted out sharply. "I fact, I would prefer to spend *all* my time in your company, Abigail."

He stopped suddenly, a deep shade of pink suffusing his

features and an embarrassed look drawing down his brows.

"If that means what I think it means, my dear Hal, then I couldn't wish for anything better," Abigail replied, beaming her delight to the world at large. "I've always wanted to learn from someone who has first-hand experience about worlds I couldn't possibly experience personally, and then—"

He reached across the table, took her hand in his and kissed her fingers gently, causing her to gasp softly. Here was the man she had been searching for for most of her adult life – a man who would understand and cherish her, allowing her the freedom to pursue her deeply held passions of exploring her own world and finding excitement in literature.

"Yes, Hal, I will," she said softly.

"Marry *me*?" he whispered, an incredulous look playing around his eyes.

"Yes, marry *you*," Abigail assured him.

"Then I'd better offer you this to stake my claim," he said, holding out a small, black, soft chamois leather drawstring pouch. "I dug the contents out of the ground myself in South Africa. Three-and-a-half carats, I believe."

Abigail pulled the tiny drawstrings to reveal a gloriously large and beautifully cut diamond solitaire in the ornate setting of a gold ring, which drew a significant gasp from her. Sliding the ring on her finger, she stood up and, in the busy tea room, she kissed him, to the applause and congratulations from all present.

This was something that didn't happen every day, so Mary bustled out of the kitchen with two fluted glasses of sparkling Champagne, as if the event had been expected.

"Happiest day of my life," Hal muttered as they finished their Champagne and settled the bill.

Hailing a cab from the rank just down the street from

Mary's Pantry, they set off back to Boulders Wood to break the news to Poppy and Florence.

"I never considered in my wildest dreams at the start of this day that, by the end of it, I would be engaged to the most beautiful, captivating lady in the world," Hal said as he sat next to Abigail in the cab and held her hand.

She sat next to him, her left hand ungloved so that she might wonder at the glorious jewel adorning her ring finger. "When did you know that you wanted to marry little me?" she asked snuggling closer.

"Within two seconds of you entering Poppy's front room," Hal said. "This feeling of … of awe and belonging overwhelmed me, as I am sure you could tell because of how tongue-tied I became. Not a usual occurrence, I can assure you."

"Well, I'm thankful it happened as it did," Abigail said, a self-satisfied smile betraying her real feelings for this wonderful, if a little unorthodox, man. "Now to break the good news to our friends. You ready?"

As the horse slowed to a gentle walk along the driveway, the happy couple prepared themselves for a warm welcome from their friends.

"When we *do* marry," Hal asked as they prepared to leave the carriage, "where shall we live? Town or country?"

"It'll need to be somewhere central, both for convenience and a reasonable distance to and from work," Abigail replied. "We need to take into consideration the cost of buying a house. I don't have much—"

"Perhaps not, but I *do* have money to buy somewhere spacious enough and far enough away from potential prying neighbours," Hal assured her. "Throughout my travels I have invested wisely in diamonds from the Kimberley Mines in South Africa, land purchases and sales, silks, gold, and other bric-a-brac, knick-knacks etc, along the way. You have no need to worry. Poppy! Lovely to see you again."

His first cousin once removed had seen them disembark from the cab and thrown the front door wide open just as they reached it. She guessed immediately that there had to be something because they had just arrived in a carriage *together,* when both had virtually dismissed suggestions of their involvement with one another.

"Come in! Come in out of this nasty chill," Poppy urged. Once they had divested in the vestibule, she ushered them into the glowing front room where Florence and Jenny were waiting, along with Mr James Hawley Weeks.

The women in the room stopped talking, eyes staring at Abigail, and mouths agape at what they noticed immediately. But then women always recognise any change in appearance in a close friend or acquaintance.

"You ... are ... eng—!" Florence blurted out without ceremony.

"This afternoon, Hal asked me to become his wife," Abigail interrupted, flashing her engagement ring. "And I accepted."

"Goodness me! Just look at that rock!" Jenny gasped in admiration at the huge diamond ring on her finger. "Is that one out of Queen Victoria's crown?"

"Mined it himself from one of the diamond mines in South Africa," Abigail told them proudly. "And had it cut and polished to give it the pristine finish that you see on my finger. I must say that I feel both proud and humble at the same time."

She grasped Hal's hand and drew his straight, almost reluctant body to her to show how she felt about this man she had known for only a fleeting moment of time. She had to pinch herself mentally to ascertain that *this* was real.

"Have you set the date yet?" Florence asked eagerly, like some young teenage girl dreaming of being a bridesmaid.

"Not yet," Hal replied pragmatically. "We have to look for somewhere sensible to live. I live in temporary bed and breakfast accommodation, and I wouldn't want us to start our married life in such a way. House hunting starts in earnest, immediately after Christmas."

"I have some friends with a property or two in this area," James Hawley Weeks offered with a shrug. "They provide the high-end market with exquisite living opportunities."

"We'll take you up on that offer, perhaps immediately after Christmas as I said, if Abigail feels it might be advantageous to us," Hal agreed on the nod from his fiancée. There was no way he could possibly, or fairly, make a definitive decision without tacit agreement from her.

"You could always stay here together, as Abigail is already here?" Florence suggested.

"Wouldn't dream of it, personally," Hal retorted quite firmly as he turned to Abigail for corroboration. "We will live together as husband and wife only when we *are* husband and wife, and I am sure my dear fiancée will agree with that."

She nodded sagely in agreement, although she would have agreed with whatever he might have said. She simply wanted to marry and settle down to spend their life as they would no doubt agree at an appropriate time. Children would arrive in due course if they were meant to; a philosophy they both agreed upon quite strenuously.

"Tea everyone?" Poppy asked. "With a slice of either fruit cake or Victoria sponge, or the occasional mince pie, all made by Mary Jane to the recipe devised by her Aunt Mary and Nanny Nell Booth."

An excited and eager chorus of "Yes, please" and "Thank

you very much" greeted her offer, all of which would be fulfilled by Mary Jane herself via the new-fangled telephone system that magically linked the main house and cottages. What a godsend *that* invention had proved to be!

Just fifteen minutes later the knocker on the front door sounded, to be followed by the creaking from one of the door's black metal hinges and a voice from the hallway announcing, "You rang milady?" supported by a quiet, naughty giggle.

"Nanny Nell! Mary!" Poppy shrieked in joy as the pair trooped into the front room, each carrying a large wooden tray. "I didn't know you were here!"

"We've come down to offer our congratulations on the engagement of the esteemed Miss Abigail Green and Mr Hal McIntyre," Nell said with a happy grin splitting her face.

"But how did you … know?" Abigail asked, puzzled at the seemingly magical knowledge at large in this fairy-tale farm.

"My friend here is the 'Mary' in Mary's Pantry, and she was there this afternoon when Hal popped the question," Nell explained. "Grandpa Ross and I just happened to drop in shortly after you had left. We guessed that this was where you would be heading. Ross?"

Her husband came in from the vestibule, carrying a bottle of Champagne and a dozen flutes to toast the newly engaged. Abigail couldn't believe the joy all her companions felt and showed at her pre-nuptials, and the trouble they were taking to make them feel part of this wonderful extended family. She had never experienced such togetherness, even when she was a nipper able to understand how and why grown-ups expressed emotion and joy for others. As she had become an adult, all she had ever experienced was a degree of aggravation of men towards women, and being reminded of her place as a woman in a man's world. *This* family was entirely without precedence or equal for her.

"Now then Mr Hawley Weeks – James – Might we explore your suggestion in a little more detail?" Poppy said. "And then perhaps we might arrive at consensus."

CHAPTER 16

The back room of the Ship Inn was poorly heated, dirty and suffered from bad lighting and ventilation, making the thick tobacco smoke hang lifelessly in the air above the group of dirty and dishevelled ruffians. Only two of them stood out as having at least a modicum of style and education.

"Are we all clear what is expected of us tonight?" a very large, massively side-whiskered and reasonably well-dressed man asked the gathered group sharply. "This operation will be the making of us all if…" he emphasised pointedly, "we *all* play our part. If not, we all lose out, those that have failed more so than all the others. Do I make myself clear?"

His threat overlaid all other words, sticking in their minds as an incentive not to fail.

"Thresher Hall has been uninhabited and unguarded for more than six months, but its inside still holds untold riches that time has invited us to take to 'safety'," he went on, causing most of those present to smirk. "Two nights hence, there will be no moon for two reasons: one, a new moon will be barely visible, and two, hopefully there will be quite thick cloud cover. We will have veiled hurricane lamps to allow a degree of visibility, but you will all need to be very careful when loading the innards of this large house into the wagons we will have with us.

"You will do the heavy lifting – in silence – while my friends hereabouts will take care of the jewellery, antiques and pottery. Once the place has been emptied of everything of value, we will drive it all very carefully to our predetermined places, ready for distribution to auction houses. Once the articles have been disposed of, we will gather at an arranged rendezvous to receive our shares of the takings. All understood?"

Mutters and mumbles greeted the man's words, allowing each to think on the part he would need to play. None of them was unsure about what might befall them should they not perform to expectation.

"You understand your role, Jonas Jamieson?" The Big Man said to his co-conspirator, once all the others had melted away to their billets to await further orders.

"Indeed, I do," the young man said, sure of what he would have to do and the rewards that *that* part would bring him. "I shall await your orders with bated breath."

"Two days from this moment then, *old chap*," The Big Man said with a smile, a mere touch of sarcasm surrounding his last words. "Make sure your young runner is up to speed and is available and ready."

"Indeed, old chap," Jonas reciprocated equally gently. "Here's to the next couple of days. Can't wait."

"Ready as I'll ever be," Tom Garside said, replying to his friend's question about his readiness to reintroduce himself to the workplace.

"That has to be a matter of opinion, old man," Joseph McIntyre said, a concerned frown revealing his thoughts on the matter. "And the onny opinions that matter are those of yon medic … and Lilly Garside. You have tended to gloss ower medical conditions and stuff in t'past, which probably led to your present condition. Any road, how's your George getting on with his delivery rounds?"

"Champion," Tom assured him. "Not onny 'as 'e fulfilled all the orders regularly and on time, but 'e's brought in more, particularly from t'west of t'county. Grand lad. In fact, he's so efficient we might 'ave to gi' 'im a bonus to keep 'im sweet."

"I'll leave that to thee, Tom," Joseph laughed. "If *thy* digs thi hand a bit deeper into thi pocket, 'e *must* be good."

"Just like to ask a minor question wi thee, if tha doesn't mind, Joseph," Tom said quietly. "It's a little bit … delicate, like."

"Broach away, my old friend," Joseph encouraged.

"How to start? I get the feeling our George is a bit … sweet on your Poppy," Tom went on.

"We've all known that for a reasonably lengthy time," Joseph said with a knowing smile.

"Well, he asked me – in confidence, tha knows – son to father, what he ought to do, because he felt she would probably knock him back if he asked 'er," Tom went on, looking over his shoulder to make sure no-one else was listening in to their earnest conversation. "What does tha think he ought to do?"

"Just what you are leading to with him, I should imagine," Joseph said seriously. "Ask … her. She's t'onny one as'll be able to give him a straight answer."

"Just wor I wor thinking," Tom replied. "And if she does knock him back?"

"Summat as what he will have to come to terms with,

perhaps," Joseph shrugged non-committally. "Either persevere or … move on."

"Persevere?" Tom asked, none too sure where that might take George.

"Leave it a bit and ask again," Joseph explained. "It may well be that, at twenty-two years old, she's not ready to settle down as yet. She might consider that there are things she desperately wants to achieve before family affairs intrude, or she may not want to pursue all that *that* entails at all. Some women are like that."

"Aye," Tom said quietly. "I suppose it all depends on what our George is prepared to do – wait or move on."

"It'll be rayt, Tom," Joseph added. "He's a fine young man and I feel sure things will work out – one way or t'other."

As they finished their conversation, who should come into the warmth of the Garside front room but … George Garside himself.

"Very parky out there!" George grimaced as he started to warm his backside in front of *their* roaring fire. "Two more regular orders today, Father. Joseph. The sorts of orders I know will grow into summat big within the next few months. So, I think you lot need to make sure I have enough produce to keep up to market demand.

"Incidentally," he added after a moment or two, "there is nobody out there doing what we are doing."

"I don't know about you two, but I must be off," Joseph said. "I've a wife and three hearty nippers to see to."

"Is everything all right now, then?" Tom asked cautiously. "You know…?"

"It is, and we've got George here and Jim and Sally Smallshore to thank for that," Joseph returned, a smile creeping up on him. "It should be bonus time pretty soon, to say thank you to our wonderful workforce."

"I'm not sure, Dad," George said quietly, once Joseph had snecked the front door shut behind him on his way out.

"Not sure about what, lad?" Tom asked, a little perplexed by his son's strange statement. "Joseph offering you a bonus?"

"No," his son explained. "Remember what we were talking about the other day? You know…?"

"What? The birthday present you were thinking of buying me?" the old man sniggered. "I've allus hankered after a watch like—"

"No," his son replied quickly. "You know … Poppy and how I feel about her."

"Aye, well. That's another story, isn't it, lad," Tom retorted, still not too sure how to advise his son. Should he simply tell him what Joseph had said? Sometimes a hard truth was all that would work, and then George would have to make his own judgement. 'Better to be honest in the short term than to be sorry later on', is what Tom's dad would always say.

"Why doesn't tha just blurt it out and have done?" he asked. "There's onny one person would then have to live wi' 'er answer. And that would be … thee."

On that wise note the kitchen door opened slowly and Tom's wife, Lilly, and his two remaining daughters sidled around the door jamb with uncontainable smiles on their faces.

"Aye up!" Tom's wary voice heralded their entry to the room. "Them faces allus promise trouble. What is it now? One of them new-fangled charabangs?"

"No trouble at all, Husband," his wife reassured him. "You need to smile because Charity's young man has asked her to marry him."

"How come I knew nothing about this 'young man'?" he replied. "And, on the contrary, it means a whole lot of trouble

– financial trouble, for a starter."

"You don't have a say in the matter, Husband," Lilly insisted loudly. "This is women's business, and as such you have precious little to do with it other than to find the money to pay for it all."

"It's how we're going to pay for it that concerns me," he explained fiercely. Answering back was not an adventure he had ever indulged in throughout his lengthy married life to Lilly Garside. "We have had a lot on us money spoken for during the last year or two to help develop and establish new ways of running our farms."

"Then isn't it about time Joseph McIntyre started to pay his share in this partnership?" Lilly spat back, indignant at being a money horse whose saddlebags were almost always next to … empty.

"That's just the point!" Tom went on, becoming irate for the first time in their nigh-on forty years together. "Proportionately, Joseph has laid out much more than we have. Who do you think financed the merger, and who insisted on contributing almost all of the outlay for his and our Lilly Victoria's wedding?"

That last revelation stopped her in her tracks and left her with mouth agape and shock rolling round her erstwhile superior face. She had believed all along that it was them, the Garsides, who had financed the whole shindig. It left her at a loss for words – that she no doubt would redress in the near future when she had had time to reflect on its import.

Charity turned and retraced her steps back into the kitchen whence she came, tears threatening to divulge her sadness at having to listen to her parents' disagreement over what Mother considered only a small thing. No doubt they would redress any disagreement before long, but suffice to say that she, Charity Garside, *would* marry the boy of her dreams – no matter how they all viewed it.

"She will marry who she wishes," Tom said, realising how much upset his uncharacteristic outspokenness had caused. He had no intension of letting his views spoil his daughter's nuptials, whenever they would undoubtedly occur, but he would not like them to cost him as much as his wife deemed appropriate. Still, if he had to haul back on the amount he ate and drank to pay for her escape, then so be it. That would then leave them onny one…

George had no intention of allowing his parents to waste their money on deciding and developing the gathering pace of his adult life. He would certainly not be waiting for any sort of an inheritance to allow him to marry the lady of his dreams, should she appear in his life any time soon. Poppy would fulfil that role admirably, but he had no desire to wait until she'd had her fill of her literary adventuring. He was ready to settle down any time soon, to raise a family and to spend the rest of his time in wedded bliss with whosoever his wife should be.

Then there was Florence, the other lovely in his life. Would he? Could he? Should he?

The night was dark. No vestige of moonlight. No moon. Only the merest flick and flash of the occasional star as heavy clouds scudded by on a freshening breeze.

Thresher Hall lay deserted in its valley, surrounded and hidden by the rolling snow-capped hills of southern Cumberland and Westmorland, affording peace, tranquillity and virtual invisibility from all prying eyes that might catch the unusual and clandestine activity around its ample size and glowering presence.

Six large wagons, each drawn by a couple of tail-swishing black shires, stood line astern on the hardened driveway either side of an impressively large pair of oaken doors that lay open to the outside. At least a dozen or so flickering hurricane lamps flitted backwards and forwards around this impressive edifice. A succession of black dressed and masked bodies entered and exited the doors as quickly as the large items they were carrying and loading into the wagons would allow.

One hour and thirty minutes and they were gone, leaving no sign that anyone, anything, out of the ordinary had been anywhere near. Even the doors had been closed and locked. The last to leave had been a small team of 'cleaners', whose job it was to persuade any visitors that the expensive contents of this ancient pile had been spirited away as if by magic.

The wagons, drawn by those magnificent beasts would be long gone by the time anyone might come near. No-one could possibly know what had happened on this cold, dark night just before Christmas.

No-one save … one.

That one had watched every move, had seen everything that had been loaded, knew the main perpetrators, and wasn't afraid to share that information.

But, with whom, and at what price?

CHAPTER 17

"Jonas Jamieson," The Big Man said as his accomplice was ushered into the rather palatial study. Closing the ledger in front of him on his equally impressive mahogany desk, he fixed the newcomer's eyes in an unblinkingly aggressive stare. "It seems we have a slight hiccup following our 'outing' the other night."

"In what respect?" Jonas asked, not understanding what The Big Man was talking about. "Is it a matter of saleability or price?"

"Neither," The Big Man explained, handing him a well-written note. "You *can* read, I take it?"

Jonas took the note and, ignoring the other man's derisory comment, he read the missive. "What about it?" he asked with a dismissive shrug. "Can you tell me, old chap, how anyone could possibly have seen what we were doing sufficiently well to make out *anything* in those conditions? There was no moon. It was as black as pitch, and we made no noise. There was nothing about that could see anything, other than a bat or some other blessed nocturnal creature."

"He categorises quite accurately what we had in our wagons, how many wagons and shires we had, and how many of us there were – even the team we left behind to tidy up," The Big Man insisted. "You tell me that there was nobody there and that there is nothing to be concerned about? For God's sake, man!"

"And what proof, apart from circumstantial evidence, does he have?" Jonas returned quite sharply.

"Read the last sentence again," The Big Man suggested. "You do know what a sentence is, I assume? Go on then!" he went on, after a few moments' hesitation. "Read it!"

"'It would be a shame if the police were to 'accidentally' stumble across all that "material" in your warehouse on the River Swale just to the south-west of Richmond, wouldn't it?'" Jonas read, almost dismissively.

"Well?" The Big Man insisted. "Seems a touch strange, don't you think, that a letter drops on my desk only a few days later, with enough detail to point a finger at somebody that knows chapter and verse about certain activities that only a few people knew anything about?"

"Go ahead!" Jonas insisted aggressively. "Point your bloody finger in my direction. If you do, you'll see pretty quickly what my response will be. I had nothing to do with this, and you have no proof to the contrary. What are you going to do about it? Go to the constabulary?"

"Find out from the people you recruited if they know anything," The Big Man replied, less aggressively. "We'll get rid of the stuff as quickly as possible."

"I assume, old chap, that you noticed that there was no demand?" Jonas suggested. "Could this be opportunistic? Somebody that got to know from someone else and guessed that the biggest dealer in the area might be involved. Namely

… you? If the person behind this is bona fide, you will no doubt receive a demand in the very near future. He might be involved with your buyers trying to drive down your financial expectations through fear of being found out."

Jonas left The Big Man stewing in his own arrogance, and a smile began to grow as he stepped out onto the pavement.

"And James Hawley Weeks' suggestion?" Poppy asked her close circle of friends. "What did you think about it?"

"In what respect?" Abigail asked, smiling still at the flashing three-carat diamond sitting atop its twenty-two-carat gold band.

"Well, perhaps we need to decide whether what he suggested is not only desirable but also feasible," Poppy acknowledged quickly. "This has to be a joint decision. I, for one, love the idea of a book launch pretty soon after our books have been published together with your review in *The Times*."

"A book launch coupled with a book reading from other folks' works would be an ideal vehicle through which our group would be publicised even further," Florence agreed. "You never know, our little secret might sneak out into a wider literary world where we can peddle our ideas even further afield. Abigail? Jenny?"

"I like the sound of that," Jenny responded enthusiastically. "This could establish a literary standard not seen before in our small society and encourage writers to hone their talents before sharing them with the rest of the world."

"Might I suggest that you two, Poppy and Florence, hone your typing skills on yon Remington typewriter I can see in the corner by the window?" Jenny suggested. "And perhaps acquire a second one so one of you doesn't have to wait until the other has finished? That way, both books will be ready for publication at about the same time."

"Excellent idea," a deeper voice joined in from the vestibule doorway. "To that end, Poppy and Florence, you might find what I carry in my arms useful."

They all turned sharply to see Grandpa Ross with a rather large package he had just deposited on a sturdy side table.

"Grandpa Ross!" Poppy exclaimed, gripping him in a bear-like hug. "Is that what I think it is?"

"And what do you *think* it might be?" he asked, allowing the mystery to grow.

"Could it be a new Remington typing machine, by any chance?" Poppy replied.

"And how do you know that?" her grandpa teased.

"It says so on the box!" Florence chipped in, clapping her hands softly in excitement.

"Can't pull the wool over your eyes, eh, young lady!" he laughed. "Can't stay. Business to attend to." With that infusion of excitement and joy, he was gone.

"What it must be like to have a loving and thoughtful and generous grandpa!" Abigail said with a happy sigh. "No reason now not to have your manuscripts in readable form within the next couple of weeks, eh?"

"Too right!" Poppy exclaimed.

"Exciting!" Florence added, with a jiggle of her feet.

"Do you have titles yet?" Jenny asked.

"Mine's a detective story called *Death in the Sun*," Poppy informed them all. "By P.P. Spence. I have decided to use my father's surname."

"And my book is a romance called *Faithfully Yours* by F.T. Smythe," Florence added with a proud smile hovering about her face.

"I can understand why the initials, and why Poppy is P.P. Spence," Jenny said. "But your nom de plume, Florence?"

"F.T. Smythe was my great-great grandfather," Florence explained. "I thought it sounded … grand enough."

"Can't wait to read them," Jenny said eagerly to Abigail's enthusiastic nodding.

<hr />

"You're playing a dangerous game, my friend," the well-educated and well-dressed man said to his less-elegant companion. "I hope he doesn't find out about your double-dealing."

"There's only one way that will happen, old chap, and that's if you tell him," his companion replied rather foppishly. "*Are* you about to tell him?"

"Most certainly not," came the answer as quickly and firmly as he had desired. Jonas Jamieson was no fool. He would not have followed the path he had chosen had he not known he could carry it off. He always calculated the risks involved with this sort of a business deal and, although nothing could be set in cast iron with shady dealings, his calculations were as close to a hundred per cent as it was possible to get.

"Now, I know that The Big Man will be approaching you very soon so you need to be ready with your offer, which will be less than the amount I have already provided to you," Jonas urged. "We don't want him to try to go elsewhere, do we? Or am I trying to teach my grandma – whoever *she* was – to suck eggs?"

"More like asking her to grope her ducks, I think," the man corrected. "I don't need you to tell me how to run *my* business. You have no need to be concerned, young man, because I do not renege on any deal I strike. I will make him an offer he can't refuse, thereby allowing you to claim a double recompense – your original from him, and a reasonable amount from me."

"Excellent," Jonas responded. "I am looking forward to that day. I am sure you have a storage facility big enough and ready enough to receive this charming – and valuable – set of commodities. I am positive also that it will all sell very quickly, especially the exquisite jewellery that forms a large part of the consignment."

Although cold by anyone's standards, the early evening air was fresh and clear enough for Jonas to want to delay his return to the hovel he called his resting place. One of the reasons for this was that he no longer wanted to live in the sort of squalor his body had endured over the last year or two. Although their relationship hadn't lasted long, living with his little 'harlot' Jenny Bott had proved to be the best place since he had escaped from home a couple or so years earlier. He hoped that the money he would earn from his latest endeavour would provide him with something better than what he had been used to.

Strolling down the main street in Richmond with his mind on his next 'project', he bumped sharply into a passer-by. He turned slightly after the jolt to say 'Sorry, ol' chap' when he realised who the 'old chap' was.

Realising the identity of his accidental assailant, George Garside lunged violently at this easily recognised passer-by and managed to latch on to his coat sleeve. "Jonas Jamieson!" he snarled. "Now I have you, at last."

Unfortunately for George, the slight, slippery snake of a person that was his nemesis cast off his coat in one slick movement and rounded the corner into a narrow snicket and disappeared. George regained his balance very quickly and set off in lively pursuit, but once he gained the snicket four different passageways splintered off from the one he was on. This gave him no chance to follow Jonas.

"Damn!" he cursed. "Slippery as a new-born elver, as usual."

Aware that it would serve no useful purpose to comb all the passageways and snickets that he knew would give him no clue as to Jonas's whereabouts, he decided to seek his horse and wagon to return home.

"Nearly had the bugger, too," George said as he stroked and untied his shire next to the closest inn where the horse had shelter, a mouthful of hay and water. He had otherwise had an exceptional day, selling his complete load of butchered meats, milk and butter.

"Nearly had him," George said to Ross as he stored the wagon, stabled the horse and brushed him down. The horse was chomping on feed and hay in his stall.

"Who's that then, George?" Ross asked as he made ready to join his family for the night.

"Yon bugger, Jonas Jamieson. Who else?" George returned, clicking his fingers in frustration. "Almost had him in the main street in Richmond. Took hold of his coat sleeve, but he managed to slip out of it and to slither down an adjacent alleyway."

"He's getting brave, isn't he?" Ross said. "Showing himself even in the half-light."

"One of these days, eh, Ross?" George retorted. "Oh, by the way, sold everything I took today – meat, milk, poultry, butter – all gone in a trice. More orders to follow, I am told. Will we be able to keep up with production?"

"Don't worry about that, my friend. I'll make sure we do," Ross explained. "Joseph has told me to let you know you will be receiving another bonus on top of your *usual* bonus next week. I don't know how much yet, but it should be worth having. This will be to recognise your hard work in enhancing our turnover."

"Excellent, Ross," George guffawed loudly. "Perhaps I'll be able to afford to ask Poppy out."

They both laughed as George strode around the stables to head for home, a happy smile on his face.

~⌒~

"Well, old chap, still a little too sturdy and slow, eh?" Jonas muttered to himself as he regained his quarters. Back-street, grimy accommodation in whatever town or city always reeked of filth and decadence, and his was no exception: dirty and dishevelled bed in corner; bare wooden table and one rickety chair that had both seen better days; one tiny, high-up, curtainless window encrusted with filth and spider droppings, and one small square of indeterminate floorcovering that used to be a rug.

"Come in!" he called to a faint tapping on the handleless door. "It's not locked." That last comment drew a smile and a faint chuckle from even *his* lips.

A young lad of slight stature with densely curly, untidy hair stepped into the room, causing Jonas to put down the small cudgel he usually kept handy for self-defence. As there was no vetting process between him and any curmudgeonly ruffian who might fancy calling, he had to be prepared at all times.

"Toby! Good to see you," Jonas said, waving him to the chair. "Our plan has been put into place and we should be receiving our just rewards in due course."

This news caused the lad to grin widely.

"What would you think to a sovereign in remuneration for all your help in this?" Jonas asked, a sneaky smile flitting around his lips.

"I would say thank you very much, sir," Toby answered, grinning even more widely. "That would be beyond my dreams." He stood up to leave but was beckoned to sit again.

"What would you say if I were to tell you that your wages would be nearer to … twenty sovereigns?" Jonas said forcefully. "Twenty sovereigns. Just think about that!"

The young lad's jaw dropped open, and his face started to quiver in shock. "But … but…" the lad stammered, not knowing what to say. "That's more money than I have ever seen. Even more than—"

"No need to elucidate, old chap," Jonas interrupted, flinging his arms wide. In his perverse sort of a way, he was quite happy to see the lad's confusion and was pleased with his gratitude.

"Would you like to stay in my employ, young Toby?" Jonas went on after a little pause.

"I should say *so!*" the lad replied eagerly.

"The next time we meet won't be in *this* hovel, though," was Jonas's parting shot as Toby almost skipped through the door. "I'll catch you when I have something for you."

CHAPTER 18

"Don't think for the life of you that's it's going to be a magical mystery tour!" Abigail McIntyre, née Green, said to Poppy and Florence. "This will be an adventure where we travel to places you have only read about. We will be travelling to London by the new-fangled railway train, by coach and four to Dover, packet-boat ferry to Calais in France, and then on to Paris. That will take the best part of four or five days, depending on how much steam the engines can muster."

"That sounds enormously exciting," Poppy gushed.

"But very tiring?" Florence added quickly with a grimace. "We've never done that sort of thing before – except for up and down the Yorkshire east coast when we were twelve."

"When Hal and I got married, we had our honeymoon doing exactly what *we* will be doing on *our* adventure," Abigail commented.

"Honeymoon?" Florence queried. "Did you eat lots of honey under the moonlight?"

Poppy laughed but shared her friend's lack of understanding of the term.

"Its origin delves back into the fifth century, when cultures represented calendar time with the cycles of the moon," Abigail explained. "It was a time when newlywed couples drank mead during their first moon of marriage. Mead is a honey-based alcoholic drink, believed to have aphrodisiac properties – hence 'honeymoon'."

"You went all the way to Paris?" Poppy gasped. "How wonderfully fascinating."

"We did break our journey at several places en route on our 'bridal tour', to visit family who couldn't get to our wedding," Abigail explained. "We set aside a month for the tour to allow for stopping off for a day or two here and there in England, and for visiting friends in France."

"The reason we will be taking only two weeks—?" Florence asked.

"Or so," Abigail interrupted with a chuckle. "We may need a few more days in various places to allow for necessary deviations and detours."

"Will we be … safe?" Poppy asked tentatively. "I mean, three ladies on their own?"

"Three ladies plus one gentleman – our bodyguard," Abigail assured them both. "Hal is an experienced adventurer and explorer and has spent a lot of his time in dangerous places that nobody has even heard of. He will be our guard and guide."

"I can think of no-one better," Poppy returned, clapping her hands quietly satisfied with their proposed security.

"We are considering setting off in the very near future," Abigail suggested. "Late spring would be better, I think. You've already clocked up three or four very successful soirées to develop and entrench the love of literature within the north of England. It is now time to diversify by bringing in the literature and culture of our nearest European neighbours which would be—"

"France!" Poppy and Florence chorused like two nine-year-olds rushing to a party for the first time.

"I need to drop our latest article for my *Times*' column into the post before updating my wardrobe in Richmond," Abigail went on. "I need to check also how many copies of your books you have both sold to date."

"I wonder if I might accompany you, Abigail?" Florence asked. "I need some things from Richmond too."

How quiet it was in the cottage once two-thirds of its occupants had departed. Time, perhaps, to add one or two more alterations to her own proposed itinerary before plans were finalised.

A sharp knock at the door drew Poppy's attention away from thoughts of railway trains, boats and … Paris. "George! How good to see you," she greeted her dear friend. "You of all people have no need to knock. I thought you would be peddling your wares somewhere in the North Riding, making a fortune for our two houses."

"My one day off," he replied. "Anyway, there is something I would like to discuss with you. Are we alone?"

"Abigail and Florence are on their way to Richmond, so you have me all to yourself," she said with a smile. "For an hour or two, anyway. Tea and a Mary-type scone – baked by Mary Jane, I hasten to add? I tend to try my hand at baking only if I have no alternative."

"No, thank you, Poppy," George answered. "I need to ask you something that's rather important to me."

"Come and sit next to me on the settee, George?" she suggested, patting the cushion next to her. "Then we can be even cosier."

"I have one very serious question to ask you, Poppy," he started slowly and taking a deep breath once he had sat down next to her. "We are both in our mid-twenties and I was wondering if you might have had any thoughts on … settling down with a chap like … me?"

A stunned silence descended into the room with this almost unfinished question that had very serious undertones for Poppy. Understanding fully what was at stake, her face had flushed to a deep pink as she struggled with the question's implication and the serious answer it demanded.

"I knew its suddenness would take you by surprise, Poppy, my dear, but—" George started, unsure as to the implication of the strangling silence his vague question had generated.

"But it's not sudden at all, dear, kind George," Poppy answered gently. "We have known each other almost from birth and I have very deep feelings for you, of which I think you are well aware. I was deeply saddened when I thought I had lost you to Annabel and—"

"Annabel was never going to marry me, as we found out later," George said. "Anyway, I only took up with her because I felt I couldn't persuade you that I loved you. Now I know the answer to that question."

"How do you mean?" she asked, not sure what he was trying to say.

"Your silence has reinforced what I thought before," he said.

"Which is?" she asked.

"That you are not interested in becoming my beloved wife," he explained, quietly disconsolate.

"It's not *that*, dear George," she replied, sadness swimming in her eyes. "I love you dearly, but I have a lot to do, to explore and to achieve that I need to devote all my attention to. I wouldn't be able to do that if we were … married. It would be—"

"No need to explain further," George butted in, hurt beyond belief by her curt answer. Standing up brusquely, he wished her good day and strode out of the cottage.

"George!" she shouted after him as she dashed to the outside door. "George! Don't go! I have to tell you … that if you could wait a couple of years…"

Her last words were lost in the howls of the sharp winds that had sprung up, taking her words and her dear, beloved George away from her, perhaps forever. She burst into uncontrollable sobs once she had regained her living room, which now felt uncomfortably empty.

"Oh, George," she sighed, all the joy for living squeezed out of her body. "Why couldn't … you … wait?"

"And he simply walked out of the door with no explanation," Poppy commented to Florence once they were alone.

"What did you expect, Poppy? Him to roll over and accept the kick to his groin that you so thoughtlessly delivered to him?" Florence spat at her friend angrily. "The likelihood now is that we won't see our beloved friend again for some time, if at all."

"I wasn't expecting a marriage proposal out of the blue like that," Poppy pleaded, her eyes still full of unreleased tears. "I thought—"

"Actually, Poppy dear, you *didn't* think at all," her friend replied. "We both know the feelings George has had for both of us for some considerable time, and I have to tell you that, had he asked *me*, I would have jumped at the chance in a trice. Unfortunately, your thoughtless action has taken him from *me*, too. Thank you, Poppy."

Florence turned away from her friend and headed for her room to mourn the loss of a dear friend whom she would have loved to spend the rest of her life with.

"Hello? Anybody in?" Tommy Spence called out as he stepped over the threshold of Poppy's cottage.

Poppy emerged from the bathroom newly groomed and freshened after her harrowing experience with both her friends. "Hello, Father," she said, greeting Tommy with a hug. "I didn't expect to see you today. Everything all right?"

"Indeed, it is," he answered enthusiastically. "I had to come to see you straight away because I have some wonderful news I need to share with you before anyone else."

"And what could that be?" she asked, glad to know that at least someone was happy on this difficult day.

"You know Jim and Sally Smallshore, don't you?" he asked, knowing that it was an unnecessary question.

"Indeed," she agreed, wondering why he should ask such a needless question. "They are the ones that live in the next cottage down from us, aren't they?"

"Sorry. Such a silly thing to ask. Of course you do," he said, trying not to exaggerate his excitement. "I have just asked Sally if she will be my wife, and … she's accepted."

This was too much for Poppy. She burst into tears and stumbled into her bedroom, locking the door behind her, leaving her father dumbfounded and at a loss as to why what he had said had caused such a reaction.

"Don't worry, Mr Spence," Florence's voice joined him in the room. "She's upset because our friend George has just asked her to marry him."

"And?" Tommy asked, puzzled why Poppy was upset at such a joyous event.

"She turned him down, and probably we won't see him again," Florence explained with a sigh and a disappointed shrug.

"Oh dear!" he said. "And my announcement must have pushed her over the edge. Shall I go and tell her—?"

"I think it might be a good idea to let her settle down," she advised. "Anyway, congratulations. I'm sure you'll be very happy. Sally is a lovely person."

Mixed emotions and questions crowded George's mind as he trudged back to his home farm. Should he have asked Poppy outright instead of being so negative? Why didn't he discuss the possibility of their being joined at a later date, instead of jumping in with both feet and stomping off in a huff? If he had stopped to listen to what else she had to say, perhaps they might have married within a couple of years or so. Now he would never know unless … he could swallow his manly pride and go back to her.

That was never going to happen. If only…

"You all rayt, Son?" his dad's voice drew him out of his reverie abruptly. "I thowt thy were off to ignore me, like. Penny for thi thowts?"

"Not worth that much at t'moment, if truth be known, Dad," George replied, deflated.

"Is tha sure tha's all rayt?" Tom asked again, a bit concerned that his lad didn't sound on top note.

"Just a bit tired, that's all. Be rayt," George said.

Tom always knew that not everything was all right with his son when he replied 'Be rayt'. As with most Yorkshire men, that phrase was a deterrent to anyone asking the question, by insisting everything *was* all right when it obviously could easily be the opposite.

"Tea's ready for thi, any road," Tom added, rubbing his hands together, showing that he was becoming excited about filling his belly with one of his wife's wonderful concoctions.

"Not that hungry, really," George said.

"Lilly!" Tom shouted for his wife as they both flung off their coats and boots in the vestibule. "Call t'medic! Our George is proper poorly!"

"What's all the fuss about, Husband?" Lilly shouted as she entered the front room from the kitchen. "Have you been on that strong ale down at t'King's Arms again?"

"Nay, Lass. It's Our George. He says 'e's not 'ungry for 'is tea," Tom warned his wife. "When wor t'last time that 'appened? When 'e wor six, and 'ad a bout o' t'measles?"

"Ee, Lad," his mother groaned sympathetically. "Tha's off to pass out if tha's not mindful. It's thi favourite an' all! Steak and kidney pie followed by 'ome-med creamed rice pudding. Sure I can't tempt thi?"

"When will it be ready, Mam?" George asked, cocking an eyebrow.

"In about ten minutes," she replied. "So, tha'd better get thissen weshed and changed out of thi mucky clothes. Otherwise, I'll send round for Ross Booth to come ower and 'ave thy share."

"All rayt," he agreed. "Be down in nine-and-a-half minutes. Then I'll 'ave some. What was that all about the other day with our Charity, then? A bit on a to-do?" he asked as he headed for the bathroom and the WC.

Five minutes later he was down, sitting at the table, napkin tucked under his chin like his dad had always done. "Our Charity?" he asked again as his mother brought in an enormous pie dish and set it in the middle of the table, its golden-brown crust breathing out gentle flumes of steam to whet their appetite.

"It was nothing really," his dad said almost dismissively. "Summat about her wanting to wed yon Charlie Oakenshaw's lad, Jimmy. She'll ger ower it soon enough."

CHAPTER 19

"You've got to be joking me!" Ross said to his brother. "And what did you say to 'em?"

"Well, I said that if they weren't out of my sight in two minutes sharp, they would never be able to walk again," Joseph retorted as he sipped his hot tea in their sitting room on their mid-day break. "They both pulled themselves up to their full five-foot-nine height, with a put-on puzzled look on their faces, perhaps ready for action."

Ross began to grin, knowing what might be coming next. "When they asked for money, did they say, 'Pretty please'?" he went on, a laugh ready to burst out.

"It was when I stood up from the bar and clenched *both* mi fists, they both began to back off. As they reached the door, they shouted that we'd be hearing from them again," Joseph finished. "Jimmy Pearson said that they seemed to be doing the rounds, asking for – nay, demanding – money to mek sure no trouble came our way."

"Protection money," Ross Senior interrupted as he wandered in with *his* mug of tea. "They demand money to 'protect' you from any ruffian interference in your business, when you're really being protected from them. It used to happen a lot in Australia. It's a racket."

"Do you have any advice as to how we might stop 'em, Father?" Ross asked. "Short of breaking a few necks?"

"The problem is that they do stuff to your property when either you aren't looking or are nowhere near," Ross Senior replied. "There is no way you can get on top of this without finding out who is behind it all."

"I have a good idea!" Ross Junior offered. "My guess is that Jonas Jamieson could be part of it, at least. It would be too much for him to be behind it all, as he doesn't have either the clout or the money."

"I would think that it's some gang from out of town trying to muscle in on local firms to be the first to establish *their* patch," Ross Senior offered.

"Any ideas on how to nip it in the bud?" Joseph said. "It will cost us to employ folks to ride shotgun on our wagons like George Garside uses. There's also the serious question of whether this gang might be armed with guns. You can only fight guns with bigger guns."

"Next time these minions come calling, my advice would be to arrange to meet the boss man somewhere convenient for you," Ross Senior suggested. "You would then have one of three recourses: either arrange to have the police in disguise with you, or you try to warn them off, or you pay up."

"The only one on that list that appeals to me is the second one," his son returned. "And that would involve taking our twelve-bore shotguns with us, along with a number of our neighbours. Because, no doubt, they will be targeted next."

"In that case we should arrange a meeting with all our close neighbours, including our workforce, to put forward our plan of action to see what they think," Joseph suggested. "It's not just our livelihood we are dealing with here. It affects everyone in our area that works the land. We can't let these parasites ruin our lives."

"Jonas has always had it in for our family, although technically he is one of us – and he's definitely not ower keen on George Garside," Ross Junior said. "*He* will certainly need protection while he's out on his rounds, as I wouldn't be surprised if Jonas targeted him first. This may even be a ploy to draw George out in to the open to have his men attack him. We can't let that happen."

"Don't forget that, whatever you need to ensure you have the wherewithal to protect everyone in our two farms, the finance is there," Ross Senior advised. "There is a time when you need to put your money where your mouth is and this, I feel, is *that* time. Don't forget also that I have people I can call on to help in case the worst comes to the worst."

"I don't know anything about these sorts of people to be able to make an assessment," Joseph replied. "I can only assume my brother Ross feels the same. Just how susceptible they would be to 'reasoned' argument I have no idea. I've witnessed Ross's reason when confronted by unreasonably truculent individuals. They usually end up in hospital. He's no patience, hasn't my brother."

Ross Senior laughed at the faces Joseph pulled to exemplify his brother's ire at being crossed, although generally Ross was a gentle gentleman. He just couldn't tolerate ruffians that had no respect for ordinary law-abiding folk, and he would even the score if he could, no matter what.

From his experience of similar situations, Ross Senior realised that, from an extortionist's viewpoint, working farmers weren't the best people to confront from two perspectives.

Usually, they didn't have enough spare money to share, and they often they had the people and ammunition with which to fight. No. This was probably a targeted affair, where someone who had an axe to grind had a motive other than financial gain. Likely to be a reasonably clever diversion, it would deflect thought away from the true intent of the author of this particular scheme.

The only likely perpetrator was clever, leaving himself several avenues to pursue or to escape should his plans not come to fruition. The solution to this dilemma would need careful thought.

Although Poppy, Florence, Abigail and Hal were due to embark on the first leg of their adventure to Europe within the next week or two, Florence felt that she couldn't leave without trying to see their dear friend, George.

The lighter and warmer days of early May were approaching rapidly, which, according to Abigail, was an ideal time to travel the glorious countryside of Northern France on their way to their final destination of Paris. Abigail had suggested a detour along the River Loire valley, where there was a vast succession of more than three-hundred magnificent châteaux, at least eleven of which were constructed by and for royalty. However, taking into account its two-hundred-or-so miles of wonderful countryside, they felt that *that* might be added to their list for a future time.

"George?" Florence shouted as she headed for the main house, having seen her friend's broad back about to disappear around its unostentatious front. "George! Over here!"

She ran to the edge of the building to catch up with him around that corner. He had seen her and, although he perhaps didn't want to speak to her, out of politeness he stopped in front of the cowsheds.

"Hello, Florence," he said, looking her directly in the eyes. "Lovely to see you."

"George," she returned, moving closer to him. "I've not seen you for weeks and weeks. Was it something I have done or said? You seem to be avoiding us."

"Been extremely busy, Florence, what with deliveries and such like," he tried to explain. "I'm sorry I haven't made the time to visit."

"I understand completely about what's 'happened', and I simply wanted to tell you that I will always be here for you." She put her arm through his and held on as he hugged her, letting all his frustration flow out.

"You know I've always loved both you and Poppy equally," he said. "Don't you? I asked Poppy to marry me because I didn't think you would be interested, thinking that you had someone else in mind."

"Nothing further from the truth, dear George," she responded. "I have always wanted *you* and, even if you were to say you weren't interested in me, it wouldn't make any difference. I will *always* be here."

"I'm ready to settle down with the woman I love, and perhaps look forward to starting a family," he went on. "Are you?"

"You have only to say the word, George," Florence said, kissing his cheek.

He turned around and kissed her passionately on the mouth, drawing a contented sigh from her. "You are going away for how long?" he asked. "A month?"

"Less than that," she replied. "I hope."

"Will you be happy to continue this conversation when

you return?" he asked. "Keeping it between you and me in the meantime?"

"Can't wait," she sighed finally as they parted.

She could feel a huge ball of excitement building inside her, warning her that she would need to be careful not to let out their secret until it had been made official – if it ever was. She had made her play; now only time would tell.

⁓

"Ay up." A rough-sounding, guttural voice accosted George Garside as he was grooming his shires outside the main barn on the Garside farm before hitching them to the wagon before his day's work. It had to be around seven in the morning, which surprised him as nobody save the farm hands was usually about at this hour.

"'Ow do," George answered. "What's tha want?" He looked up to find two ruffian-looking men not five yards from him.

"We want to see thi gaffer," the larger one said threateningly. "We've got summat to tell him."

"Well, if tha's wantin' anything, tha can ask me as I'm in charge," George returned. "What's tha want?"

"Money," the stranger said unceremoniously. "To protect thee and thy farm from 'danger'."

"We've got enough protection, thank you," George growled. "So tha can bugger off unless tha wants a thick ear."

"Oh aye?" the ruffian said drawing a grin from his mate as he moved a little closer. "And who's off to gi me it?"

"Ross!" George yelled without moving or changing his dour facial expression.

"Ay up, George," a booming voice came from the stable, accompanied by the enormous frame of Ross Booth the Younger. "What's up?"

"These two 'gentlemen' are asking if we might consider paying them to 'protect' our interests from ruffians," George explained, clenching his fists ready for a scrap. "What do you think?"

"I think we'd better ask your folks to request our local medic to come round to attend to the grievous wounds and injuries we are about to inflict on these lads," Ross snarled. He pulled himself to his full six-feet-six-inch height and walked across to join George. "What do *you* think, George?"

"Ready when you are," George said. "But try not to let too much of their blood dirty mi horses I've just finished groomin'."

The two ruffians cast hurried, worried glances at each other before beating a hasty retreat for the track outside the farm gates.

"And tell your master that if he wants money, to come and ask politely himself, and we'll deal with him in the same way!" George shouted as they hurried down the track.

"Second such visit in as many days," Ross said, slightly concerned. "Same two ruffians, I believe."

"Do they sincerely believe we're about to hand over a fist full of cash wi'out handing them a fist full of knuckles first?" George added incredulously. "Who do they think they are? More to the point, who do they think *we* are?"

"You off on your rounds, then?" Ross asked, preparing to regain his own farm. "Your operations here, my friend, are second to none, and that Sally Smallshore has made a huge difference, don't you think?"

"She has that!" George replied. "Keeps me on mi toes and very busy."

"How's your dad?" Ross asked quietly. "Any improvement?"

"Medics have seen him a few times now but have not been able to suggest anything, save rest and no stress,"

George responded. "We've got everything covered, but … I don't know."

The ride into the countryside was a slow and deliberate affair, where George's mind was filled with thoughts and concerns about his father. This new dimension did nothing to alleviate his daily problems concerning deliveries and the best way to go about ensuring the safety of both his loads and him personally. He knew he could hold his own in a face-to-face scrap, but the devious means that these ruffians might employ to catch him off guard caused him a lot of concern.

"Morning, Harry," he called cheerfully as he greeted his first customer of the day. "I've added the extra milk, butter and cream you asked for the last time I was around. All rayt?"

"Aye, lad," his customer agreed from the doorway of his store. "T'last lot went down a treat. Disappeared from mi shelves wi'in a day. So, can tha double mi order next time round?"

"Too rayt, Harry," George acknowledged, carefully noting this down in his little ledger. "Si thi next time, then."

"And can tha come twice a week as well, instead of just the one?" Harry asked. "Mekin' sure I have t'same order on each delivery."

"Cheers, Harry," George called with a satisfied grin. "Goin' to need a bigger wagon soon," he muttered to himself.

CHAPTER 20

The train ride from Darlington to York to London brought back vivid and moving memories of the time Poppy and Florence had spent in George's company on their holiday at the East Coast when they were twelve. The trains were much more comfortable, but the feelings were the same. Sitting in a wooden carriage moving along narrow metal tracks at breath-taking speeds felt unnatural yet logical at the same time.

Florence couldn't wait to feel the cross-channel ferry's deck rising and falling gently under her feet. Would that she had George's arm to grip, and the smell of his newly shaved face to draw into her nostrils as they sailed from Dover to Calais.

Mile upon mile of open, unspoilt countryside slid by with only stationary trees and the incessant, repetitive clickety-clack of iron wheels over steel-laid track to remind them they were moving closer and closer to their ultimate goal of exploring a distant foreign country, where nobody would understand a word they were saying.

Both Abigail and Hal spoke a modicum of French – probably just enough to get by – but Poppy and Florence would be completely in the dark. Still, it wasn't for the interaction with the indigenous population that they were leaving their comfort zones for, or for some adventure that might prove alien to them. It was so they might improve themselves intellectually with experiences that precious few people could ever imagine.

Poppy spent her time gazing out of the window, trying to imagine a life in a different environment in a very different country. Florence, on the other hand, spent *her* time staring through the glass at the passing countryside imagining *her* life in a very special environment with the man she loved, and who reciprocated.

"You all right, you two?" Abigail asked as they approached the outer reaches of the capital where fog lay in patches dense enough to deny them the vision of where ordinary folk simply existed. Poppy and Florence were lucky to be supported by Grandpa Ross; similar folk hereabouts wouldn't be able to afford the luxuries they shared.

"Just thinking about the next stage of our journey," Poppy returned. "Will we be heading for Dover straight away?"

"Too far in the one day," Hal explained. "We'll be stopping over in a decent hotel in London for a couple of nights. Fortunately, your grandpa has booked for us to stay in a first-class hotel called The Grosvenor Hotel, which was built in 1862 and is next door to the Victoria Railway Station. From there, we will be taking the boat train to Dover in Kent, where our ferry boat to France will await us."

"There are one or two places we must visit before we travel on to Dover the day after tomorrow," Abigail added. "We won't be rushing about, I can assure you, but we will be visiting one or two places linked with some of our notable literary figures."

Although she maintained a reasonably smiling and affable visage, Florence couldn't wait to return to her George to see what might happen next between them.

"Tell us where, pray, Abigail," Poppy said earnestly. "I would sincerely love to know which literary giants will feature in our exciting round."

"Once we are in our hotel in London, we will sit together, perhaps after dinner, and talk about who we want to see and when we shall do it," Abigail explained. "That will probably be the best time because we will need to start early. Tomorrow our day will involve a good deal of travelling around."

"Is it an expensive hotel?" Poppy asked, keen to know what level of luxury they might encounter.

"Not cheap," Hal added. "It *is* comfortable, though, and the food is good. For dinner, bed and breakfast it would probably cost around 12/6d per night per person. Good quality and good value."

"We will have a double room, of course, as we are husband and wife," Hal went on. "You will have twin beds in the other room."

"Just like the hotels we stayed in on our week in Scarborough for my twelfth birthday celebration," Poppy observed. "*That* week was excellent. Wasn't it, Florence?"

No answer. Florence still wore that same serene look, because she heard nothing, choosing to have the picture of George in her head and his words running through her mind. All of that blocked out *all* conversation from other people close to her.

"Florence?" Poppy tried again. "Are you with us? Florence?"

"Sorry," she said finally. "I was miles away, thinking about what to expect in our two capitals – London and Paris. A veritable tale of two cities, don't you think?"

"We'll talk about all of that later this evening," Abigail reiterated for Florence's benefit. "It's all planned, but we need to look at the plans somewhere where the room is not bouncing about over rail joints – points, I believe they are called."

"Twenty minutes or so I think," Hal said, consulting the pocket watch that hung by a golden guard chain from a waistcoat buttonhole that allowed the watch itself to reside in a small pocket at the other side of the line of buttons. "Then we can eat and rest, ready for our tomorrow's excitement."

Heading for the hansom-cab rank just outside the railway station, Poppy and Florence couldn't believe how busy the concourse was. Once outside, their mouths dropped at the number of people out and about. Neither could they understand where all the cabs and wagons on the road had come from.

"Is there some sort of an event happening today, what with all these wagons and people?" Poppy asked naively.

"Yes," Abigail replied. "It's called everyday traffic caused by everyday living."

"You mean it's like this *every* day?" Florence gasped in utter amazement. "It's absolutely astounding, to say the least. I bet Charles Dickens and George Eliot didn't have to put up with this!"

"Don't forget that as Dickens only died on 9th June 1870, and Eliot died ten years later on 22nd December, so it is more than likely it *was* just as busy," Abigail pointed out. "Just a little sneak preview? They were both buried in London itself."

Both girls gasped loudly and started to become quite excited at the prospect of seeing their graves. Things were becoming more tangible with the thought of being so close to two authors they both loved and admired. Standing in the shadows of well-known, well-respected and loved writers of Dickens' and Eliot's calibre came only once in a lifetime for the likes of these two impressionable young lasses who aspired to tread in their awesome footprints.

"Lost your tongue?" Abigail suggested with a smile.

"Lost for words more like," Hal added. "Something else, eh, girls?"

Their room was something they hadn't expected, bringing back powerful memories of their Scarborough escapade ten years or so before. Although more opulently furnished and larger than the ones at Scarborough's Grand Hotel, The Grosvenor seemed more ... in keeping with their current thinking and emotions. How could they have ever considered this was going to happen to them ten years or more later? Yet, here they were, now, just about to live *their* dream.

"Remember the Grand—?" Poppy ventured when they were alone.

"In Scarborough—?" Florence replied as she flopped on her bed.

"For my twelfth birthday," Poppy added as she followed suit.

"Wonderful times with Annabel and Alice," Florence said.

"And our lovely—" Poppy continued.

"George," Florence interrupted. "Wonderful."

"I wonder how he is doing?" Poppy said quietly, her mind floating back to the last time they had spoken and drawing a saddened expression to her brow. "I think perhaps I've told you that ... he asked me to ... marry him?"

"I have to tell you that ... you did," Florence added brusquely.

"I didn't tell you all the details, so how do you know?" Poppy asked, dumbfounded that her friend had somehow found out her closest, most guarded secret.

"*He* told me," Florence explained, glad that she could unburden this 'secret' that had been preying on her mind. "And..."

"What?" Poppy retorted sharply, her annoyance about to overspill and threaten their equilibrium.

"He asked *me* to marry him shortly after *you* had refused him," Florence admitted, her look of superiority beginning to irk her close friend.

"But I thought we were 'sisters'?" Poppy countered, aghast at what her companion had just admitted. "And that we were about to share him like the last time he stayed over in our cottage?"

"So we were, until recent events expunged all those agreements," Florence insisted. "Had you told *me* that he'd asked *you*, perhaps things might have been different, but as it stands—"

"I don't think we can carry on this charade, in that case," Poppy said disdainfully. "I think I won't be wasting my time trailing to Paris with this … this betrayal hanging over the planned excursion."

"You can't—!" Florence complained, aghast.

"Oh, but I can," Poppy insisted. "No money has been exchanged after London – so my Grandpa Ross has said – so we will simply about turn and retrace our steps."

As her last act of defiance and mean-spiritedness spilled over to try to wash away Florence's perceived meanness and disdain, Poppy dressed for bed in silence. The following day would hopefully see a change in both attitudes.

"Nar then, Harry," George Garside greeted his last customer of the day. "I hope tha's ready for all I've brought thee today. Seems like a lot, but I'm sure tha can tek it."

"Now then, George," Harry replied quickly. "If tha wouldn't mind unloading onto yon trolley so I can bring it into mi store, I'd be grateful."

George was extremely pleased with himself because on this day alone he had tripled his usual *weekly* order to this part of his round. Because of this, he felt it likely the trend might continue for the rest of the week. It seemed like his long days and hard work were beginning to pay off.

Just as he turned towards his wagon to replace his trolley, he felt a sharp pain in his left-shoulder blade. Screeching in agony, he turned sharply to see the triumphantly grinning face of his nemesis, Jonas Jamieson, backing away from him, having left a long-bladed dagger buried up to its hilt in George's back.

"I told you I would find you and repay your unpleasantness, old chap!" Jonas yelled as he skipped around, grinning hugely. "I hope now you are feeling a modicum of the pain you inflicted upon me all those years ago."

Not understanding George's resilience or strength, Jonas took one step too many towards him in his attempt to taunt. As George dropped to the floor, he lashed out with his right hobnailed boot and caught his antagonist a devastating blow with his toe across the side of Jonas's knee, shattering the joint and spraying blood, bone and flesh across the pavement outside Harry's store.

Screaming in agony, Jonas collapsed to the floor and tried to crawl away from the man whom he believed he had done for, begging for help from onlookers to take him away from *his* attacker.

George staggered to his feet, knife still protruding from his shoulder, and delivered three crunching, destructive punches to Jonas's face, rendering him senseless before *he* collapsed to the floor. Harry summoned a police constable who was passing by on his bicycle and rushed to help George into the store to try to administer first aid. As he arrived inside, a doctor rushed in from his surgery not fifty yards from the scene.

Onlookers guided him to George first, knowing that the unconscious body that had been the perpetrator of *this* outrage ought to wait until the innocent one had been attended to.

Swimming in an almost endless sea of unconsciousness, excruciating pain occasionally bounced George unexpectedly back into a living hell. The knife had been removed and the external wound stitched and dressed; hopefully the internal damage had been kept to a minimum.

Although he was taken to the local cottage hospital at Richmond, there was little that could be done for him other than to keep his wound clean and stable, and to make sure the stitching held until healing took over. The overriding feeling at the hospital was one of disbelief at how little blood loss he had suffered from such a deep wound that could have seen him off.

"May I go home now, nurse, please?" George asked one of the medical team in the hospital. "I feel all right, with no pain anywhere."

"That's down to the pain relief, Mr Garside," a doctor explained. "We can't guarantee it won't start again once you are at home. You most definitely won't be able to work for a week or so. What is your job, did you say?"

"I didn't," George replied. He gave the medic his job description and described what it entailed. "But I know what I can and can't do. Trust me. What's happened to the thug that attacked me? Has he been locked away?"

"I don't know," the doctor admitted. "I think he's been taken away by the police."

"Ross!" George called as he noticed his friend walking into the hospital first-aid room. "Good to see you. Did you just happen along, or have you come to see *me*?"

"I've actually come to take you home. I have a pony and

trap outside," Ross answered. "You can't stay here with all these unhealthy folk."

George smiled at his friend's attempted humour. Hit and miss in the extreme, it was mildly humorous sometimes but at others it didn't even crease the mouth corners. "That's not the real reason, is it Ross?" he said quietly. "Something's happened at home, hasn't it?"

"It's your dad, old man," Ross explained. "He's had another heart attack, and this one is much worse than the last."

CHAPTER 21

Poppy and Florence's first night in the Grosvenor Hotel was physically very comfortable and easy, but intellectually and emotionally disturbing. Their sleep was fitful and unsettled, but neither said anything even though they felt they ought to clear the air. After all, they were as close as any two sisters might be, having been through a lot together. They shouldn't let such small things get in the way of their friendship and firmly held ambitions. This experience they were sharing was once in a lifetime, which they should embrace and be very sorry to lose.

As if on cue, at half-past six, Poppy said quietly, "Florence?"

This was almost echoed by her companion, "Poppy?"

Flinging back the covers, they urgently embraced each other in a show of solidarity and mutual regard.

"I don't think we ought to cancel our lifelong ambition," Poppy urged. "Do you?"

"Indeed not," Florence said in relieved acknowledgement. "It would be a shame, having come so close, to turn around and walk away now. I don't—"

"We need no explanations or reasons to carry on, I think," Poppy assured her good friend. "After all, I don't really wish to marry yet, with all the paraphernalia *that* might entail."

"Actually, me neither," Florence agreed. "Maybe when we are closer to that ungodly age of thirty might be a better time."

"Agreed," Poppy reiterated. "Marrying, as far as I see it, is about procreation – as well as love of course. One needs to be prepared for the inevitable so that *that* can be welcomed and enjoyed at the appropriate time."

"Well said!" her friend agreed. "I will tell George when we return after out sojourn."

"If I may say," Poppy advised, "I wouldn't mention anything. Do you think it might be better to carry on – the three of us – as we did before, and let him be the one to broach the subject? Perhaps we can deal with that situation when it arises?"

"Good thinking, my dear friend," Florence said. "Who knows? He may well have married by the time we return." They both giggled at the thought, the air now cleared ready for them to re-embark upon their projected journey of a lifetime.

"When's breakfast?" Poppy asked. "I'm starving!"

"Me too," Florence agreed. "I hope it's a good one."

This time they laughed loudly, easy again in each other's company and ready to share all that this adventure would have to offer them.

A sumptuous breakfast of bread, bacon, eggs, kidneys, cold meats, kippers and kedgeree awaited them as they stole downstairs to wait for Hal and Abigail. Imagine their shock and surprise to see their guides already tucking into a much-enjoyed feast.

"Good night?" Hal asked, once pleasantries and greetings had been exchanged.

"Reasonable, I suppose," Poppy said.

"In the circumstances," Florence added.

The table for four was luxuriously laid, ready for a timely, delicious feast: pristine luxury white linen, china crockery and silver-service cutlery and toast racks. An ornate silver teapot, already offering hot beverage, took pride of place in the middle of the table, ready to disgorge its contents. As soon as they sat to table, a waiter arrived with toasted bread and a fresh jug of milk, ready for its introduction to their white bone-china teacups.

"Breakfast, madame?" the waiter asked in that precise way that all waiters take orders.

"May we have … what they are having, please?" Poppy asked on Florence's nod, indicating what their companions seemed to be relishing. Memories from when they were at Scarborough's Grand Hotel slipped easily and seamlessly to mind, drawing a contented smile to both faces. They continued the rest of the meal in silence, except for the occasional swish and clack of knife against porcelain.

"There are two things we would like you to see today," Abigail said, once they were settled in the lounge with an after breakfast cup of tea. "The one would involve a visit to a church and the other to a graveyard … or two."

"It may sound a bit morbid or even macabre, but it will be fruitful in the end," Hal added.

"Will you tell us whose graves we are to visit, or will we have to wait until we get there?" Florence asked pointedly.

Abigail and Hal weren't sure whether they would tell or not. If they didn't, they were sure that it would add to the suspense and excitement.

"Which are your two favourite authors?" Abigail asked, feeling they would agree on at least one.

"George Eliot is my favourite of all," Poppy jumped in quickly. "Charles John Huffam Dickens is a close runner-up."

"I agree with number one," Florence added. "Mary Ann Evans is my favourite too. We first read *Mill on the Floss* and *Middlemarch* when we were twelve. Secondly for me, I have joint favourites in Charles Dickens and Emily Brontë."

"George and Charles it is, then," Hal announced. "But it won't be in the flesh, I fear."

Abigail laughed quietly behind her napkin, understanding her husband's humour well, even though they had been married only a preciously short time. The two youngsters followed suit, brows ever so slightly knitted, although they weren't sure of his exact meaning.

"So, we are about to—?" Poppy asked, eager to know how this day would present itself.

"Visit two, maybe three, final resting places of some very interesting people throughout this auspicious day," Abigail explained enigmatically.

"As in?" Florence queried.

"The last resting place – as in burial plot – of some of the most excellent writers of their day – *our* day," Abigail went on. "Charles Dickens, Dr Samuel Johnson, Geoffrey Chaucer, Edmund Spencer, Aphra Behn, George Eliot, whose real name was Mary Ann Evans, William Blake, Daniel Defoe and John Bunyan."

"Goodness!" Poppy gasped, with a puzzled inclination of her head. "I've heard of them all, save ... Aphra Behn?"

"She ... was the first professional female writer," Abigail explained. "Aged forty-eight when she died in 1689."

"Gracious!" Florence gasped. "I knew it! We are making

our mark on this male-dominated world, albeit slowly."

"We will see Dickens to Behn in one place," Hal pointed out. "The others are in two different places. Eliot is in Highgate Cemetery and the others not that far away in Bunhill Fields Burial Ground, Islington."

"We have no idea where any of those places is, any more than when our next train journey will take us," Poppy exclaimed in complete surprise and ignorance. "Dickens et al?"

"In a grand edifice not far from here," Abigail assured her. "They are buried or commemorated in Poets' Corner in … Westminster Abbey. You'll like it there."

"Good heavens!" Poppy said in utter surprise as they looked up at the enormous, largely Gothic western façade of the formerly named Collegiate Church of St Peter at Westminster.

"Westminster Abbey, my dears," Hal explained, once they had let their hansom cab return to service. "Its original history goes way back to the time of Edward the Confessor, just before the Norman Conquest. Built on the say-so of the aforesaid monarch, he was buried therein very shortly after it had been finished in 1065."

"Impressive," Abigail said with a wicked smile.

"My historical knowledge?" Hal re-joined with a self-satisfied smile.

"No," she retorted. "The building."

They all laughed at Abigail's leg-pulling of her husband. Even he chortled heartily.

"Now to find the remains of our literary heroes," Hal said as he beckoned his charges to follow him towards the entrance to the Great North Door.

The enormity of the interior stopped the friends in their

tracks. Mouths open and eyes unblinking and awe-stricken, Poppy and Florence had nothing to say except to gasp their shock at what lay before them.

Realising that the girls weren't physically with them, Abigail and Hal stopped to look around to find them. She nudged her husband to draw his attention to their reaction at the grandeur that had captivated their imagination.

"This way," Abigail said once they had re-joined their charges. "On to the South Transept."

"What is that?" Poppy asked quietly, not understanding what she was saying.

"The South Transept is at the other side of the building from where we now stand," Abigail began to explain. "If you were a bird and looked down on the Cathedral, you would see that it forms the shape of a cross, for obvious reasons. The transept, where we are now, forms the cross piece of that cross."

"And why are we aiming for the other side?" Florence asked. "Can we get a cup of tea there?"

"Not really," Abigail sniggered. "You'll just have to wait and see."

Although there were lots of people shuffling around slowly, the four doughty travellers soon discovered Poets' Corner in the east side of the South Transept.

"Oh! Oh!" Poppy gasped again, stabbing her finger towards a carved stone tablet. "Look! Charles Dickens' tomb."

"And … Geoffrey Chaucer's and—" Florence urged, excited beyond belief.

"Edmund Spencer!" Poppy added with equal zeal. "Didn't he write *The Faerie Queen* for Elizabeth the First? The longest poem in the English language? I can't believe all these wonderful writers are buried here."

"Well, not *all* are buried here," Abigail interjected. "Some are buried elsewhere but have a memorial stone here. William Shakespeare, for example, is buried in Stratford-upon-Avon where he lived, and Jane Austen was buried in Winchester Cathedral. Both have memorials here."

"We don't see any mention of George Eliot hereabouts," Poppy remarked pointedly. "Is she not here?"

"No," Hal said. "When we've finished, we plan to visit another of the writers you are familiar with."

"Come on! Tell us!" the girls giggled. "Who and where?"

"Who is your favourite author again?" Abigail asked.

"Mary Ann Evans – otherwise known as George Eliot," Poppy said, to vigorous nodding from Florence.

"Mary Ann *Cross*, I believe," Abigail corrected politely. "She married John Walter Cross in May 1880 and died just before Christmas that same year. She is buried in Highgate Cemetery, not too far from here."

"My goodness!" Poppy replied, gasping at the thought. "Our favourite writers all in the same day. Can't wait, Abigail and Hal. Let's go!"

***

After a sumptuous evening meal in the hotel's restaurant, followed by coffee and a little brandy in the residents' lounge, Poppy and Florence marvelled at what they had achieved that day.

"Today has been … wonderful," Poppy sighed to enthusiastic nodding from her friend as they relaxed in the unbelievably comfortable settees. "We can't thank you enough, Abigail and Hal."

"We couldn't believe the monuments to our favourite authors that you showed us," Florence enthused, the excitement still alive in her eyes even after such a strenuous day's travelling about the capital. "Poets' Corner in Westminster Abbey was intense, but to finish off with Bunhill Fields Burial Ground, which gave us William Blake, John Bunyan and Robinson Crusoe's 'master', Daniel Defoe! It felt like we were walking among, and spending real time with, our heroes."

"For me, the *pièce de résistance* had to be Highgate Cemetery, where Mary Ann *Cross* – our favourite author, George Eliot – is at rest," Poppy added, almost glassy eyed. "I would love to have had a permanent picture of her headstone."

"Well, as a matter of fact, my dear friends, that may indeed be possible," Hal offered with a smile.

"How—?" the girls asked eagerly.

"Did you notice that wherever we've been today, I have had a little black box to hand?" Hal pointed out, mysteriously.

"And?" Poppy said, a puzzled look clouding her brow.

"That little box is a camera – my friendly little Kodak camera," he went on with a grin. "It's a magical little box that prints an image onto a celluloid screen inside that you can keep forever."

"May we look now, please?" Florence asked eagerly, hutching to the front edge of the settee in anticipation.

"I'm afraid not," he replied. "You see, the camera has the facility to imprint one-hundred images, thirty of which have already been recorded. We have several more weeks to travel through France until we have a full record of your tour. When we return, I will take the camera to a specialist company to have the images turned into what they call 'photographs'. Only then will you both have a record of what you have seen."

"I can't believe what you have done for us!" Florence uttered. "I feel quite emotional."

"Then now is the time to head to our rooms," Abigail suggested. "Tomorrow heralds the start of our European adventure – bright and early with a train journey to Dover in Kent. That is a whole new world about which both of you have no idea – and that's before we board the cross-English Channel ferry to voyage to … Calais in France."

CHAPTER 22

"He's very poorly, George," his sister, Florence, warned him as he arrived back home, his arm in a sling and a bruise beginning to form under his eye. "Cup of tea, Ross?"

"Thank you, Florence, but no. I have to get back to Boulders Wood in a moment or two," Ross answered, a concerned look in his face. "This young man needs looking after, as well. A bad injury, to boot."

George eased himself into his dad's favourite chair once Ross had departed, and took tentative sips of his hot brew, along with nibbles of the Victoria sponge his other sister, Charity, had made. This was indeed a milestone, as she had been promising to bake one for him for some time. Tom, their father, often changed that to 'threatening'.

"For goodness' sake what happened?" Sister Martha asked as she sat down near to her brother. She had been drafted in to help with tending to the house while her mother was occupied ministering to her father's needs.

"I was attacked from behind by that shady waste of space Jonas Jamieson. You know, Poppy's cousin?" George answered.

"Too cowardly to face me with his soft little fists, he had to stick a blade into my back without being seen. He'll not be doing that to anyone else for rather a long time, I am pleased to say. How's Dad faring?"

"Touch and go," Martha replied with a grimace and a shrug. "The medic reckons he *might* survive, but it seems likely that another attack *will* see him off. Mum's in bits, as you would expect."

"And what happens if he doesn't … make it?" George added, though he thought he might know the answer already.

"I assume you'll take his place as the head of this family, George," she said, answering his question very carefully. "We would all expect no less of you."

"Heavy burden to heap on my shoulders, don't you think?" he responded.

"But it will have to be done," his mother's strident voice joined in from the foot of the stairs. "There is no other choice. Quickly, Florence, fetch our Lilly Victoria from her home. Everybody else upstairs. Your father is very weak but needs you all."

"I know I don't have long," Tom muttered from his pillow-supported bed. "So, listen up, all of you. As soon as I'm gone, George teks ower t'farm. With no disrespect to all on you others, he's t'onny male and t'law dictates as 'e 'as to tek ower. Are we clear on that?"

"Aye, Dad. We knew that anyway," Lilly Victoria said quietly.

"Yer mam knows that there is a number of envelopes in t'front room sideboard, each wi' a name on it," Tom went on. "I want you all to tek your own away and open it – at 'ome, mind you. I'm sure you'll support your brother and look after your mam.

"Well? No answer?" he said sharply after a few moments' silence.

"Yes, Dad," they chorused. "We will."

"Goes without saying," Lilly Victoria added.

"And I 'ope … for once in your life you'll … listen to what I've had to say … and act upon it," he muttered as his eyes closed slowly.

He fell silent, his breathing a bit laboured as the colour drained out of his face. They all trooped out of the room and descended to the lower level, with the exception of his wife, Lilly, and George.

"He's made just the one stipulation, George," his mother said as she turned towards him. "And that is that you need to take a wife pretty soon, like, to carry on the Garside line. *We* don't think either Poppy or her friend, Florence, would be at all suitable. They are not true farming people when all they want to do is play about with books and writing. You need a proper farmer's wife that will support you in running this farm and its businesses."

"But—" George complained.

"No buts," his mother insisted. "It's your father's wish, and I have to say that I agree with him."

This set George thinking as he headed slowly for the stairs. Strangely enough, he knew that what she said made sense. What had Poppy said before they went off on their fools' errand, attempting to trace some ne'er-do-well writers' steps towards poverty and ignominy? He needed a wife to work with and support him in his endeavour to provide a good standard of living for his family and employees.

What about Florence? He hadn't asked her, but she had

volunteered to become his wife. Why had she volunteered? Could he trust her to stay with him in spite of all the difficulties she would undoubtedly encounter if he *did* marry her?

He wasn't sure whether she would be the right person to be his life partner, to support him through all the problems that might jump in front of them along the way. Writing stories? What was *that* all about? Was that the only thing of importance to her? What would she do if, or when, she became pregnant?

The pain started to encroach again into his life, with no way to dispatch it. After all that had happened to him this day, he fell into an uneasy slumber in his father's easy chair.

"George! Quick!" an urgent, panic-stricken voice bore into his subconscious, drawing him sharply out of his fitful doze. It was his mother from the top of the stairs. "Hurry!" she screeched. "I think he's gone!"

Trying to shake off the deep-seated ache in his shoulder, George lumbered to the top of the stairs and stumbled into his parents' bedroom. His father lay still and not breathing, finally at peace, a slight smile on his lips.

Dr Twist was with him, a stethoscope still pressed against Tom's chest, but detecting no heartbeat. Turning to George and his mother, he shook his head gently and began to reload his bag. "I'm sorry Mrs Garside, George," he said quietly. "He's given up, I'm afraid. I'll make sure all the necessaries are noted, and I'll bring round a detailed death certificate tomorrow. My sincere condolences."

George drew his mother to him, trying to assuage her tears and to comfort her as best he could. His four sisters swished into the bedroom to take over from him as he slumped into an easy chair, wracked with both physical and emotional pain.

"It's fantastic to have you back," Tommy Spence said eagerly to Poppy. "We have missed you. Two months is a very long time to be away from your loved ones. A lot's happened since you were last here."

"We've had such a wonderful invigorating time doing all the things we wanted to do – and more." Poppy placed a tray in front of her father on the small table by the side of the settee. Now mid-July, the weather was giving them all they desired when the sharp frosts and deep snow had almost put a stop to normal life in late winter and early spring.

"How did London catch you, with its traffic, buildings and population scurrying about its business like so many purposeful ants?" he asked, genuinely interested in what they had been doing.

"Overwhelming at times but Cousin Hal and his wife, Abigail, led and directed us to the places they knew we wanted to be," Poppy explained, eager to tell her father about some of their experiences. "The places we've seen and the experiences we've enjoyed have been world-changing."

She went on to describe their visits to Westminster Abbey and the Poets' Corner that they had no idea existed. They had been overcome by profound feelings of awe and emotion that overwhelmed them when they finally cast their eyes on their favourite author's tomb in Highgate Cemetery. Mary Ann Cross (née Evans) had died just over ten years before and her presence was almost tangible. How could her coffined body have been carried those few years before along the paths they had only just trodden?

"We had planned to spend only two or three days in London before moving on to Paris, but we spent another week there because other opportunities arose," she went on. "Then Paris and the three-hundred-and-some chateaux along the huge River Loire beckoned. Abigail has two brothers who live in Paris, so we had a ball treading the paths followed by some of France's great authors like George Sand, otherwise known as Amantine Lucile Dupin, who still lives there, Victor Hugo, and Honoré de Balzac."

"Well over an extra month?" Tommy pointed out.

"We decided on the spur of the moment that, as Abigail has aunts and uncles in Rome, we couldn't leave Europe without visiting," she explained. "It was the Grand Tour of a lifetime that we could experience only because of Grandpa Ross's generosity and because of our dear friends Abigail and Hal, who guided and chaperoned us throughout."

"My news to you is both happy … and sad," her father warned her.

"Both? At the same time?" she queried a little apprehensively.

"Happy because Sally Smallshore became Mrs Thomas Spence," he said. "Sad because you weren't there to witness that happy day."

"Are you happy, Father?" Poppy asked as she sat on the settee next to him, her arm linked through his.

"Indeed, I am, my little one," he beamed, squeezing her hand in joy.

"Then there can be *no* sadness," she assured him with a genuine smile of happiness. "Can't wait to meet my new step-mother. I'm sure we will get along beautifully."

"You also missed another fateful occurrence." His face dropped, a look of sadness overlaying his joy. "Unfortunately, Tom Garside, George's father, passed away from a heart attack. George had been set upon the day before on his rounds by a ruffian who attacked him from behind, leaving a large dagger sticking out from his back."

"Oh my God!" Poppy gasped in horror, clapping her hand

across her mouth while gripping her father's arm tightly.

"He *has* survived, but you would need to get further details either from him or his family," Tommy tried to reassure her.

"I can't comprehend it!" she went on slowly. "My dear wonderful George! Attacked? He had asked me to marry him a short while before we left for London, but—"

"You obviously rejected him," her father continued.

"How did you know that?" she replied, surprised at what only she and George … and Florence … knew.

"He wed a local lass only a few days before you returned," he explained.

"And how the bloody hell do you expect to be paid when you tried to kill or maim an innocent man pursuing his ordinary duties?" The Big Man asked a prostrate Jonas. "Hmm?"

"I expect to get what I am due," Jonas insisted. "Bear in mind that you made an enormous amount of cash out of what was effectively *my* intervention. I know I can do nothing to force you, but fair is fair, old chap."

"Fair dues," The Big Man agreed. "All right. I'll pay you what we agreed, but then our association is at an end."

"At an end?" Jonas complained loudly. "At an end? Haven't we—?"

"How do you see yourself being of use to me now, eh?" The Big Man asked rhetorically. "Thy can't even walk! For God's sake, come on!"

"Once you've shelled out my dues, I will be getting myself one of those new-fangled bath chairs, so I don't have to walk anywhere," Jonas replied, lifting himself onto an elbow.

"What did yon hospital in Richmond have to say," The Big Man asked pointedly, knowing full well what the answer would be. "Not been there, have you? Seeing the state of yon knee joint and the amount of blood you've lost, I would imagine they would want to cut it off and gi' thee a stick as well as an invalid's bath chair … on wheels."

Jonas remained quietly pensive and in a good deal of intense pain. How would he ever get back to normal like this, with no medical intervention? Even If he managed to get himself to the medic's, they would report him to the police, and then where would he be? In the cells, that's where! It wasn't until The Big Man paid him the money that he could even think of escaping this infernal cot.

"I'll be bringing you some cash in a short while," The Big Man promised as he made for the door.

"As quick as you can, old chap, please," Jonas said, with the only grain of gratitude he had shown for many a while.

Young Toby's face swam into his mind. How was Jonas to pay him what he had promised him until his supplier came up trumps? He liked young Toby and fully intended to honour his promise to him, if he ever saw him again.

"Damn! Damn! Damn!" he cursed as he tried to drag himself out of the filthy bed he was stuck in. As he moved, the blood started to ooze alarmingly through the torn sheet he had wrapped around his knee. This wasn't going to work. He would be able to manage better with only one leg!

"Boss?" a youthful voice reached Jonas from the doorway. "What can I do to help?"

"Toby?" Jonas groaned. "That you? Am I glad to see *your* face! Give me a hand to sit upright, will you, please?"

"My God!" Toby grimaced when he caught sight of the catastrophic damage that had been caused to Jonas's knee. "That needs seeing to. Should I go and fetch a doctor?"

"No," Jonas growled, clenching his teeth to try to stop the

pain. "They'll draw the police, and we wouldn't want that, would we?"

"Doctors aren't obliged to tell anyone else that's not a medic," Toby said quite baldly. "If they did, they'd be denying the oath they took when they agreed to become a doctor."

"You sure on that?" Jonas said, unsure where the lad had got *that* from.

"I am," the lad assured him. "Happened to Mum once when she found herself on the end of some gorilla's fist."

"What did you do about the gorilla?" Jonas asked, a new light of respect growing in his eyes.

"As he turned to leave our pit, I split his head open with the broken leg of our bed," Toby said quite dispassionately. "Left him there to bleed, and we took up somewhere else. No idea whether he survived or not. Didn't care."

"Fetch him then, lad, would you? The medic?" Jonas asked slowly. "I don't think I can stand much more of this, even if it means the coppers calling."

Toby turned and rushed out of the hovel just as Jonas passed out on the bed.

~

"That does it, then," Florence said. "I was convinced it might be the last we saw of him when we chose our tour rather than stay with him."

"But … *Alice*?" Poppy croaked, almost in tears. "Didn't he realise that Annabel's sister, of all people, might bring history back to haunt him? Annabel went off with some other chap. Doesn't he realise that twins often replicate what their brothers and sisters do?"

"We have to leave him to his own devices and future now because he's married to someone else," Florence insisted. "We have the rest of our lives to see to, don't you think? We owe it to ourselves to be successful with our writing. It's what we promised each other all those years ago, and we must stay true to that promise."

They sat together for a while in their front room, the glorious early-afternoon summer sunlight streaming through the window, urging them not only to remember with fondness their recent adventure, but also to make them wish they were back there. The romance of their two European capitals, the hustle and bustle of the Champs Elysées in Paris, and the sight and feeling of young lovers around the Trevi Fountain in Rome, brought back the joy and pleasures they experienced in both cities.

"Champs Elysées or Trevi Fountain?" Florence asked her friend.

"The latter," Poppy replied quickly. "How could you not just love seeing all the coins being skimmed into that water at the meeting of those three roads?"

"The travertine stonework also was something to die for, don't you think?" Florence offered, sipping her steaming tea. "Ever thought of having a miniature Trevi constructed here in the back garden?"

"Would be divine, but perhaps a bit impractical and unnecessarily expensive?" Poppy observed. "I would dearly love to be back there at this moment with those sights and sounds and smells! That exquisite Italian food!"

"Those gorgeous Italian males!" Florence cooed, eyes closing in ecstasy.

CHAPTER 23

Tom Garside's funeral was a sombre affair, even by the usual standards of the time. The children of the family weren't even sure that it would take place, such was the state of his inconsolable wife, Lilly.

It came to light on the eve of his entombment that Tom and Lilly had never really found time to wed, theoretically rendering all the children illegitimate, which mattered not one jot to any of them. The estate would never leave the family, and as George would inherit it all as Tom's undoubted male heir, it could only flourish in his hands.

The last year or two's problems with Tom's health had meant that this arm of the joint business between the Garside farm and Boulders Wood had stalled somewhat. This urged George to move forward quickly so that their business didn't become irretrievably stagnant. He and Joseph McIntyre met regularly to discuss and put in place innovations that Tom and Joseph had agreed upon. Under George's stewardship, all reasonable developments in modern farm husbandry were considered seriously.

After a year of marriage, George's wife, Alice, fell pregnant and gave birth to identical twin girls. Unfortunately, George's joy was short-lived as Alice died shortly after her confinement.

In his late twenties, he was widowed with two beautiful, if demanding, daughters to bring up alone. Fortunately, his mother had decided that this was to be her lifetime's project as she had always loved babies. Now was her chance to feel useful and hopefully have as much effect on their little lives as she'd had on her own children.

Charity finally managed to achieve her goal of marrying her beau. She had no wish to glory in the opportunity that her beloved father's death had presented to her now that he was no longer with them to object to her becoming wed. This usually led to offspring appearing on the scene, which often persuaded the new mother to cease taking part in the work that might take her from raising them as she wished. Tom's objection to wasting money on wedding receptions definitely went out of the window, as Lilly loved the pomp and ceremony that a daughter's wedding usually brought.

The writings that Poppy and Florence had undertaken after they had returned from their Grand Tour, both individually and collectively, had significant success, with plaudits heaped upon them – although at a shilling each, no ordinary working person could afford to indulge. Very few people could even read and understand their erudite stories that seemed to be about a life beyond their comprehension. The girls' lives, too, had become cocooned, taking them almost outside the range of reality.

Now getting on for *their* late twenties, their lives' path had taken them in in a very different direction from that which they had shared with 'their' George almost twenty years earlier. They had tasted few of the realities and none of the emotional pains that had bedevilled *his* recent existence and seemed to inhabit a world that was entirely alien to his.

"When was the last time we saw and talked to … George Garside?" Florence asked, as winter began to cast its chilly claws into *their* world. Although they rarely noticed or felt its icy grip within their warm and inviting cottage, the first snows threatened, dragging in wickedly cold winds as harbingers of what would follow in their wake.

"I have neither idea, nor desire to recall, although it is obviously quite some time ago," Poppy uttered, coldly indifferent to his life or to the history they had once shared with him. "Why do you ask?"

"Don't know, really," Florence answered almost defensively. "Only he must be having a hard time bringing up two youngsters on his own."

"I neither know nor care," Poppy said, returning to her writing. "The words *bed* and *lay* and *make* spring to mind."

"I think it must be at least a year ago," Florence surmised quietly as if sharing a long-hidden memory with herself.

"Thinking of offering yourself to him again?" Poppy asked caustically.

"That's not fair!" her friend retorted defensively. "I wouldn't have thought you could be so sarcastically hurtful. You've changed a lot, Poppy Spence, since we returned from our grand tour. One could be forgiven for believing you had become cynical about—"

"Enough!" Poppy snapped sharply. "Please believe me when I say that George Garside no longer features in my life, or even in my thoughts."

"Can I take it, then, that you have no intention of doing what your cousin Hal and his delightful wife, Abigail, are attempting to do?" Florence pushed even harder. "They want to have delightful children. If they do, I will consider changing to writing for youngsters like them."

"My life is now devoted to a higher ideal, as I have no doubt you might have noticed," Poppy went on, almost as if standing on an imaginary soap box.

"Does it mean nought to you that even your father has decided that he wants to be father to a child he can help bring up?" Florence said finally, before moving into the kitchen to make a pot of tea.

"How do you mean?" Poppy asked, following her.

"Don't pretend you didn't know that his wife is now with child," Florence sneered. "Or perhaps you didn't, from the surprise on your face? You haven't seen them lately, have you?"

They sat in silence once Florence had brought each of them a cup of tea and a cream scone into the sitting room.

"The problem is, as far as I can detect, that you haven't taken time to draw into your life the things that most human beings would give a king's ransom for – family love and affection, and spending time with those whom one should keep close," Florence insisted. "Don't let those things go by before it is too late, my dear friend. George has always been our friend and, for me, always will be. I will be visiting him and his family very soon, whether you like it or not."

~⸱~

"George?" A familiar voice wrapped itself around him, assuring him that here was someone that cared.

"Florence?" he replied, turning to face the newcomer as he loaded his deliveries for the day. "Seven o'clock in the morning? I wouldn't have expected you here at this time. I thought you'd still be wrapped in your cosy blankets and eiderdowns."

They laughed together as they hugged, glad to feel each

other's warmth after such a long time.

"A year … eighteen months?" George queried. "Seems like a lifetime since we last saw each other. Did you keep your promise?"

"About our marriage?" Florence answered, more than a little uncomfortable with *that* particular question. "Yes … and … no…

"Two little girls, eh?" she went on after a moment or two's hesitation. "Busy man. I am truly sorry to hear about your bereavement. Alice was a lovely lady. Brought back lots of memories from when we were children together."

"Very true, but one has to move on despite all the sadness we might suffer," he said. "Lovely to see you again, but I have a schedule to stick to. Any chance you might come around some time when we can have a real get-together?"

"Would you like to come round to ours?" she offered. "We're always there…"

"Not really," he said almost immediately. "I would rather you came to me … just you. All right? Can I give you a lift back home?"

"Not really," Florence assured him. "The walk will do me good but thank you any way."

She understood perfectly what he meant as she retraced her steps to the cottage. What could have been, eh? Those two beautiful youngsters could have been hers had she not taken that unprecedented step of spending the two months following their intimate conversation about their possible future together. 'Mrs George Garside' still had that attractive ring to it. Perhaps one day…

"Florence!" a strong male voice came to her as she and a carriage arrived at the cottage almost simultaneously. "Out for a walk in this weather. You must be a fit young lady."

"Dr Spence!" she called back. "How good to see you – and Mrs Spence, Sally. Please come on in. The cottage will be warm by now."

"For goodness' sake, Florence!" Tommy urged. "How long have we known each other? Please call me Tommy."

"Poppy!" Florence called once they had embraced the warm interior and shut out the threatening snow. "Someone here for you!"

"Father! Sally! It's so good to see you," Poppy gushed as they hugged. "When are you due?"

They divested and sat comfortably in the sitting room while Florence made tea and scones in the kitchen.

"My doctor here tells me it will be another uncomfortable two months or so yet," Sally said with a deep sigh. "Can't wait!"

"Seems a while since we have seen each other," Tommy said. "I wanted to be the first person to congratulate you on the success of your novel – *Death in the Sun*, wasn't it?"

"And 'P.P. Spence'?" Sally added. "How 'afternoonified' is that!"

"I have also started to read the serialisation of your grand Tour in the *Times*," Tommy added. "Bit later than expected, perhaps, but it is fabulously exciting. Do you know the writer?"

"Abigail McIntyre is my cousin Hal's wife, and a great friend who literally took us on our 'adventure'," Poppy explained. "We had an absolutely wonderful time, upon which I will not elucidate. You will have to wait upon each weekly instalment in the *Times*.

"Florence has her book out now, too," she went on after a moment or two's tea sipping and scone chomping.

"It is called *Faithfully Yours* by F.T. Smythe," Florence explained.

"But why the different names?" Sally asked, as she had no

inkling as to why they didn't use their own names. "I have never read much because of our previous working life."

Both girls explained the rationale behind their choice as to the whys and why-nots, which made Sally want to dip into this wonderful world of storytelling. Perhaps she might follow suit? Maybe first things first, though?

～～

"Have you noticed anything different about our functioning over the last few months?" Ross asked George in their weekly farm meeting. "Like … demands?"

"I've noticed that yon ruffians haven't been back with either their demands for money or to carry through their threats of retribution," George stated with a knowing smile. "And we both know why, I think, don't we?"

"Seems like it," Ross said. "Any idea where yon Jonas Jamieson has secreted himself these days? I believe the police would still like a word or two with him."

"None at all, old chap," George replied with a grimace. "I've only just got the full use back of my hand, arm and shoulder. More than a year it's taken. I've heard on the grapevine that he is paralysed in one of his legs because somebody shattered his knee joint with a hefty boot. He now either walks – slowly – using a walking stick or has been seen in an invalid's bathchair. Pity, eh? As for anything else? No idea. Good riddance, I say."

～～

"He must come and stay with us!" the man's mother insisted.

"No! He most certainly will not!" his father contradicted fiercely. "This is *my* house, and he will *not* enter, even if he uses the only vehicle I will recognise – a coffin! If you allow his miserable criminal body through my door, I will throw him out personally and inform the local constabulary immediately. As far as I am concerned, he no longer exists. Our sixteen-year-old daughter, Millie, is one-hundred times the human being he reckons to be, and she will be the one to inherit my – our – wealth, such as it is. She will no doubt find an exemplary spouse with whom she will produce grandchildren for us."

"Let's not plan too far ahead, Ernest, or make Millie's choice for her," Louisa warned. "Despite the upbringing he has had, Jonas was not the son we thought we would have, and—"

"A thief and toe rag, to boot," her husband added, "and that's … criminal."

On his way out to his work, he passed a nondescript lad loitering on the corner whom he dismissed as such as soon as he had cast his perfunctory glance at the boy's scruffy body. Once around the corner, the teenage lad sauntered towards the house the man had just left. Knocking on the door, he took four steps backwards and waited.

The curtain at the window next to the front door moved slightly to reveal an older lady wearing a slightly worried expression. "Who are you?" Louisa mouthed. "And what do you want?"

Her daughter, Millie, joined her.

"I have a message from your son, Jonas," the lad replied.

The curtain closed and bolts shot back on the door, revealing a narrow gap that was secured by a single chain to stop it from opening further.

"My name is Toby, and I'm a friend," the lad explained. "He asked me to bring you this note."

Handing over the message in an envelope, he stepped back again to allow her time to read its contents.

Mother dear, it started. *Toby is a good lad who helps me a lot.*

Please believe him when he tells you what has happened to me.
If you could see your way to send me some money – any amount
of money – I should be grateful. Please be so good as not to tell
Father of this communication. Yours in agony, your son Jonas.

"Young man," she beckoned the lad. "What pray has happened to him? He has to be desperate to call again."

"He is, ma'am," Toby explained. "He's had a serious accident to his knee, which prevents him walking unaided. He spends a lot of his time in a broken bathchair in severe pain."

"We'll get our coats and come to him," Louisa said quickly as she turned to her daughter.

"No, ma'am, please," Toby said holding his hand up as a sign for her to stay where she was. "He specifically ordered me not to allow you to do that. He said if you could allow him some money, I was to accept and leave with it in the envelope you have in your hand. He also said that if you were to say no, I was to turn away with thanks and leave, Ma'am."

"How much does he need?" she asked, seeking support from her daughter.

"He said I had to leave it to your judgement," the lad answered slowly. "You need to bear in mind that he hasn't eaten for almost a week."

Millie returned from the errand with which her mother had charged her with a black-chamois drawstring purse to hand that her mother took from her. Taking out five sovereigns, Louisa dropped them into the envelope and handed it to the lad. Turning to her daughter, she looked once again at the lad to see his back disappearing round the next corner down from their house.

"You realise, of course, that it could all have been a trick by that boy to get you to part with however much you gave him," Millie offered.

"I had to take that chance," Louisa replied. "After all he *is* your brother and my son, no matter what your father insists. Not a word to him, mind!"

CHAPTER 24

George was shocked beyond belief to have met his friend Florence again after all that time – something he hadn't expected to happen. He was exceedingly grateful, too, for her having taken the trouble to call. It couldn't have been easy for her. Why hadn't he visited her – and Poppy – before? After all, they had been very close friends for many years, much closer than male and female friends were usually expected to be.

He sat in the semi-darkness in his bedroom on the settee that he and Alice often shared after a long day's work, spending a wonderful couple of hours in each other's company before sleep ambushed them. Those times he would always cherish. And now? As with most things in life, the good, memorable ones didn't last. First his dad, then his lovely wife. What would hit him next? Perhaps better not become too involved or too close to anyone else for fear of—

A guttering hurricane lamp flickered alarmingly, desperately trying to warn him that a refill was urgently needed before total blackness overwhelmed him completely.

A light tap at the door drew him sharply out of his deep

reverie. He opened the door to see his remaining sister, Florence, wrapped in her dressing gown and a thick blanket to ward off the low temperatures.

"Problem sleeping?" he asked, ushering her into his room. "Me too. So much stuff rushing around in my head, really, Florence, that I have no way of managing it."

"You also need to realise that now mother has taken it upon herself to become surrogate mother to her grandchildren here, and Charity has her own household to manage, we are desperately short of labour to keep afloat our part of this grand joint effort with Boulders Wood. There is just Sally Spence and me left to manage the dairy on our own, and Sally won't be with us too much longer, I think."

"Don't worry, Sister, we will start our hunt for replacement staff tomorrow – today, even," he said, seeing that it had just crept past midnight. "When we get interested parties, would you be able train them?"

"Don't forget also that I have a young man who has just been put out of Davis's failing farm in the valley," she pointed out.

"Looking for a job?" George asked.

"Indeed," Florence muttered, as she stifled a yawn. "Sorry to have to put all of this on your shoulders, Brother, but we can't carry on being *this* overworked. If—"

"Don't … worry, Sis," he reassured her. "That's what I'm here for. Bring him round tomorrow and we'll see what we can do for him. Now, off to bed or you'll not wake up in the morning."

He kissed her cheek and hugged her like a brother should, thanking her for bringing it all to him. Another problem or two to see to! What the hell good was sleep anyway?

Sleep was elusive for him further into that night. Daily

problems flitted in and out of his consciousness and he couldn't get his friend, Florence, out of his head. What should he do? Should he have waited to marry her, as they had discussed before she went away on their grand tour? And what about Poppy, the other love of his life? She was sure that she loved George, but how important was that love to her? He could understand that she wanted to fulfil her dreams, but love was all important, wasn't it? Yet here they were now, getting on for two years down the line, and she had achieved so much with her literary ambitions. She had said to wait a couple of years or so, but now he would never know, as she wasn't interested any more. Or was she?

Was Poppy's life to be turned upside down again? Hadn't she taken her decision and reconciled herself to becoming a well-read and revered author, come what may? Although she accepted gratefully that her life was a universe away from those of many other young women, was it what she wanted – needed – for the rest of her time on this hallowed earth?

On their European Tour all that time ago, she had spent a wonderful two months achieving her life's ambitions to provide herself with the basis for the rest of her time as a writer of worthwhile and cutting-edge literature that might, perhaps, be remembered for the right reasons. Yet was her mind now telling her that what she was achieving wasn't enough?

Her two months away had convinced her that her professional writing had helped to put away *all* thoughts of an intensely personal life. But had it? If it had, why did she spend so much time since returning thinking about George – the man she had always considered that one day would be hers?

"Can't sleep either?" Florence asked her friend as she

entered the cottage sitting room close to four in the morning.

Poppy was sitting in *her* easy chair near a roaring fire, a cup of hot steaming tea to hand. "Restless, so I decided a nice cup of tea and a chair near the fire were of the essence," she agreed. "Tea's only just mashed. Bring yourself a cup, and we can chat for a while."

Although not yet snowing, that keen northerly wind had warned that much colder wintry weather might be on its way.

"Been thinking a lot lately about our Tour what seems like years ago. Do you know what I miss the most about Paris and Rome, apart from the buzz and the intellectual stimulation and the sights?" Poppy said, once Florence had gained *her* comfortable armchair with her cup of tea.

"The males?" Florence suggested smartly.

"The sunshine and warmth," Poppy corrected, ignoring her friend's coarse response. "I should love to be there at this very moment."

"Did I tell you that I went to see how George is getting on after his rather rough and dangerous altercation with Jonas Jamieson?" Florence announced rather starkly after a moment or two's embarrassing silence.

"Actually no, you didn't," Poppy answered, seemingly uninterested in what she had to say. "What you do with your own time is your affair. I have not seen him – nor would I want or need to – since before we went on our grand tour. Whatever George Garside does doesn't interest me at all. Don't forget that, unknown to us, he did marry Alice while we were away. Twin relationships, eh? Twin choices at marriage, albeit months apart?"

"It was good to see him, although he does look somewhat harassed and overworked, what with his father passing away, his wife dying in childbirth, his mother looking after his twin girls and his sister leaving the workforce to get married," Florence emphasised. "Oh, and his top employee marrying *your* father and now being with child, of course."

"Do we have to have these … 'competitions' to see who can be the most unpleasantly hurtful, Florence?" Poppy asked once her friend's diatribe had sunk in. "We used to be such good, close friends. Do you know what – or who – has caused what can only be termed as a rift between us?"

"Could it be one George Garside?" Florence replied quickly, not needing time even to think about her answer.

"George has set his thoughts and feelings before us on more than one occasion," Poppy pointed out. "Each time they have moved away from true friendship to a closer relationship to marriage. That has involved both of us at some stage. I know that we both have had … deeper … feelings for him, and he for both of us. Is it time that we left those feelings in the past, perhaps where they should stay?"

"I still love him, Poppy," her friend said candidly, "and I could say that only to you. Although I sometimes say otherwise, I am not sure whether I should *want* to marry him."

"There comes a time, I feel, when a man has to make a forthright, lasting commitment to a woman without letting anything or anyone else intervene," Poppy countered. "Unfortunately, our friend George has not done that, and I for one don't think I can accept it. Whatever you decide to do, whether marry him or not, will make no difference to the value of your friendship to me."

Tears began to well in Florence's eyes as she hugged her one true friend, knowing that their competition over George Garside was at an end. "What does today promise, my dear friend?" she asked.

"Abigail will be here at eight to discuss a list of people who would like to attend our next soirée," Poppy pointed out, her face quickly sloughing off her dejection and allowing her usual joy to re-emerge.

"Would that be eight o'clock this evening?" Florence queried, a rigorous bout of limb and body stretching slowing down her words.

"Actually, as it now six o'clock in the morning, that would be in a couple of hours' time," Poppy assured her, a wicked smile lighting her face even more. Florence's expression changed to one of urgency as she realised she had only two hours to ready herself, not allowing for breakfast.

"Abigail! Hal! Please come in quickly," Poppy urged her friends. "Unfortunately, even though this is the centre of our universe, I have never experienced anywhere else where the four seasons' weather might happen within one day. I've never seen two happier people anywhere. Would you say that married life suits you … both?"

"Couldn't agree more," Abigail responded. "It will soon suit three of us, too."

"Three?" Poppy puzzled. "How—?"

"Come on, Poppy!" Florence urged, a smile and quizzically raised eyebrows trying to nudge her friend's sense of humour into the room. "How many of them are there in front of us now? If we add another, what would—?"

"Ah! Yes!" Poppy giggled, once that magic light had sparked into life in her head. "So, you are going to deliver a small Abigail or a Small Hal – or both? It seems like everybody in the world is producing offspring."

"Goodness me!" Abigail exclaimed in shock surprise. "One at a time will be enough, I think."

Hal sat in his favourite armchair, happy to allow his three women do all the talking, unless he was invited to speak. Although everyone agreed it was a man's world, Hal definitely knew better. What was the saying? 'Behind every rich and successful man there is a more powerful and knowledgeable woman prodding him in the back, directing his operations'?

"I absolutely adore this room," Hal said, once they were settled with tea and scones. He could eat those scones at any time of day or night. "It always welcomes and warms you in such a way as to make you believe you are the only person on this earth. It also lets you know that you have no option but to call regularly."

"It doesn't mean, my dear husband, that you'll be getting any more scones because of what you are saying, otherwise you would never walk away," Abigail warned with a beaming smile.

They all laughed at her forthright appraisal whilst nodding sagely at Hal's reaction to it.

"We have our usuals for the next soirée," Abigail announced. "James Hawley Weeks, the publisher Jenny Wilton, all of us and several quite well-known writers – three youngish females and one male."

"James Smythe-Spence, Alice Bryce, Zena Polinska, and one other," Hal added. "No idea who the 'other' is yet."

"Spence?" Poppy queried.

"No relation as far as we are aware," Abigail assured her. "We could check with your father, if you would like us to."

"It's all right," Poppy acknowledged. "I'll speak to him the next time I see him. Coincidence, I should think."

"I've left all their details in this folder," Abigail said as she deposited said folder on the table. "Please write to them all as soon as you can, letting them know what you expect from them individually. Your letters should also include precise details of the event."

"I think I need to congratulate and thank you for your series of articles in *The Times* about our Grand Tour," Poppy said to Abigail as they relaxed by the fire. "I feel like we are famous already."

"Although I never planned for this, I have been told that those articles have been instrumental in boosting our readership by a significant amount," Abigail answered with a satisfied smile. "My editor even offered me a raise and a permanent place on the staff."

"Good heavens!" Poppy gasped. "That makes what I have to say even more urgent."

"Sounds pretty serious to me," Hal observed with a serious bout of nodding.

"More intriguing than fundamental," Abigail added.

"Florence and I would like you to become our agent and manager," Poppy said quite seriously. "And … you must state your price."

"That was Grandpa Ross's advice," Florence said with a giggle. "We have no idea about any of that officialese."

"What do you say, dear Abigail?" Poppy asked urgently. "Perhaps a good idea to continue writing articles for *The Times* as well. I don't know. It's up to you. If you wish, you could leave the decision-making until after Baby Abigail or Hal has made an appearance into our wonderful world? I hate to keep on saying this, but it's up to you."

"Then our answer is an unequivocal … YES!" Abigail retorted with a joyful punch of the air.

"That falls in with our plans very well indeed," Hall said with a chuckle.

"Plans? How do you mean?" Poppy queried.

"When the baby arrives, I had decided to haul back on

doing too much with work – what with all that traipsing about to secure stories," Abigail replied. "Working from home with my trusty Remington typewriter would allow us to spend more time with our – what do you call them? – nipper. Because of your offer, Hal could help me with the organisation and the running about."

"I hasten to add that it would not involve 'running about' physically," Hal insisted with an emphatic scowl. "I gave up running about a lot of years ago, I can assure you. My legs do perfectly well with what they were perfectly designed for."

They all laughed at what would turn out to be a very equitable arrangement.

CHAPTER 25

"You have three choices, Mr Jamieson," the hospital doctor advised Jonas as he sat uncomfortably in the hospital consulting room. At last after all this time, he had decided to see if these medic chaps might be able to relieve at least some of the pain and discomfort that his injured knee was causing him..

"And the three choices are, old chap?" Jonas asked, unable to rationalise his usual sniggering smirk, even now.

"This is one of the most serious cases I have seen in my entire professional life," the doctor acknowledged, a clear look of concern in his eyes. "Choices? Either leave it as it is, plastered and patched, or submit to an operation to set the bones and tendons back in place, or amputate just above the knee. The first option is touch and go because infection might well set in. The second will offer a better prognosis but is still dodgy. With the third, although the problems and pain will eventually disappear, so will at least half of your leg, leaving you with difficulty getting about. Oh, and possible infection from the knife wounds."

"Eenie, meenie, minie, mo. Not a lot of choices that will provide the best outcome, eh?" Jonas said, in a quandary as to which way to crawl. "Whichever I choose will still leave me severely injured with no chance of returning to normal. About the top and bottom of it?"

"Indeed," the doctor agreed. "I hate to admit it but it's almost flip-a-coin time. I'll leave you with your son here to decide if any of these options turns into a solution. Hum?"

"Well that's novel!" Jonas muttered.

"What?" Toby asked, puzzled. "You having three choices?"

"Nay, young Toby," Jonas joked. "Your being my son!" He laughed almost giddily at the thought that he looked like he was old enough to be father to a seventeen-year-old. He was a good and attentive lad was Toby, but Jonas's son? Never in a million years!

"Call us a hansom then, old man," Jonas urged his young friend. "I think we need to shake off the genteel scents of this unholy place, eh, Toby? Then it's back to our glorious stately house in the country to encourage Jeeves the butler to shake up a goodly meal before we retire to bathe and visit our new pristine white sheets."

"You have a very strange sense of humour, Boss," the lad said, not really understanding Jonas's language or humour. He definitely was a 'one off', was Mr Jamieson. All Toby Bott wanted to do was to make sure he was safe, even if he had to stay up all night to make sure his boss was free from threat. "Have you decided what you will do with your leg?"

"Well, one thing's for sure," Jonas assured him, "no lame-brained quack is about to sharpen his scalpel on *my* bones. I might as well hot foot it to Zululand and have one of their witchdoctors look at it."

It was all Toby could do to stop himself laughing at the

picture Jonas had just painted. He knew full well that his boss wouldn't let anything get him down or stop him from earning what he called 'a crust'.

"I have an acquaintance that knows a good deal about bones and joints and will give me the once over," Jonas said. "He has had one or two run-ins with his medical bosses concerning his predilection for a small glass or two of mother's ruin, which obliged him to relinquish his medical qualifications until he gets rid of the habit. He was one of the best bone practitioners around, and still has those skills, I am convinced. So, if you'd be so good as to avail me of your services tomorrow, we will take a trip to see him."

"You can rely on me, guvnor," the lad promised. "I'll be here bright and early."

"Try not to make it *too* early, old chap, or I for one won't be so bright," Jonas said, making the lad laugh raucously.

"By the way, be so good as to reach me the tin box that you see on the table over there," he went on as he shuffled onto the decrepit old bathchair to try to get comfortable. Once in his grasp, he opened it and handed the lad a small black cloth, drawstring bag.

"What's this for, Boss?" the lad asked, puzzled why he was handing over such a strange object. "It feels a bit heavy. What's in it?"

"Open it and see," Jonas suggested quietly.

Following instruction, Toby tipped its contents onto the crumpled bed and gasped. "Money?" he managed to gulp eventually. "What's all this for? What do you want me to do with it?"

"Firstly count it, old boy, if you wouldn't mind," Jonas said, "and tell me what you think. You *can* count, I take it?"

"Of course I can – and add and take away, and read and

write," the lad insisted, a little put out at the perceived jibe. That didn't last for long when his count reached twenty sovereigns. "My God! Why have you given me all this? What have I done to deserve it?"

"You are the only one to have stood by me and to have helped when I needed it the most," Jonas responded. "Do you remember that rather large job we worked, out Thresher Hall way on?"

"Aye, I do," Toby replied, a gathering smile showing the memory was true.

"Well, this is part of your share for our night's work," Jonas explained. "You are now in my employ, young sir, and we can look forward to more of that, mark my words. I should like you to help me with my mobility issues, both as personal assistant, and for when I move from this evil-smelling cowshed into something a little more ... salubrious. You up for that?"

"Too right, Boss," Toby agreed. "Too right."

"Are you sure you're all right with this evening?" Poppy asked her dear friend, Abigail McIntyre. "Although not too obvious yet dressed in your finery, you can't be *too* far away from gracing the world with another dear little 'nipper'."

"Three weeks and five days to be precise," Hal announced. "Give or take."

"I'm fine, dear Poppy," Abigail assured her. "As long as I don't spend too long on my feet, the baby won't want to show its face just yet. Your other guests should be arriving pretty soon."

"Everything's ready," Poppy said quietly. "James Hawley Weeks is here already. Couldn't keep away from the spread Mary Jane has provided. She's a real magician, that young lady.

Do we know anything much about our guests for this evening?"

"Yes, we do, but I'm saying nothing. I will allow them to do their own talking," Abigail said, her twinkly eye sparkling. "They are Alice Bryce, published author; Zena Polinska, published Polish author; James Smythe-Spence, aspiring author who is not related to you; Jude Dryden, poet, and a mystery young person – male or female I don't know – called George Ellis."

"Intriguing," Florence muttered, a slightly wicked look playing around her eyes.

A resounding rattle of the door knocker drew attention sharply to the vestibule, encouraging Hal to stride over to allow access to whomever so desired it, to find—

"Grandpa Ross!" Poppy exclaimed as she hugged him. "Didn't expect to see *you* here tonight! And … Father! This is so unexpectedly wonderful to have you both come to one of our humble soirées."

"Nothing humble about a group of writers talking about their writing and sharing their wisdom with like-minded folks," Tommy Spence said, embracing his daughter. "I have to say that I feel somewhat excited at what's about to embrace *us*. What do you say, Ross?"

"Couldn't agree more, old chap," Ross Senior agreed. "It's been my undoubted pleasure to watch this young lady blossom and grow from a gauche nipper into the beautiful, intelligent woman we see before us now."

"Enough!" Poppy laughed "You'll embarrass me. Please excuse me. It seems like my guests are arriving all at the same time. I must away to welcome them in."

Once outer clothing had been removed and hung up in their spacious vestibule and introductions settled, the guests were led into the dining area where there was the most unbelievably sumptuous spread of food of all sorts to be enjoyed by everyone. It was a distinct wonder that any discussion would be had at all, other than that which was interrupted by the sighs and groans from food meeting palates.

"I'm sorry I'm a little late," a small voice accosted Poppy as she was enjoying Mary Jane's wonderful food while talking about writing in general with the young writers Jude Dryden and James Smythe-Spence.

"Don't worry about it," Poppy replied as she turned to greet—

"Florence? Are you here—?"

"To talk about *my* writing, Poppy dear," George Garside's youngest sister explained. "My nom de plume is 'George Ellis'."

⁓

"Fabulous evening," Ross Booth gushed as he congratulated Poppy and Florence on their wonderfully successful event. "The food was excellent, for which we owe our deepest gratitude to our magician Mary Jane. The incidental conversation while eating was kept to a minimum by delicious food, and the in-depth talks around the fire in yonder sitting room couldn't have been more interesting."

"The dark horse for me?" Tommy Spence added. "George Garside's youngest sister, Florence. I never knew she wrote. How exciting to hear what she had to say! What with all these youngsters, I think it safe to believe that our literary future is secure in their hands for years to come."

"I was so excited to hear everyone's views," Abigail noted. "Particularly our young ladies; Zena, all the way from Poland, Alice Bryce who is already published, and Florence Garside, a wonderful local talent."

"Zena Polinska has lived in this country from birth,

actually," Poppy explained. "She is the daughter of an exiled literary figure who was hounded out of his home country by those who either don't know or don't want to understand what he might have to say. Their loss, our gain."

"I think you've made a hit with the chaps, dearest Poppy," Florence pointed out when they were sitting quietly on their own with a cup of tea in front of a glowing fire, and everyone else had gone.

"How do you mean?" Poppy said, not sure where this was leading.

"Well, we had our usual in James Hawley Weeks," Florence explained. "You could do a lot worse than choose him. He may be a little older than you, but he is rich, has an enormous country pile, and carries a great deal of influence in many quarters."

"Do you also include Jude Dryden and James Smythe-Spence in that list, by any chance?" Poppy asked. "I'm not too sure about Jude the poet, but—"

"I thought James was dishy … and intelligent," her friend added. "How about—?"

"Another cup of tea!" they both chorused with a whoop and a grin.

"Soon time for bed," Poppy added. "We have a busy day tomorrow."

⁓

"And what do you want?" Jenny Bott said to her caller. "I thought you were dead. Might as well have been for all the good you have been to me. Promises, promises! Just like all men – a lot to say but never any substance to back it up. A right state you're in now, as well! Bathchair?"

"Hang on a bit, Mam!" a familiar voice introduced the appearance of a young man she knew very well.

"Toby? What are you doing here at this time?" Jenny asked, surprised to hear her son close by. "Aren't you supposed to be at work?"

"I *am* at work!" he exclaimed. "I work for Mr Jamieson here."

"You work for—?" she snarled.

"Do you remember that money I gave you a while ago, along with several bags of groceries?" Toby interrupted. "That was from the wage that Mr Jamieson pays me. Who do you think pays your rent for this flea pit?"

Knowing the response she might make, she stopped talking. Jonas's treatment of her on many occasions had been questionable to say the least. There had been times when he had treated her like a lady; better than she had been treated by most other men she had come into contact with.

"Open the doors please, and I'll get him inside with his carriage," the lad said, to a guffaw from his employer.

Once inside, Jenny made a pot of tea while her lad sorted out Jonas's comfort.

"Now then, Jenny Bott, my girl, I have a proposition for you," Jonas offered. "I know how good you are with the few cooking implements you possess, and how you have always tried to keep clean the hovels you always had to inhabit through lack of finance."

"What of it?" she replied, not sure she wanted to have any sort of a conversation with this man.

"I now have a reasonable – legitimate – source of income that will not only pay for me to live comfortably, but also will allow me to employ your lad as my personal assistant. The next proposition might be a difficult one for you to accept, given my behaviour towards you on occasion."

"Spit it out man!" she exclaimed. "For God's sake!"

"I have purchased a house of good order for us all to live

in," Jonas went on.

"Now just a minute!" Jenny Bott jumped in. "I am no longer—"

"No strings attached," Jonas interrupted. "You will be my housekeeper and Toby will be my personal assistant to run my necessary – *our* necessary – errands and attend to my personal needs. You can see that I don't move very well these days. I will also pay you for your work. What do you say? Put all my indiscretions behind us for the general good?"

"And what happens when you lose your temper, as was your wont?" she asked pointedly.

"As you can see, I have no physical capability to carry out any threats. You can ignore anything derogatory I might utter," he assured her.

"Listen, Mam," Toby said. "You – we – won't get a better offer anywhere else. We'll be able to live decently as we ought in proper, clean conditions. What do you say?"

"I'm not so sure, lad," Jenny said after a bit of thought. "What if—"

"Life's full of 'what ifs', Mam," Toby advised her honestly. "Now we will have something to live *for*. Whatever Mr Jamieson says he will do, he *will* carry out to our mutual benefit. Come on, Mam, what do you say?"

Chapter 26

"How long have we been together, Ross?" his wife, Nell, asked, with more than a little annoyance edging her question.

"Probably fifteen years or so?" he replied quietly.

"And didn't you think I would be able to cope with what I have only just found out?" she added. "I thought we had agreed to share everything. We did, didn't we?"

"I didn't want to worry you," he responded apologetically.

"A serious lung condition, did the doctor say?" she asked, trying to squeeze as much information from him as she could.

"Comes of working too long with those damned sheep in Australia," he added "Fibres and dust from the wool, you see."

"And?" Nell went on, not willing to let it drop. Important questions needed equally important straight, honest answers. "Are you going to … die?"

"It apparently all depends on my – our – lifestyle from now on, I suppose," he offered.

"And by that you mean?" Nell pressed him for a quicker, more understandable answer.

"I think climate has a lot to do with it," he tried to explain. "Apparently, the warmer the better."

"So, we need to move to a much warmer, more clement climate," she said. "Top and bottom?"

"Top and bottom," Ross agreed. "Probably somewhere like Southern France or North Africa, or the Canary Islands in the North Atlantic, off the coast of Morocco, or even the Balearics. We have to look into it."

"How do we go about securing a place to live in Southern France, then?" Nell asked seriously. If anyone knew, it would be Ross.

"There are agencies that can sort out stuff for you," he returned. "You'd have to leave it to me. I'll ask around and get some ideas as to where on the French Mediterranean coast would be a good place to live. We have no problem with anywhere costly, so the sky – sorry about the pun – is the limit."

"Once you have somewhere in mind, we will need to look into it," Nell insisted. "That, of course, means holidays – and lots of them."

"Joseph and Ross don't need us for the running of the business," Ross pointed out. "We simply need to make sure there is always sufficient capital in the farm's bank account to cover all eventualities. That will be no problem."

"And Poppy?" Nell asked.

"That's already taken care of," he assured her. "Always has been. Always will be … automatic. Besides, now she has her father to look after her financial affairs."

"She has an agent and manager now, as well," Nell added. "Abigail and Hal are the best they could hope for. Bear in mind also that her writing is beginning to take off, giving that extra lift to her position."

"Mediterranean France here we come, then!" Ross replied with a genuinely relieved grin.

"Yet still no young man on the horizon?" Nell queried. "Whereas it seems likely that Florence and George might head towards each other … eventually."

"I have no doubt that everything will turn out fine for our Poppy," Ross decided with a nod. "Mark my words."

⌒◠⌣

"I love these stamped envelopes bearing messages from people that live perhaps far away," Poppy said, having been alerted by the clack-rattle of the cast-iron letterbox by the side of the cottage's front door. "It's always exciting when, confronted by a letter, you have no idea of its contents until it is opened."

She broke open the seal on the envelope's flap to reveal a beautifully hand-written letter from James Smythe-Spence, one of her regulars to both their intimate and much larger soireés throughout the year. They had spoken briefly on a number of occasions but never in private or alone.

"Do you remember James Smythe-Spence from our soirées?" she asked Florence. "You know, the one whom every-one thought was my brother?"

"How could I forget!" Florence sighed. "A more handsome and striking man I have never seen before. Why?"

"Well, he has invited us to the family estate in the West Riding, near Keighley," Poppy replied, a slight frisson of excitement taking control of her limbs.

"And?" Florence said. "What is there in Keighley to excite up-and-coming authors like us?"

"Perhaps you had forgotten, my dear Florence, that a family of wonderful writers lived there," Poppy urged. "The Bell Family?"

"Never heard of them," Florence said dismissively, but knowing full well who they were.

"Come now! Surely you remember the Brontë sisters?" Poppy gasped in surprise at her friend's dismissal of such important writers who had figured largely in their studies. "Those wonderful story-tellers Charlotte, Emily and Anne who chose to be called Currer, Ellis and Acton to hide their gender? They lived at the parsonage in—"

"Haworth," Florence interrupted dispassionately. "And?"

"Haworth is in the same area as Keighley, don't you know?" Poppy added, wondering why her friend seemed so … disinterested.

"Tell me, my dear friend, is there something on your mind?" she went on. "You seem to be … preoccupied."

"I suppose I'll have to tell you," Florence retorted. "You'll find out sooner or later."

"Come on, then!" Poppy urged, needing to clear the air because Florence had had such … pensive times in the past. "Out with it."

"Our dear friend, George has asked me if I will become his wife," Florence admitted, looking directly into Poppy's eyes.

"Why, that's wonderful news!" Poppy gushed, genuinely happy that her good friend had received the request that she had wanted for such a long time.

"But aren't you—?" Florence answered, unsure of the response that Poppy had almost flung at her.

"Delighted for you?" Poppy reassured her, drawing her friend's resisting body to her own. "I am very happy that you have finally got what you have waited for, and, no, I am not jealous or annoyed. I stopped wanting dear George as a husband quite some time ago."

"Aren't you afraid that this could mean the end of our

writing friendship?" Florence said.

"I will always be where you will have access to *me*, no matter where your life takes you," Poppy reassured her earnestly. "You will also be able to pursue your writing in the full knowledge that you will have a husband who obviously loves you and a family home that he will provide for you.

"That having been said, will you accompany me to Keighley to stay for a while at Spence Hall?" she finished.

"I don't think so," Florence said quietly. "I need to spend some time with George to see if that's what *I* really want."

"Really want?" Poppy gasped in disbelief. "But I thought—"

"That I had accepted?" Florence responded. "That his asking was a *fait accompli* and that I would fall into his arms without question?"

"Well … yes," was Poppy's simple answer. "Didn't *you*? Metaphorically speaking, of course."

"I told him that I would think about it and give him my answer in a week or two," Florence explained, a somewhat confused look in her face. "I owe it to him to give him my answer … soon."

"But won't he—?" was Poppy's confused answer.

"Find someone else?" Florence suggested. "There *is* no-one else. He wasn't sure he should have married poor Alice, because—"

"He wanted *you* all the time," Poppy butted in, beginning to understand. "Then, shouldn't you accept immediately?"

"It's not quite as straightforward as that," Florence tried to explain slowly. "There are his daughters to consider, although George's mother, Lilly, is very happy to continue looking after them. Then the question arises as to whether *I* want children."

"Don't you?" Poppy's question stopped her friend in her tracks.

"The unequivocal answer to that is – I … don't … know!" she replied, a look of fear descending into her eyes. "It's a question I've never considered, in truth. I love the idea of loving the man, but *serious* lovemaking can, inevitably, lead to serious repercussions."

"A lot to consider, then," Poppy said. "That can only be resolved by talking to your soon-to-be husband, perhaps?"

"Are you going to accept James's invitation to Keighley?" Florence went on after a moment of quiet thought.

"Indeed I am," her friend said, beaming widely. "I love the conversations we've shared, and I can't wait to visit the Parsonage at Haworth, if only to see Emily and Anne's final resting place in St Michael and All Angels churchyard. Can't believe they were only about thirty years old."

"Why *did* they die so young?" Florence asked, wondering why she thought that Poppy might know.

"Fifty years ago it was thought that, following several family deaths – mother and two siblings – it might be because of melancholy and grief," Poppy explained. "Today it has come to light that they suffered from consumption that is easily spread from one family member to others."

"When will you visit James Spence?" Florence asked, taking little notice of what she was saying. "Your birthday?"

"Don't know yet," Poppy said. "Haven't decided. Probably sooner rather than later. Maybe—" She stopped in mid-sentence to the clacking of the doorknocker.

"Father!" she called as he slipped into the vestibule. She hugged him as if there were no tomorrow. "It's been a while."

"I just popped in to let you know that you are now sister to a little baby … girl whom we are to call … Annie," he retorted with joy in his eyes and tears streaming down his cheeks.

"That's wonderful news!" she gasped as *her* eyes followed

suit. Like father like daughter, eh? "How is Sally?"

"Tired but well, I think," he said.

"Did you deliver your—?" she asked.

"No fear!" came back his unequivocal answer. "I would have been too nervous. She had little Annie in Richmond Hospital after a longish labour that we were both glad to be over – her more so than me."

"Annie Spence, eh?" Poppy muttered. "Rather prophetic, don't you think, bearing in mind that that could have been my mother's name, given half a chance. A sister? I'm looking forward very much to welcoming her into our family."

"And how are you getting on?" Tommy asked. "Soireés going well?"

"Indeed, yes," she replied. "In fact, I'm going to visit the parental home of one of my friends who has been to the last one or two, by the name of James Spence. No relation, I think."

"James Smythe-Spence by any chance?" Tommy asked. "Young chap of about your age? Light-brown hair and a ruddy complexion?"

"That's right," she said, a slightly puzzled look growing in her face. "He is rather good looking, and I thought—"

"They live in a mansion called Spence Hall somewhere Keighley way on, in the West Riding," Tommy went on.

"How do you know all this?" Poppy puzzled, slightly alarmed at what he was saying.

"His father is a textile magnate with a factory in the town that makes woollen clothing," Tommy went on. "He is my much older brother, Jacob. Consequently, James would be your cousin."

"Oh," Poppy gasped, rocking back in her chair, flabbergasted at what she was hearing. "He told me he didn't think we were related."

"Probably didn't know that I am your father," Tommy advised her. "Your mother and I were kept a secret until just recently when you and I discovered each other. Father and I never saw eye to eye on anything he didn't either like or subscribe to. Left to him, you and I would never have discovered each other. He could be persuasively unpleasant when he wanted to be. OK then, my sweet girl, I'll away, back to bringing up your sister and looking after her mother. See you soon, hopefully."

"Well, that's a setback," Florence said, turning towards her friend to gauge her reaction. When she saw *no* reaction, she was surprised.

"What?" Poppy said, uncertain as to her meaning. "Are you thinking that I am disappointed because I was about to marry that chap?"

"No … yes … I don't know, my friend," Florence vacillated. "I thought—"

"Lovely man and good to talk to but … husband?" Poppy sneered. "I don't think so! I haven't met the man I would like to marry … yet. I definitely *do* want to see how he lives, though."

CHAPTER 27

"Although I wasn't present on the actual day your arrival graced this earth, the 30th July 1869 is indelibly imprinted on my mind," Tommy commented to his daughter. "The fact that you are visiting part of my family today in the West Riding of Yorkshire on the anniversary of your birth reinforces the reason why I wished to accompany you, Poppy."

"I am looking forward to it, Father," she replied, wrapping her arms around him in one of her many shows of affection. "Wouldn't Sally have liked to be with us?"

"She would, but there are too many things to do with a new baby, and she is still feeling a little tired from her ordeal," her father said, consulting his silver pocket fob watch. "Twenty minutes should see us approaching Keighley's railway station, I believe, and then we need to cross to the branch line up to a village called Oakworth, where we will be picked up and taken to the Spence family seat."

"Two nights in a country house that is not the centre of a farm!" Poppy said enthusiastically. "With Haworth not far away? Heaven! I hope they have hired Mary, who was our cook at Boulders Wood for two days."

Tommy laughed, realising what good fun it was to be with the young lady he hadn't seen or even known existed for at least the first eighteen years of her life. Now he was living his dream of spending as much time as he could with her. He also would have many years to look forward to with another young lady who would grow up to be like Poppy, hopefully. He couldn't have wished for two more beautiful human beings than his two daughters, Poppy and Annie.

"The countryside hereabouts is delightful but rugged," Poppy observed as she gazed at the greenery, moors and hills. "Not sure whether I'd want to live here, except to be part of its literary heritage. Will we be able to visit Top Withens where *Wuthering Heights* is supposed to have been set, and the parsonage at Haworth, and the two Brontë graves in the local cemetery?"

"I don't see why not," Tommy agreed. "After all, your cousin *is* part of your literary group, isn't he?"

"This is a lovely little station, Ingrow (West)," Poppy stated as they walked. "Just like those we passed through when Grandpa Ross and Nanny Nell took my friends and me to the East Coast for my twelfth birthday anniversary celebration in 1881."

"Not heard about that one," Tommy said as they walked on to the platform. "I think the next station after this one – Damems, I believe – is only just over half a mile away, so why don't you tell me about it? The one after Damems – Oakworth – where we will alight, is about another mile and a half, which gives us plenty of time to explore your adventures along the coast where Scarborough, Bridlington, Staithes and Whitby lie."

First-class travel had improved in the thirteen or so years

since Poppy and her dear friends had travelled from their home to York and then on to Scarborough. It seemed that the railway companies had paid a good deal more attention to comfort than they had in earlier days. Significantly less claustrophobic, much more comfortable seats, and very much lighter than their earlier experiences, the two intrepid travellers enjoyed their jaunt along the Keighley and Worth Valley branch line.

Once she had relayed her feelings about her birthday anniversary celebration at age twelve, Poppy settled to take in the view, soak up the atmosphere and rejoice in what delights this area steeped in literary joys was about to offer her.

"The train's slowing, I think," Poppy said in a warning to her father.

"Our destination approaches, I believe," he said, drawing his belongings to him. "Oakworth."

"This station is much bigger than the one before it – Damems, wasn't it?" Poppy added. "That was tiny. Much smaller than my cottage, and no mistake."

"It certainly was," Tommy replied with a laugh. "I'm looking forward to the next few days with you, my little one.

"I think that expensive-looking brougham standing on the road the other side of the station buildings must be our vehicle," he pointed out. "The one with the gold-coloured edging to the carriage. My brother always had ostentatious standards. Come on, then! Let's away before the train takes us to Haworth."

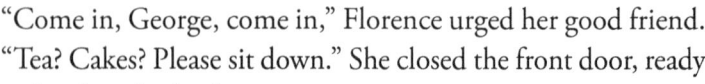

"Come in, George, come in," Florence urged her good friend. "Tea? Cakes? Please sit down." She closed the front door, ready to head to the kitchen.

"How could I ever refuse," he replied jovially, a smile

decorating his face. "No Poppy here today?"

"She's gone off to Haworth in the West Riding with her father to visit her uncle's country mansion for a few days," she explained. "He's a textiles baron, apparently, with factories where they make clothing out of sheep's wool."

"Did you not want to go with her?" George asked, surprised because he knew they usually did most things together.

"I'm glad she's gone with her father because there is something I need to talk to you about," Florence said quietly. "I think you probably might guess what I want to say."

"My offer of a little while ago that you said you would consider seriously?" he acknowledged, hoping for the best but expecting the worst.

"Yes," she said.

"Yes what?" he asked, a little puzzled, not understanding what she meant.

"Yes, I will," she assured him, a slight smile dancing around the corners of her mouth. "Yes, I will … marry you."

He was taken aback by the answer he did not expect. "Are you really serious?" he gasped, as he sat back on the settee with a bump. "That's not what I expected you to say. You are really, really serious?"

"Well, you may be surprised, but are you … pleased?" Florence asked, now a little uncertain because of his response to the most serious she had ever been.

"Florence, my dear, beautiful lady, of course I'm pleased!" he exclaimed with joy. "I couldn't be more pleased. In fact, I'm overjoyed. Mr and Mrs George Garside! That does have a certain ring to it, doesn't it?

"Talking about 'ring'" he added quickly, drawing a small box from his pocket, which he opened and offered to her. "I've had this for quite some time, just in case I got lucky. I know it's what you like so—"

"George!" she exclaimed with delight, taking the solitaire diamond with sapphires surrounding it set in a gold ring. "This is—" She burst into tears before she could finish.

Recognising her deep emotion, he took the ring gently from her and slid it onto her engagement finger, saying, "I love you, Florence. Always have and always will."

He kissed her passionately and, sliding his arm around her unprotesting shoulders, he drew her unresisting body to him. "At last," he sighed. "Happiness, finally."

The driveway to the Spence country estate was similar to the one at Boulders Wood as it wound its way through a dense forest of mature oak and beech trees. Probably five times as long, the drive allowed the visitor to see the house only when the carriage had negotiated the last sweeping bend. Then, there it was – a magnificent early-Victorian pile that oozed charisma and expense. It put Poppy in mind of the Victorian Grand Hotel in Scarborough with its many chimneys, and she gasped at its ostentation and size. Sympathetically designed and expensively built, it persuaded the onlooker that it was everything that Boulders Wood was not.

Poppy gasped loudly again as they approached the porti-coed door, taken utterly by surprise. The door opened slowly to reveal a liveried footman waiting to greet them and to usher them into the large, lobbied area to await a family member to receive them.

"Thank you, George," a young man's voice broke the silence as they entered. "I'll take it from here. Poppy, so good to see you, and…?" he offered.

"Good day, James," she replied. "This is my father, Thomas."

Pleasantries out of the way, James led his guests into the living room, where they were greeted by Tommy's brother, Jacob, and his wife.

"Hello, Jacob. I hope you are well," Tommy said, even though his brother neither acknowledged him nor offered to leave his easy chair to greet him.

Jacob rang a little handbell with gusto, bringing a sour look to his dour face.

"This is my daughter, Poppy, and I am pretty sure you know who I am," Tommy continued.

His last comment was designed either to sting his brother to life or to be a precursor to an early departure. His thoughts were interrupted by the quiet entry of a serving girl bearing a silver tray with bone-china teacups and saucers and plates, a domed silver teapot and silver-service implements, along with a plate of broken biscuits that seemed to have experienced better days.

"My wife you know, and my son I believe at least the young lady has already met," Tommy's brother mumbled gruffly. "Sit down and have some tea. It's Earl Grey."

"No, thank you," Tommy insisted. "We drink only proper tea and eat real home-baked, buttered scones."

"Let's get to the point then," Jacob growled. "My son tells me he would like to marry your … girl, and—"

"Not possible, I'm afraid, for two reasons," Poppy interrupted, annoyed at being ignored and treated as some count-at-nought chattel. "Firstly, I am his first cousin, so it's not possible legally. Secondly, and more importantly, I … don't … want … to. Shall we go, Father?"

"Indeed, my dearest, we are going to get nowhere here," Tommy added, turning towards the door, his arm under his daughter's. "We can take a return train to Keighley and book a hotel for the night. Tomorrow will see us at home among real family and *friends*."

"It seems like we are to be offered no lift to the station," Tommy observed once breathable fresh country air was reinvigorating their lungs. "Still, it's only just beyond the gates at the end of this driveway. I think we'll be able to manage a brisk walk. Don't you?"

Arm in arm, with a smile on their faces and a joyful briskness to their step, they reached the end of the drive and the short road into Haworth in no time at all.

"See the Black Bull Inn on the corner over there?" Tommy pointed out at the top of the steep Main Street. "*That*, I believe, was the ale house brother Patrick Branwell Brontë frequented – too often, I presume, and just round the corner here is—"

"The parsonage where they all lived not fifty years ago!" Poppy gasped. "But I thought—"

"That we were on our way to the railway station to catch a train home?" Tommy replied with a grin. "What? And miss one of the highlights of your visit? That was never about to happen, my dear."

"How do you know all of this, Father?" Poppy said, almost not believing what she was seeing.

"You have a sterling friend from whom I gleaned all the information we would need before we set off," her father explained. "And she bears the name … Abigail McIntyre."

"The wonderful Abigail!" Poppy clapped joyfully. "Would it be possible very quickly to have a look in the church's graveyard?"

"To see where three out of the children of Patrick and Maria Brontë were laid to rest?" he asked. "Saint Michael and All Angels is just next door. Shall we…?"

"We have two choices now," Tommy explained to his daughter as they waited on Haworth's station platform. "I know that the line between here and the next station along – Oakworth – has to cross a somewhat 'unsafe' viaduct at a place called Vale Mill, whatever that is."

"The choices, then?" Poppy puzzled.

"Train, and hope the viaduct holds up," her father replied. "Or take a carriage to Oakworth and then a train from there."

"Look!" she urged. "Train's coming! Come on! Time to be brave!"

Chapter 28

"Unsuccessful, then?" Florence said as Poppy sat down for breakfast.

"In what respect?" Poppy returned, not quite sure what her friend was trying to say.

"Your stay and your business with James?" Florence tried to explain. "You didn't fulfil any of your expectations. Did you?"

"And what expectations are you hinting at? Marriage? Enjoyment of the two days away with my father?" Poppy retorted. "The former was never on the agenda, but the latter lived up to expectations … and some! I had a fantastic time with my father, and I couldn't have done without his guidance and company."

"Oh," Florence said, seemingly deflated. "So, you *weren't* looking for a husband?"

"You know perfectly well that James and I are first cousins and so couldn't possibly contemplate marriage legally, even if I wanted to – which I *didn't*," Poppy insisted.

"But what about James?" Florence persisted.

"He was astounded – and speechless – when he discovered

that we were family," Poppy sniggered. "He hadn't been told. At all."

"Does that mean—?" Florence asked quietly.

"Will you never listen to and believe what I say?" Poppy snapped. "I … don't … want … George! Is that good enough for you?"

"In that case, if you're sure, I have news for you," Florence said almost dismissively. "George and I have decided to become husband and … wife."

"That's what you've wanted all along. Isn't it?" Poppy replied. "It's nothing to do with me. As a matter of interest, can I take it you won't be staying here?"

"Very true," Florence said, matter of fact. "George will be setting up an office to cater for my writing projects. I will be using a publisher other than Jenny Wilton and an agent that is not Abigail McIntyre."

"When will you be leaving, may I ask?" Poppy enquired of her friend. She had no idea how or why their close friendship had stalled of late, nor could she foresee a resolution to Florence's perceived intractability.

"George would like us to marry sooner rather than later," Florence explained in an almost throw-away manner. "It could be anytime within the next couple of months. No shenanigans about custom or protocol. We may even have a private affair at some registry office … somewhere."

"Can I take it that your present attitude towards me means I may not even be … invited?" Poppy asked with trepidation.

"It's up to you, Poppy," Florence ventured. "If you *want* to come…"

Unable to sustain any more of her former friend's indifference, Poppy slipped her coat on and left the room quietly, heading for Boulders Wood as she fancied friendly conversation with her nanny and grandpa to tell them about the time spent with her father in the West Riding's wonderfully brooding countryside.

"It was unbelievable, Nanny," Poppy enthused, over a mug of hot tea and one of Mary Jane's buttered scones. "Father's relations lived in a wonderful, palatial house in enormous grounds, but the inside was dour at best, matching the demeanour of Uncle Jacob, his wife and son, James. Ostensibly I was there to be vetted, leading to approval or disapproval as James's soon-to-be … wife. Can you believe it? Father and I left within fifteen minutes of having arrived to spend time doing what I had set out to do – visit Haworth Parsonage where the Brontë family lived and died, and the church's graveyard where they were interred. That experience was wonderful in the extreme, and one that will stay with me forever."

"How did you find your friend Florence when you returned?" Grandpa Ross asked carefully.

"She is distant … disinterested … dismissive … and decidedly disappointing," Poppy said, a tear threatening to reveal her deeper feelings. "All linked, I fear, with her impending marriage to our dear friend, George Garside. I think that she may find all that has to offer her somewhat problematic and difficult to cope with."

"All the more reason why she will need your continuing friendship," Nell answered cryptically.

"What do you mean, Nanny?" Poppy noted.

"The association with her marriage to George Garside seems to be something of a rushed affair," Grandpa Ross explained. "You see, her father and mother cut her off without issue, leaving her with no alternative but to re-kindle her relationship with our good George."

"But why? She could have stayed here with us, with me," Poppy insisted. "She didn't have to make such a quick decision without talking things through with—"

"Have you ever thought that that's what she might have wanted all along?" Grandpa Ross added. "I assume it's not a marriage of the *other sort* of convenience?"

"She wouldn't do that," Poppy assured him quickly. "She has always loved George, as we both did, but was taking her time deciding since he last asked her."

"And you, Poppy lass, what do *you* want to do?" Nell asked, unsure of the direction Poppy's ambition might lead her, bearing in mind that they – Nell and Ross – would not be around too much longer.

"I shall carry on as I am now," Poppy said with a smile. "I have my ambitions to attend to, to which I have pledged all my efforts. I will develop them until I have achieved what I have dreamed about since I was twelve. No doubt marriage may happen if it raises its head. If not, then so be it. It's not going to govern my life."

"We ought to tell you that we intend to move house again in the near future," Nell said quietly.

"Where are we heading this time, Nanny Nell?" Poppy asked, her face taking on a softer hue.

"The South of France, we think," Nanny Nell replied, the glimmer of a smile hovering around her features.

"France is such a beautiful and exotic place, particularly around and in Paris," Poppy extolled. "But I don't think it will be there, because it's not that dissimilar to the South of England. However, I know from talking with Abigail and Hal that the South of France is much warmer than here, particularly in the winter months. So, where in the south?"

"I have just discovered," Nell said, casting a glower at her husband, "that your grandpa has developed difficulties with his lungs from working too long with sheep."

"Sheep?" Poppy sniggered, but not knowing why. "What? Did he share living accommodation with them?"

Her nanny and grandpa laughed at the image that conjured in their mind. "We have heard," Nanny Nell went on to explain, "that the South of France on the Mediterranean coast is very good for people with lung problems. You remember the condition that your Brontës suffered from?"

"Consumption, wasn't it?" Poppy ventured tentatively.

"Indeed," Grandpa Ross said. "Depending on how bad the condition is, it is said it can be cured, or at least alleviated, by constant exposure to good and warm air."

"By constant exposure you mean … permanent?" Poppy asked hesitantly.

"Unfortunately … yes," Grandpa Ross agreed. "Could be a matter of life or death, really. Heaven or hell, in fact."

"Are you just thinking, or have you started to do something about it?" Poppy wondered, rather concerned that she wouldn't have much longer to share his company.

"We have booked to stay in a luxury hotel in Nice for a month or two, close to where our Queen spends *her* winters," Ross explained. "That will give us time to look at what appropriate properties are available. I have to warn you it will be a permanent move. It'll also give you the chance to join us for periods, should you wish."

"When?" Poppy queried, very concerned at the news about her grandpa's health.

"Very soon," Nanny Nell responded. "As soon as we've tied up loose ends here."

"Is today removal day?" Poppy asked her friend, noticing suitcases and bags lining the lobby at the front of the cottage. "I'll give you a hand when the carriage arrives."

"There will be no need, Poppy," Florence responded quietly. "George will be bringing his wagon, and *he* will do the loading."

"Will this be the last time I see you?" Poppy inquired, finding it hard to hide her feelings. "Best part of twenty years since we met and became the closest of friends. In fact, you're the only person I could ever call a true friend."

"Except George, of course," Florence replied, quietly but coolly.

"We're not about to part as … enemies, are we, my dearest friend?" Poppy said, almost in tears. "I—"

"Will always be my bestest friend, dear Poppy!" Florence burst out, drawing her friend to her bosom as tears flowed from them both, unstaunched because of their heaving emotions.

"You know you will always be welcome here in the cottage that we designed and where we planned everything we have achieved … together," Poppy sobbed. "I'm happy for you to go, if that's what you want, but also very sad if you decide to stay away. I will ensure that your books and possessions will remain in your room, which no-one else will either touch or even look at. Your bed will always be made, ready if you need it."

"Would you allow me to come on occasion to work with you here on some of the joint projects that we might plan?" Florence asked tentatively.

"You must keep your key to the door, just in case you need peace and quiet at any time away from the hubbub of normal, everyday family life, particularly where children are involved," Poppy suggested, still holding on to her dear friend.

Silence crept upon them for a while as each tried to control her emotions on this stressful day that signalled the parting of their ways, at least for a time.

"Cup of tea time, I believe," Poppy urged, as she pulled away from her friend. "And a piece of homemade Royal Victoria sponge cake from Mrs Beeton's 1861 *Book of Household Management* recipe."

She was interrupted by the metal clacking of the letterbox that was attached to the outside wall next to the front door. Hearing that, as she left to access the kitchen, she decided to collect whatever it contained later when Florence had gone. The noise was followed moments later by a rattling of the door knocker, announcing someone else's desire to gain entry.

Florence opened the door. "George!" she cried, flinging her arms about his neck and burying her face in his shoulder.

"Hold on, old girl," he urged. "You've been crying. Why on earth would you want to do that, particularly on the day we move in together?"

"George!" Poppy cried, her cheeks tear-stained as she carried a laden tray into the lobby. "My, how good it is to see you."

"You've been crying, too, Poppy!" he exclaimed, mystified as to why there was so much emotion.

They all took to their customary chairs as silence descended, while Poppy poured tea and sliced cake – one of George's favourites; but then, weren't they all?

"Why the upset?" he asked, once he had tasted and sipped.

"You wouldn't understand, my man," Florence said to the nods of her good friend. "It's a woman thing. Emotions, and all that men don't share with their womenfolk. Don't worry. It's all settled now. Some things we have agreed to leave here so I can attend to the projects we have already started. They are important to us both, and should be carried through to completion."

George loaded his fiancée's necessities into his wagon and set off back to his farm, while Florence remained to sort out the tidying of her writing wherewithal before she, too, departed on her short walk around to her new home in Garside Farm.

Having plenty of time to think en route, she wondered whether she really did want to take this step. Once that wedding ring was nestling on her finger, there was no turning back either from the pressures of living on a working farm amidst all the toing and froing throughout the day – and night – or the possibility of being with child. How would she cope with that almost certain inevitability?

Poppy sighed as she turned to the note that had been pushed through her letterbox, with simply *Poppy* written on the front. Flipping the envelope backwards and forwards, she finally decided to investigate its innards.

It read:

Dearest Poppy. Just a note to ask if I might see you. You have been on my mind since our latest, wonderful evening together, even though we were not alone. Please write to me at the above address. Jude Dryden.

This note set her back on her heels mightily, as she would never have expected that from him. She read it several times to detect any hidden meaning, but none could she find. Did she really want to meet him on her own? What could be the possible result of an almost clandestine assignation? Did she find him attractive?

She was intrigued.

CHAPTER 29

"Getting to be a little concerned about our Poppy," Ross said to his brother, Joseph, one morning as they were breakfasting together after three hours working in the fields.

"How do you mean?" Joseph asked. "And what time do you get to follow her exploits?"

"That's just it," Ross explained. "I don't need to follow her because she rarely leaves that blessed cottage. Florence has been gone a while now and no-one else visits, except for her father, Tommy Spence. I'm concerned."

"She's following the path on which she set out many years ago," Joseph replied. "She's old enough to decide her own future, you know, Brother – a bit like all adults, really."

"She's a woman who lives on her own with precious little male company," Ross added. "She doesn't even seem to hold many of those author gatherings these days. It seems that since Florence's departure and marriage, they haven't been seeing much of each other."

"How do you know all this?" Joseph asked, oblivious to Ross's ways of knowing.

"I visit her and, believe it or not, I talk to her," his brother commented. "And it seems like I'm t'onny one as does. In fact, I shall be nipping down to t'cottage straight after mi snap. Fancy coming?"

"Don't have the time today, I'm afraid," Joseph said, taking his plates and stuff into the kitchen. "Perhaps later in the week when stuff slackens off."

"Well, I'm off to see her now," Ross insisted, once he had cleared away his breakfast things.

"Oh ho! What's this?" he muttered as he approached the cottage from the wood's side. "Front door wide open?"

He stepped quietly over the threshold to the sound of muffled squealing and thuds. Opening the sitting-room door, he saw a bloodied and bruised Poppy on the floor with a man's hands around her throat.

Ross said nothing, but he grasped the thug's hair in one hand and lifted him from the floor, turned his body around and delivered a murderous, crunching fist to the attacker's face, bursting asunder his nose and mouth. The attacker's look of utter shock and terror was wiped away with another face-altering blow from the same fist.

Unconscious on the Persian rug, the attacker oozed blood from his shattered and unrecognisable face as Ross stamped on both his hands with his enormous, heavy farming boots.

Poppy all but collapsed into Ross's arms.

"Now then my beauty, what's this all about?" he asked as he tried to soothe his niece's distress. He sat her down next to him once he had straightened the upturned settee. "Who is this … this cowardly lump of sad humanity?"

It took a few minutes to recover her senses enough to say, though a swollen mouth and cut lip, "He is called Jude Dryden, and he is supposed to be a poet. I received a note from him a while ago saying he would like to see me. He was at one of my – *our* – soirées a while ago, and I thought he wanted advice on how to proceed with his writing. He came in all smiles and then, unexpectedly … this. What are you going to do with him?"

"My only concern is you at the moment," he assured her. "This pile of cow dung I will tie up and leave outside while I take you to the house to have Mother minister to your injuries, which are, as far as I can make out, not life threatening. Then I will wait until he wakes up to taste the blood in his mouth and experience not being able to breathe through a shattered nose. Nobody is ever going to get away with manhandling *my* Poppy."

"Oh Ross!" she sighed deeply. "What have I done to deserve this?"

"I think that this is the result of your being related to me and to being closely associated with George Garside," Ross warned. "This has the stamp of Jonas Jamieson about it. I will find out when I speak to this lump, although he may not be able to enunciate terribly clearly. Can't wait to catch his reaction."

~⌒~

Life for Florence had been … different since her marriage to George. With very little spare time in which to either visit or work with her now-distant friend, Poppy, Florence had begun to perform many of the functions most married women do without the help of serving staff. Money in the Garside household wasn't flexible enough for that sort of luxury.

Her writing materials had been barely disturbed, and the books she had planned to read had remained untouched in their dust-gathering bookshelves. She loved George with all her heart but wasn't sure that the baggage that came with married life was what she had bargained for.

The most difficult adjunct to her otherwise testing family life in a household a million miles away from her ideal was the fact that she was with child. *That* brought its own problems. Morning sickness that lasted almost all day, with severe abdominal pains, had turned her life upside-down. She couldn't help but think at times that *this* had been the most ill-conceived decision she had ever made.

"George?" Florence ventured quietly as he arose at six o'clock to start his day's work.

"Yes, my lovely?" he replied, sliding his arm around her shoulders in their over-sized bed.

"Don't go in today … please?" she answered. "I don't feel well enough to face the day on my own. Stay with me?"

"I would love to, but I'm afraid I have no choice," he explained. "We don't have anyone else to deliver our orders."

"Couldn't one of the other workers do it?" she pleaded.

"We don't have any other workers," he insisted, a look of sadness in his eyes. "I'm sorry, my sweet lady, but I don't have any option. Can I get you breakfast or a cup of tea?" he offered as he continued to dress for his busy day. "I'll try to be back by mid to late afternoon."

This day wasn't going to be as enjoyable as normal, with almost twice the number of orders as usual and worry about his wife's health preying on his already overworked mind. What was that concept that one of his business contacts had floated by him the other day? Holiday? If only…

A glorious, golden sunrise cascaded over him as he stepped over the front door's threshold ready for his initial ride to Northallerton. His ride to his first delivery usually cleared his head ready for a busy day, but this day was different. He had a nagging and annoying feeling crawling about at the back of his mind that caused him a degree of disquiet, and it wouldn't leave him. It was as if he were being warned about something unexpected that was about to happen, without knowing where or when.

Family? Friends? Business associates. He couldn't imagine, probably because he didn't possess second sight and could not predict the future. If only this day was over and he could re-join his family as quickly as possible.

⁓

"Pretty comprehensive, those injuries, don't you think, Mr Booth?" the policeman observed.

"They are all he deserved, Sergeant Shaw," Ross refuted. "He had already beaten my niece and was trying to throttle her. I had to drag him away and render him unconscious to save her. I punched him only twice – just enough to settle him down. He is lucky I didn't finish him off."

"Any reason he should have done what he did?" the policeman asked.

"What, apart from getting away with attacking a defence-less woman in her own home?" Ross replied angrily. "He was a member of her literary group, for goodness' sake, if that helps. But I don't think that has anything to do with it."

"Any … sexual interference?" the policeman continued.

"If there had been, his groin would have suffered a signif-icant trampling as well!" Ross growled. "So, no, there wasn't."

"What do you think, then?" Sergeant Shaw asked, at a loss as to why Poppy had been attacked.

"I believe I know who is behind this," Ross said. "We have had problems with him for many a year and now he's disappeared, despite having been in police custody at the time, given that he *was* in hospital after George Garside had given him a kicking."

"Jonas Jamieson by any chance?" the policeman offered.

"Indeed so," Ross agreed. "He disappeared from hospital, though I don't know how because he couldn't walk with a shattered knee joint. Oh, he's behind it all right."

"This young lad – Jude Dryden? – has no previous, but I'll be having a word with him to ascertain his connection, if there is one, with yon Jonas Jamieson," the sergeant stated. "If we can find him."

"I hope you find him before I do—" Ross said.

"Be careful, Mr Booth," the policeman warned. "If you dish out your vigilante punishments willy-nilly, I will have no alternative but to arrest *you*."

"And if you do find him before I do?" Ross challenged him.

"I will arrest him and wheel him in for a heart-felt chat," the police sergeant assured him. "He is wanted for the stabbing of Mr George Garside, if nothing else."

⁓

"Why did he attack me, Uncle Ross?" Poppy asked, once her uncle returned from the police station. "What had I done wrong to him?"

"You had done nothing to deserve *that*," Ross explained. "But do you remember a few years ago, when you and Florence were accosted in the wood by an individual called—?"

"Jonas Jamieson!" She spat out his name in disgust. "But it wasn't him that—!"

"I believe this Dryden man was paid to get you on your own," Ross said. "Joining your soirées was a perfect way in for him to get as close to you as possible without raising suspicion. Young man asks young woman to meet, and boom boom! Had

I not been there, we would have been grieving right now."

They sat in silence for a while. Poppy's sad face was very much in evidence.

"I think we need to vet all the people who apply to attend any future events you organise with care and thoroughness," Ross said to Poppy's nods. "That is, if you decide to continue, bearing in mind that you no longer will have Florence by your side. It would then be up to you alone."

"Not sure," Poppy responded, saddened by all that had happened. "This has really knocked my confidence in my abilities."

"It's nothing to do with your abilities, my sweet pea," Ross assured her. "They are unaffected. What *has* dealt a blow is your confidence in *other* people to do what you want them to do within a trusting environment."

"I don't feel I can ever trust others not to disrupt, or even do what Jude Dryden has done," Poppy sighed. "I need people to be trusting, open and spontaneous in their actions and I can't be on tenterhooks all the time. That would be counter-productive at best, and destructive at worst."

"Then the decision is yours," Tommy Spence's voice joined them from the doorway.

"Father!" Poppy reacted eagerly as she flung her arms about him.

"Have no fears, Poppy," Ross advised as he moved towards the door to leave father and daughter. "I will get to the bottom of it to allow you to rebuild." He clicked the outside door behind him as he strode off to catch up with his daily toil.

"I heard about what happened, my dear, and came as quickly as I could," Tommy Spence said. "I also caught what Ross said about taking time to rebuild. Would you like to come and stay with us for a while, to allow that to happen?

You would be more than welcome to have your own room where you could write and read to your heart's content…"

"I don't know, Father," she retorted.

They sat down together on her wonderful settee that her attacker had wantonly damaged with splashes of her blood staining its back and arms. Her beautiful Persian rug had taken the full brunt of the blood *he* had shed at the hands of her Uncle Ross. It was now ruined.

At that moment the outside door burst open, crashing into the wall behind as George's sister, Florence, bounced into the vestibule.

"Poppy! Come quickly!" she shouted almost hysterically, tears streaming down her face. "You've got to come! Our George's Florence … she's … had a miscarriage, and now she's not … breathing. The doctor's on his way but—"

"I have my carriage outside," Tommy urged. "We will come. Hurry!"

CHAPTER 30

On a cold, rainy and miserable Saturday morning in late August, a cortège slowly left Garside's farm, led on foot by a tall, thin gentleman bearing a mace and dressed in black. He was wearing a shiny, black top hat with long black ribbons flowing behind in the breeze. The family had refused the ostentation of similarly dressed mutes to walk alongside the hearse, drawn by two mighty black shires, and two carriages each drawn by a pair of similar shires.

George Garside had lost his second wife in childbirth, but without issue. Sadly, he had not been present at her passing and learned about it only when he returned home in the late afternoon of the Friday, a week before.

The elm coffin, as was the custom, lay in Garside Farm's parlour for five working days to allow relatives, friends and acquaintances to pay their respects and to celebrate the life and passing of Florence, wife to George Garside.

The family had vigorously resisted the undertaker's attempts to persuade them to opt for clouds of black plumes, a solid and magnificent oak coffin, and more shires than were necessary to pull hugely ornate and ostentatious carriages and hearse. They wanted only to lay Florence to rest in their local churchyard with the least fuss possible in a death-obsessed society.

George was in despair at having lost two wives whom he had loved in his way in such a short space of time. How could he now continue to grow old without the woman he loved at his side? With due deference to his parlous situation, Ross and Martha had taken on the task of providing the afternoon tea at Boulders Wood, with Mary's Pantry as outside caterers once the ceremony ended.

Because there had been no local church in the area for many years, the service was held over the grave with the family and friends under umbrella cover – except for George. He stood, bare headed, at the edge of the deep black hole into which the glorious elm coffin was lowered to the absolute sorrow and sadness of all onlookers, to the words of the *Book of Common Prayer…*

'We therefore commit this body to the ground … earth to earth; ashes to ashes; dust to dust; in sure and certain hope of the Resurrection to eternal life…'

George stiffened as the distance between him and his beloved Florence widened, taking her away from him forever. Tears began to course down his cheeks, as his feet remained fixed, immobile on the wet, grassed land.

Florence's mother and father did not attend, despite having been warned about all the arrangements via a hand-delivered message.

The reception at Boulders Wood was a sombre, quiet affair where little was said but much food and drink was consumed. The quietest of all was George, followed by his good friend and support, Poppy. *His* was a hurt *she* experienced keenly.

Between accepting condolences from time to time, reminiscences crept in unexpectedly as if they had been prompted by another involved party – Florence. That was the only way either of them could survive this crushing blow to their emotional state.

These were memories they shared from as far back as age nine and ten, the time Poppy, Florence and George became inseparable friends. Whatever one did was shared by all three, and it seemed that none of them could function properly without the other two.

George was grateful to Poppy for her support and understanding at this dire, crushing time when he could easily have descended into a dark pit of remorse and self-pity.

"We've been through some dreadful episodes in our life, my dear friend," Poppy said to George, "and some very uplifting high plateaux."

"Like the time we were attacked by your Grandpa Joss's long-lost brother—" George replied, his face contorted into a grimace.

"And our adventures to celebrate my twelfth birthday on the East Coast with Grandpa Ross and Nanny Nell," Poppy interjected, drawing a smile to his lips and a glint to his eyes. "Two of our dear friends from then are no longer with us."

"I still can't help but blame myself for Florence's death," George changed direction.

"How do you work that one out?" she gasped. "How could you possibly take the blame for … that?"

"She asked me not to go to work that morning and I refused because I had too much work on," he explained quietly, painfully, his eyes filling with remorseful tears. "And I suppose she would still be here if we hadn't got … married."

274

"You mustn't reproach yourself," Poppy urged. "It can only end in deeper sorrow. Don't forget, she was my friend too. Perhaps I ought to have done more to support her. Carry on in this vein, George, and you *will* succumb to a very deep and destructive depression."

"Every time I feel like this, dear Poppy, would it be all right to come to the cottage to … talk? You are the only person I can relate to these days. Folks aren't my thing. Never have been," George said.

"My door is always open to you, George. You know that," Poppy stated as the last guest made to leave.

"We believe we have found him," Ross muttered to his brother as they cleaned their harvesters ready for winter's onslaught.

"Found whom, pray?" Joseph asked, not in tune with the strange and obtusely obsessive language his brother used these days. "The fairy at the end of the rainbow?"

"You've been reading too many stories to your children, Brother!" Ross laughed. "Remember the thug that attacked our Poppy a while back? Jude Dryden was his name, I believe."

"Ye … es," was Joseph's drawled response. "What about him. Wasn't he the one that a rather nasty, life-changing accident when he ran into your … fists?"

"Indeed, he was," Ross agreed. "He gave the name of his master to Sergeant Shaw in exchange for a more lenient sentence. It turned out that I was right about his employer – Jonas Jamieson."

"And your response to that nugget of information?" Joseph asked, concerned at what his hot-headed brother might have devised.

"I intend to seek him out to—" Ross went on, to be

interrupted by his brother.

"Deal with him in the same way you dealt with his hench-man?" Joseph offered, knowing his brother well. Ross was a firm believer in the law of retaliatory retribution, which would give him the right to inflict as serious an injury to the assailant as the assailant had dealt to his victim. Unfortunately, that notional 'law' had been meant only for those injured in the first instance.

"No," Ross insisted firmly, eyes flashing. "I would simply drag him off to the law enforcers to let them deal out their punishments – legally."

"Not a good idea to leave it entirely to them to enforce their laws without public interference, then?" Joseph argued. "By taking action, Brother, you might incur the wrath of that force that has been set up to protect *all* its citizens. Don't you think?"

"Mr Booth! Mr McIntyre!" A deep voice hailed them from the driveway as they walked back to the house for a cup of tea and a bite to eat. Ross spun around to see Detective Sergeant Shaw climbing out of his police carriage.

"I'll go and sort out the tea and sustenance," Joseph suggested. "Don't be long."

"Sergeant Shaw, how good to see you," Ross said on a firm handshake. "How can I help you? Would you like to come in for a mug of tea and a bite?"

"Would love to, but I have a few more calls to make," the policeman explained. "Just a brief one. We have definite, solid information that your Mr Jonas Jamieson was behind the attack on your niece. He paid—"

"The ruffian I stopped in the act. And now you are about to arrest him?" Ross queried. "Only...?"

"We don't know as yet exactly where ... he ... is," Sergeant

Shaw admitted.

"Well then, I can help you because I know exactly where he lives," Ross offered. "And rather than become involved, I'll give you chapter and verse so you can collar him and put him where he belongs for as long as the judge deems fit."

"I am very much obliged to you, Mr Booth," the policeman said, a satisfied smile creeping up on him. "Will you be able to come to the station to provide us with a statement?"

"Indeed, I will," Ross replied. "Tomorrow be all right?"

CHAPTER 31

Poppy sat in her study in her cottage, a half-written page on her desk before her and a faraway look in her eyes as she gazed out of the little window into the indeterminate distance over the fields and woods. Her second romantic novel was close to conclusion, but continuing bouts of reminiscence and nostalgia periodically interrupted her story flow. She couldn't help but think about her two dearest friends who no longer spent time in her company.

Two years had passed since that dreadful day when her closest friend and associate, Florence, passed from the gloriously wonderful experiences and adventures they had shared. She missed her company dreadfully. She missed the friendship they had shared since they were eight years old, from that memorable Christmas at Boulders Wood when they shared a room and founded their close friendship.

Her other close friend, George Garside, had lost Florence as his wife in childbirth when she was experiencing a miscarriage, alone, without him near. The last thing Poppy had heard from George was his plea to allow him access to her should he need her support. That request came at the gathering for afternoon tea at the funeral.

She missed him desperately. Why had he not called when she was open to his visits? Still, life couldn't remain in limbo, and she owed it to herself to pursue her ambitions to their ultimate conclusion.

The front door opened slowly, encouraging Poppy to walk through to the sitting room, knowing that whoever had just entered was allowed to be there as only a key would grant entry. In the middle of the sitting room, of all people, stood … George.

"I knew you would come as soon as you were ready," she said quietly, as they embraced. "I knew it."

"I had to be sure it was you I really wanted," he acknowledged, holding her tightly to him. "I had to be sure I really wanted to spend the rest of my life with you, now that I can devote all my time to the woman I really love and have done so all my life."

"Yes, I will, my George," Poppy said confidently. "I *will* marry you."

"At last," he sighed deeply. "At last!"

FRANK ENGLISH
AUTHOR

Born in 1946 in the West Riding of Yorkshire's coal fields around Wakefield, he attended grammar school, where he enjoyed sport rather more than academic work. After three years at teacher training college in Leeds, he became a teacher in 1967. He spent a lot of time during his teaching career entertaining children of all ages, a large part of which was through telling stories, and encouraging them to escape into a world of imagination and wonder. Some of his most disturbed youngsters he found to be very talented poets, for example. He has always had a wicked sense of humour, which has blossomed only during the time he has spent with his wife, Denise. This sense of humour also allowed many youngsters to survive often difficult and brutalising home environments.

In 2006, he retired after forty years working in schools with young people who had significantly disrupted lives because of behaviour disorders and poor social adjustment, generally brought about through circumstances beyond their control. At the same time as moving from leafy lane suburban middle-class school teaching in Leeds to residential schooling for emotional and behavioural disturbance in the early 1990s, changed family circumstance provided the spur to achieve ambitions. Supported by his wife, Denise, he achieved a Master's degree in his mid-forties and a PhD at the age of fifty-six, because he had always wanted to do so.

Now enjoying glorious retirement, he spends as much time as life will allow writing, reading and travelling.

Other books for adults he has written:

Jack the Lad	Published 2016
Jack	Published 2016
Hit the Road Jack	Published 2017
Welcome Back Jack	Published 2017
All Right Jack?	Published 2019
Carry On Jack	Published 2020
Where to now, Jack?	Published 2022
Hidden Secrets	Published 2021

Children's books he has written to date:

Magic Parcel: The Awakening	Published June 2010
Magic Parcel: The Gathering Storm	Published March 2011
Magic Parcel: A New Dawn	Published August 2012
18 Mulberry Road	Published September 2011
25 Primrose Walk	Published January 2013
Autumn Adventures	Published September 2013
Winter Tales	Published September 2014
Towards Spring	Published September 2016
Juniper's Tale	Published August 2018
Honey	Published January 2019
The Story of Lemuel Pecker	Published April 2019
Josephine's Journey	Published June 2019
Holly's Prize	Published April 2020
Garnett's Grand Getaway	Published May 2020
Sara's Astonishing Story	Published June 2020
The Boys in Black	Published August 2020
The Magic Whistle and the Tiny Bag of Wishes	Published October 2020
Half Moon Farm	Published March 2021
The Spirit Tree	Published February 2022

Lightning Source UK Ltd.
Milton Keynes UK
UKHW010630310722
406618UK00001B/65